Watch Out for the Big Girls 3

Watch Out for the Big Girls 3

J. M. Benjamin

URBAN
BOOKS

www.urbanbooks.net

Urban Books, LLC
300 Farmingdale Road, NY-Route 109
Farmingdale, NY 11735

Watch Out for the Big Girls 3
Copyright © 2017 J. M. Benjamin

ISBN 13: 978-1-62286-490-4
ISBN 10: 1-62286-490-5

First Trade Paperback Printing June 2017
Printed in the United States of America

10 9 8 7 6 5 4 3 2 1

This is a work of fiction. Any references or similarities to actual events, real people, living or dead, or to real locales are intended to give the novel a sense of reality. Any similarity in other names, characters, places, and incidents is entirely coincidental.

Distributed by Kensington Publishing Corp.
Submit Orders to:
Customer Service
400 Hahn Road
Westminster, MD 21157-4627
Phone: 1-800-733-3000
Fax: 1-800-659-2436

Watch Out for the Big Girls 3

by

J. M. Benjamin

Prologue

Edge nodded to the sounds of Meek Mill's *Dreamchasers* CD as she looked at the address she had been given for a second time. The last thing she wanted was to invade the wrong house and foul up the one job that would change her life forever. The reality of being home still hadn't set in, but the old, familiar feeling of putting in work was coming back to her like an adult riding a bike for the first time in years.

For a second, Edge thought she had heard the sound of shots going off. She peered out of the rental car's windows. She didn't see anything out of the ordinary, so she brushed it off. Once she was convinced the coast was clear, she slipped on her black leather gloves, opened the driver's door, and exited the vehicle. As an extra precaution, she looked left, then right, before making a beeline to the two-story home.

Diamond had given her a picture of the intended victim, so she knew what, or rather who, she was looking for. Diamond hadn't told her anything about the victim other than that she had compromised their operation.

Edge had been familiar with the Double Gs before she had gone to prison. She and Diamond used to have mixed views on what the organization represented, which was why Edge was surprised to discover that Diamond had become a member. Edge had been hearing about the Double Gs while she was away and she found it difficult to believe that Diamond was a part of the stories.

Nonetheless, Edge was grateful and appreciative for Diamond's contribution to her release, no matter what the cost.

Edge had always been a woman of her word, so when Diamond told her she was ready to cash in on her debt forty-eight hours after Edge had gotten out of prison, Edge accepted the job respectfully. She was sure it would be an easy enough task to fulfill: kill one woman. What Edge was not sure of, though, was whether she wanted to be a Double G. She knew she had to give the idea some more thought. All that Diamond had briefed her on sounded good but, still, the part about Diamond having feelings for and dealing with the head of the organization didn't sit well with Edge. She couldn't see herself taking orders from someone who had Diamond's heart when she still loved Diamond herself.

Edge shook off the thoughts off and focused on the job at hand. The first thing she noticed was the door ajar. Edge's spider senses went off. She got that tingling feeling she always got whenever trouble or danger was around the corner. Edge cautiously pushed open the door. She checked to see if there was any forceful entry but she didn't see anything to support the thought. Edge took one last look back before slipping into the home and closing the door behind her. Immediately, she heard the commotion coming from upstairs. The way the top level was designed, Edge could see shadows in the distance on the top part of the wall and ceiling.

The story of my fuckin' life. She realized it was not going to be an easy task at all. She knew turning back was not an option, though. She had committed to a job, and she intended to carry it out or die trying.

Edge made her way over to the steps. She took the first three in one motion and scaled the side of the wall. She had her .40-caliber in one hand and her 007 blade in the other, both of which she was equally skilled with. The farther she got up the steps, the louder the voices grew. Edge couldn't make out what was being said, but she could tell there were both men and women in the room. *Think, Edge.* She was tempted to bum-rush the room, but she laughed off the idea. *Bitch, this is not the Wild West,* she reminded herself. All types of ideas ran through Edge's mind. Her thoughts were interrupted by the unmistakable words that came out of the room and bounced off the hallway walls.

The words were enough to cause Edge to plant her back flush against the wall. She took a deep breath. There was no doubt in her mind she had the right address now. She knew it was either now or never. Edge took another deep breath.

"One, two, three," she counted; then she barged into the room like she used to do when she was on the force before she turned crooked. The room was completely caught by surprise as Edge appeared with her two silencer-equipped .40-calibers blazing.

Smoke was the first to spin around and draw his attention to the sound of the room door slamming up against the wall. He managed to raise his pistol, but not fast enough. The two shots let loose in his direction were enough to slow him down. Both bullets tore into his chest: one just mere inches away from his heart; the other ripped straight through it. His gun fell from his hand, and his body followed as he stumbled backward, right before he plunged to the plush carpet.

Still a little shaken by the sudden presence of Edge, Clips dove across Felicia's bed for cover, but not before one of the three shots Edge sent his way ripped through his right triceps. *Who the fuck is that?* he questioned as he fumbled and made a failed attempt to cock his weapon. The shot to his arm prevented him from fully cocking it. He could feel the blood oozing out of the back of his arm.

Edge heard the sound of his weapon attempting to be cocked, but she paid it no mind. She let off two more shots toward the bed area as a diversion. She knew Clips was hit, and she could smell his fear as she stepped over Smoke's lifeless body sprawled out on the floor. She and Felicia made quick eye contact as she passed her. Edge could tell by the way she looked at her that Felicia had no idea who she was. Wasting no time, she made her way to the other side of the bed, where Clips lay.

"Who the fuck are you?" Clips growled as he tried to raise his gun to no avail. His breathing was now out of control, and he began to feel lightheaded after he asked the question. He was losing a lot of blood, and he knew it. Tears escaped the crevices of his eyes as he blinked uncontrollably.

Edge stared at him with no remorse. "I'm the last bitch you'll ever see," she calmly replied, right before she dumped two shots in Clips's face and another two in his lower abdomen.

Clips's soul exited his flesh before it slumped over and lay on the floor.

Edge walked back over to where Felicia was. At that point, Felicia didn't care who Edge was; she was just thankful that she had shown up when she had. She was sure she knew all of the Double Gs members, and she figured Edge was one of the newest recruits.

"I don't know who you are, but—" That was as far as she got before Edge emptied the unused .40-caliber into Felicia's already bloody face.

"And you never will," Edge spoke under her breath.

She pulled out the phone Diamond had given to her, snapped a picture of Felicia's dead body, and sent it. A thumbs-up emoji immediately appeared on the cell phone screen.

Edge shoved the phone back into her pocket and then exited Felicia's home.

Chapter 1

Her hair was silky, woven like a ball of yarn, and it was the color of dark, thunderous clouds. It held tight as a crown around a round, full face. For a woman of age, her skin was smooth and radiant as if she were preparing to give birth. A shade of blackberry sat on the windows of her eyes, which heightened the rosiness of her cheeks and emphasized the fullness of her lips.

Very few people lived to give that description of one of the most notorious gangsters ever to grace this earth. For Mirage, the thought of uttering that description was a warrant to execute a death wish.

Mirage knew her position and played her role well. Driving wasn't just her job; it was a passion she had come to love and respect. Every Wednesday, she found a way to treat herself to a simple wash and set. She didn't have time to be away from her mistress for any longer than an hour. Her role was too important to go unaccounted for for any length of time. In the twenty years she'd been employed by her mistress, she'd rarely looked her or her closest allies in the eye. She'd come to recognize each of them by voice alone. Mirage rarely spoke to any of them, and she'd never once had to identify them by name.

Despite her position, she saw her family rather frequently. She had a daughter, who decided in her thirties that she would finally go to Spelman and study chemistry and biochemistry in an effort to become a creator of green-friendly products that were less dependent on oil and other precious resources. Her grandchildren, nine-year-old twins, enjoyed the luxuries and privileges that came with attending a private school that emphasized the importance of mathematics and sciences.

For Mirage, her daughter and grandchildren were her legacy. She made a special effort to rarely speak of them in the presence of her mistress. The less Queen Fem knew of their existence, the greater their chances were of survival. Realistically, she knew Queen Fem probably had them under surveillance and could destroy her whole world without a moment's notice. She knew the risk when she accepted one of the most dangerous jobs in the world. Her daughter and grandchildren motivated her to be more flawless than Beyoncé.

"Tell me something," Queen Fem spoke to her from the back of the black Phantom she rode in.

"Yes, Mistress," Mirage addressed her boss.

"If you were in my shoes, would you play your position any differently than I have?" Queen Fem quizzed her.

Mirage was dumbfounded. She'd never given too much thought to her role beyond being a well-paid stunt driver who could navigate any vehicle through any challenge Queen Fem found necessary.

"No." Mirage was firm in her answer. She knew that was the best way to gain and keep Queen Fem's respect. "Starr knows what she must do, and if she didn't, you would've killed her the first chance you got."

"I suppose you're right," Queen Fem replied without any emotion whatsoever. At least, not on the surface. But on the inside, she was troubled. Starr had been the cause of her many sleepless nights in recent months. The Double Gs had been receiving more heat and static in one year than they had ever since she had founded the organization.

Queen Fem took a deep breath and sighed. She began to relax as she peered out the window. A warmness appeared across her face as she took in and enjoyed the scenic route through Las Vegas. She switched her mind from her troubling thoughts to much more peaceful ones. They were replaced with the view of multimillion-dollar homes they passed by. They gave her ideas for an architectural undertaking she wanted to start and complete before her journey on this earth came to an end.

"Every now and then it is good to hear constructive criticism and to receive a second opinion." Queen Fem patted Mirage on top of her hand as she continued to take in the scenery. Next to Starr, there was no one else Queen Fem loved and admired more than Mirage, which was why she both respected and valued her opinion and views on certain things.

"You're right," Mirage answered. "You spent years growing and cultivating the Double Gs to be the women they are. You have too much dirt on the most powerful people for anyone to cross you and live long."

Mirage knew her mistress wasn't worried in the least. She knew and understood her second most important role, her "secret" job. Queen Fem loved and trusted Mirage enough to let her guard down slightly and be a woman. Queen Fem could be soft around Mirage and show her almost every emotion she had reserved for her common-law wife.

"Stay" by Rufus featuring Chaka Khan sedated the two of them. Mirage had always admired and respected the soul singer. *Truthfully, in addition to being a social activist, the legend has it in her to be a Double G if she desires to wander a different path,* thought Mirage.

"Turn that up for me." Queen Fem smiled and relaxed some more. The late-seventies soul hit reminded her of a time period that she had long ago buried in the back of her mind and heart. She could remember it as if it were just the other day when her first love would cruise Highway 15 in one of his many sports cars, blasting the song. It seemed like so long ago, when she was a different person living a different life. She couldn't help but think about him and how he had played such an intricate part in the birth of the Double Gs. It was the one thing that she and she alone knew, something she would take to her grave not as Queen Fem, but as Carlita Banks, from her pre-Queen days.

Without warning, an image of Lewis Steele appeared in her mental movie. It had been a long time since she had thought about him. Queen Fem tried to shake his handsome face out of her mind, but the image refused to remove itself. She grimaced as the images turned into what she had stayed away from for so many years.

As the limo switched lanes, so did Queen Fem's thoughts as her last memories of Lewis Steele took over. Her heart skipped a beat, and her stomach fluttered with butterflies as the uneventful evening illuminated on the glass of her window as if she were at a drive-in movie. His laugh echoed in her mind through his smile.

Queen Fem smiled and closed her eyes. Rather than try to keep fighting it, she embraced where her mind was trying to take her. As she traveled back in time, it was as if she could feel Lewis Steele's spirit and touch in the limo.

Lewis's hand slithered farther up Carlita's dress as Al Green filled the car with his melodic voice. He slid her panties to the side and began fondling her. She spread her legs wider and pushed his hand deeper under her dress. She slowly gyrated her sex to match Lewis's fingers fondling her. She could feel her juices oozing down her inner thigh and Lewis's fingers. Her body quivered. She removed Lewis's hand from between her legs and reached over into his lap. Within mere seconds, she had his rock-hard dick out of his briefs and in her mouth. She could feel the horsepower of the car as Lewis accelerated on the gas. The sudden speed turned her on. She attacked Lewis's dick with her mouth. She licked alongside his pulsating veins then took him back into her mouth and deep-throated him. Lewis placed his hand on the back of her head and guided her as she bobbed up and down on him while he navigated the Maserati with his other hand.

"Yes, baby," he cooed. "Right there—" The impact of the hit broke his concentration and cut his words short.

"What the hell?" Lewis boomed. He quickly pulled his hand from Carlita's head and gripped the steering wheel just in time to gain control of the car and avoid crashing.

Carlita had now risen up and was fully alert. "Lew, what's going on?" she cried.

Lewis peered into his rearview. His eyes widened as the headlights of the car behind them rapidly approached. Before he could answer Carlita, the back of his Maserati was rammed for a second time. This time the impact was more forceful than the first. The hit caused Lewis to spin out of control. Within seconds, the sports car was skidding down the road.

The last thing Carlita remembered before blacking out was staring into Lewis Steele's deep brown eyes.

Queen Fem's eyes shot open. The chain of events to come after that rehashed a sharp pain that she hadn't felt in a long time. Priding herself on being a fearless individual, she was hesitant about letting the vision continue. The last thing she wanted was for Mirage to see her in a vulnerable or weak state and she knew thinking about Lewis Steele would put her in one. She had built herself up to be a super woman, but Lewis Steele was her kryptonite.

"Are you okay?" Mirage asked, seeing the disturbed look on Queen Fem's face.

"I'm fine," she offered in a subtle tone. "Just sorting everything all out in my head," she added.

Mirage smiled. "I know. That's what you do."

Queen Fem matched her smile. "Yes, it is."

Mirage's words resonated in Queen Fem's mind. They made her realize just how far she had come as a woman. It also made her reflect on the many women she had built up, inspired, and motivated who were once considered weak victims and slaves to men. It was because of her strength she'd been able to grow and expand her empire, laying the precursor for the life she enjoyed now. Queen Fem closed her eyes for a second. And, just like the first time, the painful memories resurfaced. She couldn't fight them. This time she embraced them.

Carlita jumped out of her unconscious state. Once she regained her vision, the first thing she saw was a young white male hovering over her. His words alarmed her of the imminent danger she was in.

"His bitch is woke," the young white male chimed.

"Good. Bring her black ass over here," one of the five men surrounding Lewis Steele commanded.

"Come here." The young white male roughly grabbed a fistful of her hair. She screamed out in agony as he dragged her over to where Lewis lay.

She immediately burst into tears at the sight of her lover. She noticed one of the men standing over Lewis's body, zipping up his pants. Lewis was covered in his own blood. Both of his eyes were nearly shut and swollen. His mouth leaked of blood and his lips were busted. Blood oozed from the top of his head where an open gash existed. The stench of strong urine caused Carlita to gag. She nearly vomited.

"Why are you doing this?" Carlita yelled. "What do you want from us?"

*Her words caused more laughter among the men.
"Aw, she really doesn't know," one of the men mocked.*

*"I bet she doesn't know about this, either," another one
of the men chimed in.*

*She looked up and over at the man. She noticed the
red velvet ring box he held in his hand. More tears
spilled out of her eyes. She knew the red velvet box was
the reason behind the special question Lewis intended to
ask her.*

*"Give me that!" She reached out and tried to grab the
box from the man's hand. Instead of accomplishing
what she set out to do, she was compensated with a
backhand across the face. The blow sent her tumbling.
She landed on her lover.*

*"You stupid bitch," the man spat. He moved in to
deliver another blow but was stopped in his tracks.*

*"That's enough," another man calmly stated. "Let's just
see if she knows anything," he continued.*

The other men nodded in agreement.

*The man then kneeled down in front of Carlita. He
began stroking her hair and the side of her face. Carlita
cringed from his touch.*

*"Now listen carefully, sweetheart. You can save your-
self and your soon-to-be fiancé if you just do us this little
favor and tell us what we need to know. Understand?"*

Carlita nodded.

*"Good girl." He smiled. "Now, Lewis here has some
very important information that could do a lot of people
some harm if it falls into the wrong hands. Before that
happens, we'd like it back. The problem is Lewis refuses
to tell us where we can find this information. And since
we know he doesn't have a lot of friends and doesn't
really trust anyone, we figured you'd be the only person
who would know, and he would tell in case something
like this ever happened."*

She listened attentively. Her mind was racing a hundred miles a minute. For the first time, she stared at the man kneeling in front of her. She recognized him from the party they had just left. She did a quick scan and realized she recognized all of the men from the party. The only difference was that at the party they wore police uniforms, versus the plain clothes they wore now.

Carlita cleared her throat. "Honestly," she started out with, "I don't know anything."

"Man, fuck this!" one of the men yelled. "We wasted enough time already. The fuckin' nigger didn't tell us shit, and now his bitch is playing stupid too. If we kill both their asses, they can't use the information anyway."

"I'm with Johnny on this one, Luke," one of the other men joined in.

The remaining men nodded in agreement as well.

"Everybody just chill the fuck out," the man known as Luke ordered in his calm tone. "Honey, are you sure you don't know anything about a black book of names, a ledger, anything?"

"I swear to you, I don't know nothing about nothing," she assured him.

The man known as Luke rose up. "That's too bad." He frowned and then turned his back on her.

"Kill 'em," he nonchalantly stated.

The man known as Johnny wasted no time. He raised his weapon and pointed it at Carlita. Her eyes widened with fear. The shot to the head knocked her backward. She felt the additional two shots rip into her body just before darkness came.

Queen Fem let the tape play out in her mind. It was the first time since she had gotten out of the hospital many years ago after her near-death experience that she had so vividly thought about what had happened to her that day. She smiled to herself at how blessed she was to have survived that day. And it was all owed to Lewis Steele. Because of him, Carlita Banks was one of the most notorious and powerful women on the West Coast. She opened her eyes and peered out of the limo window for a second time. She took in the view of Sin City.

"Before it's all over with, I'm going to own Las Vegas," she turned to Mirage and said. A half smile appeared across her face.

"Yes, you will," Mirage agreed, offering a smile of her own. She grinned slightly at the calm and reserved demeanor of Queen Fem and the rarity of the smile that appeared on her face as the limo exited the ramp.

Chapter 2

Monica would have never thought that she would be in the predicament she was in. She was supposed to have cut ties long ago with Prime. But she didn't. Since, as a Double G, she had to pretend not to have any interest in men, she had been missing the feeling of penetration from a man, and Prime had reawakened that feeling in her body.

This is just what the doctor ordered, thought Monica. It had been years since she had felt a man inside of her, until she had slipped up and fucked Prime during her Double Gs initiation. She had crossed so many lines and broken so many rules as an agent and Double G, and sex had been the cause. The last person to make her body come close to feeling the way it was now was Starr, but Monica did not believe that it could compare to how Prime felt inside of her.

She cooed at the thought of how he had her cumming repeatedly and moaning, squirming, and clawing at his muscular back. With each downward stroke of his manhood, she slipped deeper and deeper into a sex coma. For that moment, it made her forget just how forbidden her actions were. It felt to her how a good bag of dope would feel to an heroin addict. Prime was her drug and Monica was addicted. She was in too deep and she knew it.

Besides the fact that, as a Double G, she was not allowed to have any sexual contact with a man if she wasn't instructed to do so, there was another matter to consider. The man who was the cause of her sex running like a broken faucet was a criminal. She couldn't figure out why she was risking everything—her job, her life—by sleeping with him. It was a question Monica had asked herself since the first time she had slept with him. The last time, she had only gone to talk, to end the secret sexcapades they had been having.

She remembered, as if it were yesterday, that night when they had first officially met at the club. She remembered how, while Prime was freshening up, she sipped on a few glasses of wine. Two drinks later, she felt lightheaded and needed to lie down. Having never visited the club before, she stumbled into a wrong room before finding her way to the bedroom upstairs. Prime had just gotten out of the shower and was drying off. The two locked eyes. She slowly drifted from his eyes to his chest and then to what lay between his legs. Her long stare caused Prime to drop the towel and approach her.

She made an attempt to exit the room, but she failed at breaking free of Prime's hand, which was now gripping her wrist. Before she knew it, he had her dress hiked up and her panties pulled down, bent over on his bed and sexing her like the young teen he was. It was a way Monica had never been fucked before, and she liked it. In the beginning, she had blamed it on one too many glasses of wine, but she quickly abandoned that reason because she knew exactly what she was doing and had done.

Since Starr had been locked up, Monica spent more time with Prime. And each time he brought her body to a sexual bliss, one higher than the next. She had crossed the line in so many ways; and if she was ever discovered, she could lose not only her job, but her freedom or life as well. But her sexual appetite and the need for something more in life clouded her judgment, and she let it lead her. She knew the type of man Prime was, just as she knew the type of woman Starr was, but they each did something different to her, something she longed for in two different ways. Now, she was caught up and had some decisions to make.

"Mmm, Monica, you make me feel so good," Prime claimed.

"Do I really?" At this point, she had flipped him on his back and had her thick body straddled across his beautiful, rock-hard body and was squeezing her pectoral muscles as tightly she possibly could. She leaned forward, kissing his perfect lips; and she'd slipped his rock-hard dick inside of her when his phone rang. He didn't bother to answer it.

She kept riding him, but she began to feel guilty because she knew the more she let him sex her, the more dangerous her situation would become. Still, it was as if her pussy had a mind its own. "You feel so good," Monica admitted.

"I love fucking this juicy pussy," he chimed.

Monica burst out laughing and gyrated harder on his thick, stiff manhood. She was mere seconds from coming again.

She looked into his beautiful brown eyes, and he leaned up. He kissed her and whispered in her ear, "I'm coming, girl. Come with me."

She kissed him back and did just that.

"Come on, baby, let's shower so I can get you home."

"Naw, baby, remember? I drove my own car."

Monica looked him in his eyes but said nothing for a few minutes. She placed her hand on his thigh and kissed him on chest. "I need to ask you something."

"What's up, love? You know you can ask me anything." Prime smiled.

"How do you feel about me, about us, this?"

On the inside, Prime's mood changed, but on the surface, he maintained a straight face. He realized that Monica was falling for him. And that's exactly what he wanted and needed. It was all a part of his plan.

"Monica, you know I'm diggin' you, but you know you can't afford to let them bitches find out you're still dealing with me," he reminded her.

Monica grimaced. "As far as Starr and 'em, that's almost over and done with. I'm leaving the Double Gs. But I'm just not sure how I'm really going to go about it."

"I don't care how them bitches would take it. We grown and I want to be with you." Prime laid it on thick.

Monica flashed a nervous smile. "I'm glad to hear you say that." Monica paused. There was something that had been weighing heavy on her mental for the past several weeks and now was as good a time as any to let Prime know.

"I'm pregnant," she blurted out abruptly.

The room instantly became silent. Her words had caught Prime off guard. He didn't know what to say.

Monica felt like a fool. *I knew I shouldn't have said anything. How could it ever work?* Monica regretted her words. She felt the sudden urge to leave. She rose up but was stopped in her tracks.

"Wait." Prime grabbed her by the waist. A huge smile crept across his face. He grabbed her up and began planting kisses all over her face and neck, and then he dropped to his knees and kissed her stomach.

Monica beamed. He kissed her gently on the lips and pulled her close in a warm embrace. Monica wanted to stay there, in his love, forever.

This shit don't get no better than this, Prime thought. He was already thinking of ways to use the news to his advantage. "Damn, why you ain't tell me before?" Prime questioned her. He was still trying to internally process the disturbing news.

"I didn't know how. I was just gonna get rid of it, but then, I mean, I don't know," Monica rambled.

"You don't have to do anything alone. I got you," Prime offered. The more he thought about it, the more he saw an opportunity. "Don't worry; we'll figure it out together," he assured her a second time.

Monica laid her head on his chest and snuggled in closer to him. True, she had feelings for Starr, but she realized that she had stronger feelings for Prime. Despite being a gangster, he had been more of a man to her and for her than any other man had been. She knew her situation was a messy one, but in her mind, she believed that somehow, someway, she'd be able to clean it up.

Chapter 3

When Correctional Officer Dylan Williams crawled out of the cell, the first eyes he met were up above on the other side's top tier. Starr looked down and blew a kiss at him, smiling as he rolled over on his back reaching for his scattered clothes. Low giggles were released behind hands covering mouths as he struggled to get dressed while lying on the floor in the middle of the pod. He was unable to stand up. A bloodstain trailed behind him. Each of the four girls quickly escaped the cell and split up in different directions.

Dylan struggled to make his way over to the poker table to try to use it for support to stand up. Kathy heard the commotion and exited the cell. Looking down at Officer Dylan, she stood behind Starr in shock. Starr waved her back into the room. Dylan dragged himself all the way to the bubble station and banged on the glass, whispered something into the speaker holes, and then collapsed before passing back out. The word "lockdown" was repeatedly announced until the riot squad rushed in.

Starr and Teya made eye contact. Starr gave her a nod of approval before they shut their cell doors. Teya had proved herself to be both reliable and trustworthy. Starr was impressed at the way she had executed the plan to teach the crooked officer a lesson he'd never forget.

Knowing all that she knew about Teya on the outside and how she moved in the federal holding facility, Starr had a good feeling about her. Teya had been on Starr's radar for quite some time since she first saw her and her female harem up in Club Panties. One day Starr had watched the cameras from her office as Teya sat back in a VIP section, low-key, and let her ladies work the club. Starr was impressed by the way she lay in the cut while her team of voluptuous escorts did their thing. That was enough to make Starr find out more about her. She knew Teya was in her late twenties, was her own boss, was West Coast bred, loved to turn up in strip clubs, and was into women: sexy plus-sized women particularly. She was aware of the fact that she was locked up for a bunch of trumped-up charges revolving around pimping and transporting underage girls across state lines. And within the facility, she had a reputation that exceeded her. Starr believed she knew enough to consider her for an initiation. Teya was considered to be a certified female in the streets who didn't take any junk from men or women, and that's exactly what Starr was looking for. She felt she would prove to be a worthy candidate to become a Double G, and that feeling was confirmed now that Teya had carried out her orders and instructions to a T.

Chapter 4

"Are you sure you know what you're doing?" C Class asked Prime after tossing his duffle bag in the back seat and hopping in the passenger side of Prime's new Porsche. "It's not too late to change your mind, bruh. I know you want to get these chicks back, but is it really worth the hassle?" You could hear the genuine concern in his tone. C Class had been thinking about it the entire time he was in California handling business for them. It bothered him that Prime had become seemingly obsessed with the the Double Gs. C Class also didn't like how much time Prime was spending with Monica. He had never doubted Prime before, and he believed and trusted that he had a plan when it came to her, but he didn't trust Monica as far as he could see her.

"Man, fuck them bitches!" Prime barked at C Class. "They don't run fucking Vegas!"

C Class held his palms up. "My bad, bruh. You know I didn't mean no disrespect. But, like I was saying, trusting that chick Monica like that is crazy. I mean, she is one of them—"

"I got this," Prime spat. His tone became more stern as he navigated his new black Panorama out of the airport area. "I'm not gonna let a bunch of dyke chicks run around our fucking city like they some puppet masters, treating niggas like puppets for their own enjoyment and gain. I'm nobody's fucking puppet, ya dig?"

"You said a mouthful, bruh. I just wanna make sure you got everything under control like you normally do. Especially that chick." C Class's attention was drawn to the airplane that roared overhead, as it prepared to land at McCarran International Airport.

"I know, fam. And, trust me, I got everything under control, including that bitch." Prime smiled as he and C Class headed outside the airport. "I got her right where I want and need her."

Ever since Prime had peeped that Monica was up to something and revealed to him how the Double Gs had sent her to set him up, on point was all he had been. He believed he had Monica in the perfect state of mind: vulnerable. After she revealed her pregnancy to him and expressed how she was considering keeping it, Prime was already conjuring up how he could utilize his potential baby's mother. He wasn't even sure he was the father, but none of that mattered. The only thing that mattered was using her to infiltrate Starr and the rest of the Double Gs.

Their new bond had strengthened with each day they risked getting together. Prime had every intent of being there the way he believed Monica needed him to be. He knew that mattered the most to Monica and it was something she deemed priceless, so Prime stood supportively by her side. He was still laughing inside at the raw emotions Monica displayed at his house. There was no doubt in his mind that he had tapped into both her heart and mind after she revealed he would be the father of Monica's firstborn.

The Gucci Mane ringtone returned Prime to the present. He retrieved his iPhone 7 Plus from his hip clip. He recognized the number and put it on his car's Bluetooth.

"Yooo?" he answered.

A deep sigh followed by a gust of hot air from one of Prime's young boys came through the speakers. Prime peered over at C Class.

"Li'l bruh, what's good?" The concern could be heard in Prime's voice.

"Big bruh, shit crazy," the young boy began. "Got some news you ain't gonna like." His words blared through the Porsche's speakers.

"Talk to me." Prime could already feel his pressure rising.

"Is this a clean line?" the young boy asked with skepticism in his tone.

"Nigga, fuck you think?" Prime barked. "What's the deal? What ain't I gonna like?" an irritated Prime questioned.

"They found Clips and Smoke at one of them Double Gs bitches' crib."

The mention of the Double Gs caused Prime to whip his steering wheel to the right and pull over. Both he and C Class possessed the same peculiar facial expressions.

"What the fuck you mean, they found Clips and Smoke at one of them Double Gs bitches' crib?" Prime had already assumed the worst, but he needed clarity on what he was being told.

"Somebody killed them," the young boy announced. "And the chick who lived there too," he added.

Prime's jaws tightened. "How the fuck did that happen? And why the fuck was they there?" Prime's question was directed to the young boy, but he was looking at C Class as he spoke. C Class shrugged, clueless.

"I'on know, big bruh. That's what everybody wondering. Thought you may have known," the young boy answered.

Prime shook his head. He gripped the steering wheel tightly. *Fucking Double Gs,* he cursed to himself. "Which one of those bitches' house was it?" he then asked.

"The girl Felicia."

"So, this bitch kills two niggas who've been playing with guns and doing home invasions since they knew how to walk and talk before they managed to kill her. That's what you telling me?" Prime couldn't believe his ears. Both Smoke and Clips were known shooters, and they had a laundry list of work they had put in. He found it hard to believe that one chick could take out both of them at the same time before dying herself.

"That's the crazy thing, big bruh," the young boy corrected him. "From what we hearing, whoever pushed them killed the bitch too."

Both Prime and C Class became wide-eyed. *A setup?* was the first thought to come to Prime's mind.

"Yo, where y'all at?" Prime wanted to know.

"We at the spot close to Freemont."

"A'ight, tell everybody to sit tight. Me and C'll be through."

"No doubt," was the last thing they heard before the call disconnected.

"Yo, what the fuck!" C Class was the first to say. "What the fuck was them niggas doing at that dyke bitch crib? And how they let a motherfucka get the drop on them like that?"

They were the same questions Prime wanted answers to. He did a quick process of elimination. Outside of his issue and dilemma with the Double Gs, the only real major problem he had in the city was with Freeze and his crew, but the last time the two saw each other there was a mutual unspoken peace treaty between them. Prime counted Freeze out for being behind the murders of two of his top earners and shooters. Only one other thought came to mind that made any sense to him. *A double cross?* It was the only logical answer Prime could think of.

"It gotta be them bitches!" Prime exclaimed. "It gotta be," he repeated and then whipped back into traffic heading toward old Las Vegas.

Chapter 5

Edge sat at her favorite pizza shop on Las Vegas Boulevard in the old area of the city, eating a large chicken and onion pizza and some Buffalo wings. She had been sitting for nearly a half hour at the agreed meeting spot, since she had arrived early. Two slices of pizza and five wings later, in walked Diamond. Edge's eyes cut over toward the doorway. She could actually smell her as soon as she stepped in the establishment. It was the same Chanel No. 5 Diamond had been wearing since she'd known her. When the door flung open, the light breeze from the outside entered and carried the fragrance inside and throughout the pizzeria. She watched as Diamond strutted over to where she sat. Edge stood to greet her.

"Hey, you." She opened and extended her arms.

Diamond flashed a half smile and leaned into Edge's invitation. The exchange was brief, but enough for Edge to get a full whiff of Diamond's scent. The reality of being a free woman and being able to hug someone she had thought about for many years had not yet set in. With all that had been going on, Edge hadn't had the chance to think or even feel anything about anything other than the mission Diamond had sent her on straight out of prison.

The last time the two had seen each other it was quick and to the point: no hug, no pleasantries. But now that Edge had handled what she had agreed to for Diamond, by killing someone without question or hesitation, she was able to focus on other things, like

Diamond. Although their agreement was simple and fair (get her out of prison, and in exchange she'd agree to put somebody in the dirt for Diamond), Edge wanted more than just to be a one-time hit woman for her ex. *That was a small price to pay for freedom,* thought Edge. But she and Diamond had history, and none of it was business related. It was all strictly personal. And Edge was already contemplating how, if possible, they could rekindle that after all these years.

"Hungry?" Edge asked.

"No. I'm fine, thanks." Diamond sat in the booth space directly across from her.

"What? You used to love Johnnie's pizza and wings," Edge recalled.

"That was a long time ago," Diamond rebutted. "Things change," she added.

"I see." Edge grimaced. Her first attempt had been shot down within five minutes of their meeting.

Edge had chosen the particular eatery thinking it would make for a great icebreaker, since it was once one of Diamond's favorite places to eat at. The two of them had so much history surrounding the establishment. It was Diamond who had actually turned Edge on to the pizza joint. Both their first date and one-year anniversary had been spent at Johnnie's. Whenever they celebrated something, they usually did it over food from Johnnie's. And Johnnie's had been the peace offering for many nights Edge and Diamond had beefed.

Edge studied Diamond, who sat stone-faced with her fingers interlocking. She realized Diamond was not the woman she remembered her to be. Aside from still being beautiful and thick in all the right places, everything else about her was different. Since the first time Edge had laid eyes on her when she had gotten out of prison, she noticed the difference, but she charged it to it being the way she handled business. The Diamond she remembered smiled and laughed a lot and was only serious when she was in the courtroom or the bedroom. The one who sat across from her now seemed like someone who didn't play, laugh, or joke about anything.

Diamond actually reminded Edge of herself. She credited that to Diamond's involvement with the Double Gs. Throughout the years, she had been hearing a lot about the organization and the way they operated, which was why she was surprised when she discovered that Diamond was part of the group.

There was an awkward silence that sat in the air. Diamond was the first to break it. "I didn't get to tell you, but I appreciate what you did." She had no facial expression and showed no emotion when she spoke.

"A deal is a deal, right?" Edge responded with the same demeanor.

"You could've gotten out and said fuck me," Diamond replied.

Edge chuckled. "I know things change, but some things don't." She stared Diamond in the eyes when she responded to her.

If anyone knew her, she knew Diamond did. She wanted Diamond to know that even though Diamond had changed, she hadn't. She was a woman of her word back then and a woman of her word now. Again, Diamond was both expressionless and emotionless; but, this time, Edge saw a familiar look in her eyes. It was a look Diamond always made whenever she believed what Edge was saying.

Diamond reached into her Gucci bag. When she pulled her hand back out, she possessed a manila envelope folded in half. Edge watched as she put it on the table and slid it in her direction.

"What's that?" Edge looked down at the envelope, already having an idea what it was.

"It's for you," Diamond offered.

Edge shook her head. "Nah, I'm good."

"Don't be prideful. Take it, E," Diamond encouraged her.

Her words rubbed Edge the wrong way. *Yeah, she definitely different,* thought Edge. She slid out of the booth's seat and stood. "Our business is done. Thanks for everything."

"Edge, wait." Diamond grabbed her by the wrist. "I didn't mean any disrespect. It's just—"

"It's cool. No need to explain. I get it," Edge said dryly. She broke free of Diamond's grip. "It's not personal, just business, right?" She spun around and made a second attempt to walk away, but Diamond grabbed hold of her again.

"No, that's not it. Please, sit back down," she insisted.

Edge turned to face Diamond. She peered down at her. "For what, D?" Her tone came across as a little harsh, but Diamond excused it.

Diamond grimaced. "Because I asked you to."

Edge ran her hand down her face. She let out a gust of hot air and shook her head, before sitting back down.

"Thank you," Diamond offered.

Edge just nodded. She never could resist Diamond or tell her no.

"I'm sorry," Diamond then said. The sincerity could be heard in her tone.

"Thanks," Edge accepted.

"I wasn't trying to be a bitch or nothing." Diamond paused. "Things are just complicated. You know. But you don't have anything to do with nothing, so you don't deserve how I was coming."

"I was thinking the same thing," Edge agreed.

That made Diamond laugh. "Same ol' Edge."

Edge made no reaction to the statement. "You didn't have to try to play me like I was some hired help or a charity case." Edge let Diamond know how she felt about the envelope she slid across the table.

"Honestly, the money was not to offend or try to buy you. It was a welcome home and thank you gift. I figured it would help in whatever your plans were now that you're home. You know I've never intentionally or deliberately tried to make you feel any type of way. Especially over no money," Diamond reminded her.

Edge pondered the statement and agreed. Diamond had always been straight up with her and played fair no matter what the case. For that moment, Edge felt as if she were sitting across from the old Diamond. "I know that."

"Good." Diamond lit up. "Now take this shit and put it to good use." Diamond slid the envelope back across. For the first time since the two had been sitting up in Johnnie's, Diamond flashed a huge smile.

Her smile was enough to ease whatever tension there was between the two. Edge reached over and took the envelope. She stuck it in her back pocket.

"So, what are your plans, now that you're out?" Diamond wanted to know.

Edge thought about the question. Other than wanting things to reignite between her and Diamond, she had none. "Nothing," she abruptly responded.

"Well, would you be interested in something?" Diamond wasted no time asking, hearing how Edge had nothing on her agenda.

"I don't think that Double Gs shit is for me," Edge replied, thinking Diamond was trying to recruit her.

"I know. That's not what I had in mind," Diamond corrected her.

Edge was surprised. She was sure that's what Diamond was referring to, but she was glad she wasn't. "So, what did you have in mind?"

"Let's ride and talk," Diamond suggested.

This time it was she who stood. Edge followed suit. Before heading for the exit, Diamond picked up a slice of pizza. "And, don't get it twisted. I still love me some Johnnie's pizza." She winked at Edge, before sashaying toward the door.

That's the Diamond I know and love. Edge smiled and strolled toward the open door Diamond held for her.

Chapter 6

The City of Las Vegas's temperature had risen, once again, thanks to the Double Gs. The media was broadcasting nonstop about the assassination of Officer Douglass, the government's key and only witness against the Double Gs, at the memorial service of Douglass's wife and daughter. Every law enforcement agency was in overdrive. That seemed to be the normal mechanics for the past few weeks.

Agent McCarthy was in shock as he sat in the hospital's waiting room watching the news. When the nurses came in and interrupted him watching it in his daughter's room, so they could wash her up, he rushed out to the common area where visitors waited, hoping the television was not occupied by something else. When the breaking newsflash first appeared across the screen of the TV in his daughter's room, he thought he was both seeing and hearing things. *Public executions? Outrageous!* He was still pissed behind the disturbing news. Although it wasn't stated or confirmed, he was positive the Double Gs were behind the hit.

He was still trying to wrap his brain around the fact that they were so bold and able to kill Officer Douglass in broad daylight with all of the cameras covering the service and all of his colleagues swarming the area. But he wasn't all that surprised considering the deaths of other agents and officers at the hands of and orders from the organization. Images of Agents Mullins and Craven illuminated in his mind.

For as long as he lived, he'd never forget Agent Mullins's brains blown out the back of his head as he lay slumped over the steering wheel, and how Agent Craven had been thrown to the back seat of the unmarked car from the impact of their crash. McCarthy shook his head in disgust remembering how the Double Gs had left a gender sign on Agent Craven's crotch, mocking the federal government. And now he would never forget today as the media continued to report the demise of Officer Douglass.

That would have never happened on my watch, McCarthy told himself as his eyes remained glued to the television. He was all too ready to get back to work and finish what he started. There was so much going on right now, and he believed that, without his expertise and knowledge, a lot more would follow. In his entire career, he had never seen anybody get away with killing so many law enforcement officers like the Double Gs had. As far as he was concerned, they were winning and the good guys were losing. He didn't think Agent Reddick was smart and levelheaded enough to strategically respond well to all that was happening. He thought him to be too impulsive. Agent McCarthy was sure now more than ever that more law enforcement officers would get killed. He felt no one could put a stop to the Double Gs reign of murder and mayhem but him, even if it meant putting his own life on the front line. He had no choice left, he felt. No one knew more than him about Starrshma Fields and the organization, he believed.

While watching the recurring story about Douglass's murder, McCarthy couldn't help but notice the newsflash at the bottom of the television. The words POSSIBLE GANG-RELATED EXECUTIONS ON OUTSKIRTS OF LAS VEGAS followed by TWO MEN AND ONE FEMALE FROM DIFFERENT GANGS FOUND DEAD IN HENDERSON HOME caught his attention. For some strange reason, he had a gut feeling that the incident was related to the Double Gs.

I hope it's not who I think it is, he thought, knowing that his deepest plant in the Double Gs organization resided in Henderson. *It can't be,* he told himself. *She's too good and has been undercover too long to have been found out,* he wanted to believe.

McCarthy pulled out his phone and texted the number only he had access to. Usually after five minutes, she'd respond. Fifteen minutes went by, and still he had no response. "Shit," McCarthy cursed under his breath.

This can't be happening, he thought, already beginning to think the worst. His agent deep undercover, Agent Marsha Briggs, known to the Double Gs as Felicia, was his best kept secret next to his latest plant in the organization.

His train of thought was interrupted by the nurse who was assisting his daughter. McCarthy made his way back to his daughter's room, where he found her sound asleep. He tiptoed in and kissed his baby girl on the forehead.

Ten minutes later, Agent McCarthy exited the hospital.

Meanwhile, in the middle of nowhere in North Las Vegas, Agent Reddick was leading a task force on an independently owned airfield. After several sightings and anonymous calls and tips, the small aircraft carrier that hovered over the memorial service during Officer Douglass's murder was traced back to the open dirt field. For hours, Reddick rendered instructions and positions until he was sure he had the stand-alone aluminum dome-shaped building surrounded. The last thing he wanted was for another agent or officer to lose their life behind him being careless, unprepared, or disorganized. He realized he had underestimated the Double Gs. It was something he didn't intend to do again from here on out.

He put his lips to the front of his walkie-talkie and pressed down on the longer side button. "On my command, all teams move out!" he yelled into the walkie-talkie.

He could see agents spilling out of vehicles rushing toward the aluminum dome. He and three other agents hopped out of the jet-black Denali with weapons drawn. Reddick ducked low looking from right to left, shifting his block from side to side. The other agents spread out and followed suit. By the time Reddick reached the oval-shaped facility, his agents had the place surrounded.

Reddick scurried over to a spot just shy of the front entrance. He put his hand in the air and used his fingers to communicate with his fellow agents. He held three fingers up and began to tuck them one after the other. When he tucked the third finger, all at once all of the agents bum-rushed the inside of the facility.

Jake was wiping his hands off with yet another oily towel, which he instantly dropped while throwing his hands up at the sight of what seemed like over a hundred assault rifles and handguns being pointed at him.

"Don't move!"

"Let me see your hands!"

"Hands in the air!"

Those were some of the shouts that were directed toward Jake Stolkoff by the agents, who by now had infrared beams covering his body from head to toe.

"Get on your fuckin' knees! Now!" Agent Reddick yelled, running up on Jake. He didn't even bother waiting for Jake to comply. Instead, he threw his arm around his neck and swept him off his feet with the swipe of his right leg.

Jake went crashing to the dirt ground. Pure, unadulterated fright filled him. He hadn't seen the news during the last four days and had no idea of what had taken place at Officer Douglass's family's memorial service, let alone his alleged connection and involvement.

"Wh . . . what'd I do?" Jake voice was shaky.

"Shut up, asshole!" Reddick barked. Kneeling down, Reddick put his right knee in Jake's back, pulled out his handcuffs, and then roughly grabbed hold of his left arm. In seconds he had Jake cuffed and on his feet.

"Suspect's been detained, everything's clear," Reddick spat into his walkie-talkie.

"Suspect?" Jake Stolkoff's eyes widened. "You got the wrong guy, mister," he offered.

"Didn't I tell you to shut your fucking mouth?" Reddick yanked him by the handcuffs.

Jake let out a cry from the tightening of the handcuffs around his wrists. He watched as the agents all dispersed and exited his private property. Within minutes, an SUV zoomed up and Reddick tossed him into the back of the Denali.

Twenty minutes later, Jake Stolkoff sat handcuffed to a metal table in a federal building, while Agent Reddick stood up against the interrogation room's wall with arms folded.

"Look, I told you, she had on a blond wig and big, dark sunglasses. It coulda been any one'a dem," Jake expressed in frustration while being detained and harassed in the small room he was being held in downtown in the old Las Vegas area. He had just spilled his guts about everything he knew about the day Officer Douglass was killed.

By now, Agent Reddick concluded that he was telling the truth. Jake was just paid to do a simple job for the Double Gs. He was hoping that they had slipped up and left some type of evidence, but catching a break like that was wishful thinking. The reality was that Jake committed no crime on his part and, once again, the Double Gs had outsmarted them. Not even the FAA could tag him for any violations. The airspace wasn't restricted. On top of that, during the investigation it was confirmed that the bullet found lodged in Douglass's head did not come from the air, but from a strategic sniper position from a safe and far distance.

Once again, there was no leads. Agent Reddick was sure that Chief Officer Mobley would remove him from the Special Crime Division. He scratched his balding head and looked down at Jake, and then back over at the two-way mirror.

"Get 'im outta here!" he yelled with an attitude.

Chapter 7

No matter what season it was, Freemont Street never seemed to change. There were only two versions of it: "day" and "night." The daytime was horrible for the people who lived even close to the lengthy, rundown drug strip. And nighttime was much more terrifying. For Esco and Freeze, it was their home. It was their foundation. It was the first location where they opened up and built on their own, besides the projects that Freeze's father once controlled. But Freeze didn't want to hide in the shadows of the respect that his father left behind, so he made his own mark by taking over the first street that his old head, Frenchie, taught him how to work. It was the same street they all once lived on, the same street the cops dragged him away from to lock him in juvenile hell. Ironically, it became the same street that became the most prosperous to him. It was home again.

The sun was just beginning to set. Esco sat in the driver's seat of the brand new all-white BMW X6, rolling up a blunt of Kush. He kept his tongue pressed down on his lip as he broke up the multicolored buds and sprinkled them along the Dutch leaf in an evenly thin line. He then took the edges of both ends in his fingertips and held the center of the gutted cigar to his lip before twirling it around in a thin coat of spit. The blunt was sealed, ready for ignition.

Freeze was sitting in the passenger's seat counting stacks of money that was just dropped off to him by one of his workers. No matter what, he always double-checked.

"Shit's crazy," Esco blurted, distracting Freeze from his count. Freeze let it slide, but he didn't acknowledge Esco as he continued. "I know you heard what happened at that pig Douglass's family service," Esco continued.

"That's good for his bitch ass. I wish I woulda popped 'em. Them bitches just keep getting in my way," Freeze retorted, still counting the folded stacks of cash. He flipped each bill and separated them, putting them in order and making sure they were all facing the same way. He liked all of his bills a certain way: all of the presidents' faces upright. "How many times I gotta tell these li'l niggas . . ." he expressed in frustration while shaking his head.

Esco waited for the red-hot car lighter to pop back out. When it did, Freeze's hand beat him to it.

"Chill. This shit's brand new. You're gonna fuck up the book value. Use ya damn lighta."

The blunt hung from the corner of Esco's lips as he cracked a smile. Sometimes he just liked to test Freeze's nerves. He pulled the blunt from his mouth with his left hand and patted his pockets with the right. After fishing for it in his sweats, he finally lit up. The first pull was always the best to him. He inhaled in a long, deep pull, closed his eyes, and held his breath until his lungs tried to force the smoke out against his will. He set the lighter next to the fun on his lap.

Freeze waved away the secondhand smoke. "Crack the window. Fuckin' with you, the police'a roll up and we'll get knocked off!"

"Stop complainin.' We own the fuckin' police. You must mean the feds. But, trust me, if they roll up on us, I suggest you take a long pull'a this shit too 'cause it means we ain't neva gonna see the streets again."

Freeze couldn't help but crack a smile at hearing the truth. He liked when Esco challenged him. "You're right.

That was just the best excuse I could come up with. I just ain't tryin'a catch no fuckin' lung cancer. And you fucked up my count. It's your turn." Freeze scooped up all of the money from his lap and dumped it over Esco's gun. He then reclined his butter-soft leather seat, pulled his Raiders fitted hat low over his nose, folded both arms behind his head, and closed his eyes.

Just as he fell into relax mode, he heard a squeaky sound that he didn't like. The noise was rapidly getting too close. He instinctively reacted.

Li'l Rodney mistakenly pulled his raggedy bike directly up to the passenger window of the X6 and almost immediately pissed himself as he stared down the barrel of a chrome Desert Eagle .45. "Whoaaaa shit!" he yelled.

"What the fuck do you want? Why you runnin' all up on my shit like that?" Freeze asked the fourteen-year-old, who was wearing a hooded sweatshirt and whose eyes were bulging.

Li'l Rodney could barely speak. "I . . . I . . ." He almost forgot the reason he came.

"Think fast, li'l nigga!" Freeze reinforced as he thumbed back the hammer and tightened his index finger around the trigger.

The sound of the hammer sliding back only erased more of Li'l Rodney's short-term memory by each second. His mouth hung open. The triangular barrel never wavered away from his nose. "I . . . I . . . ummmm."

"Nigga, spit the shit out already 'fore you get ya head blown from here to that stoop behind you," Esco yelled across Freeze through the thick clouds of weed smoke.

Freeze's eyes were empty as he studied the young boy wondering about his intentions. And then it finally registered.

"Oh, shit! That's right!" Li'l Rodney was so excited to remember why he was there that he released the right grip of his handlebar while leaning the bike to his left, balancing it as he reached into his back pocket.

Kabwooooooong!

Both Esco and Rodney flinched as the entire X6 shook from just the echo of the miniature cannon's explosion. Li'l Rodney fell off his bike and rolled onto his stomach, balling up into the fetal position as Freeze calmly exited the X6 with the smoking gun still exposed.

"Get up. You ain't hit," he softly stated as he kicked Li'l Rodney.

Li'l Rodney rolled over on his butt and backpedaled away, planting the palms of his hands and the heels of his worn-down Timberlands on the concrete. "Don't kill me! I'm just deliverin' a message," he cried out, extending an open palm forward as if it would somehow stop a bullet.

Freeze had missed the first shot on purpose. He didn't trust Li'l Rodney's quick movement. He always felt if he would be assassinated, it would be by some young, dumb punk who an older person brainwashed. To Freeze, that would be the only way. "So, what's the message?" Freeze asked, looking down.

Li'l Rodney looked around for the piece of paper that fell from his hands when the shot rang out. "It's around here somewhere. I dropped it."

Freeze was frustrated now. He pointed the gun directly at Li'l Rodney's head, this time not intending to miss. Li'l Rodney sensed it and panicked.

"No! No! It's right there! Look!" Li'l Rodney pointed behind Freeze. The envelope lay under the bike frame. Li'l Rodney kept his hands high up in the air as he further explained, "Some older guy said it came to his house. He paid me twenty dollars to deliver it to you."

Esco hopped out of the vehicle and jogged around to the sidewalk to retrieve the letter. He took one look at it and screwed his face up while passing it to Freeze. "Yup! It's for you. Let li'l dude go. C'mon, we're out."

"You can't just run up on people like that, shorty. Next time somebody offers to overpay you for a job that they could do themselves, either let them do it or run away with the money. If somethin' seems too good to be true, it probably is." Freeze let himself back into the X6 while tucking his pistol back in.

Li'l Rodney didn't get back up until the X6 pulled off and was far down the street. That's when he stood up, brushing himself off. He was pissed. "Bitch-ass nigga!" he mumbled under his breath. Although they had pulled off, in his mind, he was still afraid that if he said it any louder, Freeze would've heard him and turned back around to finish the job. He jumped back on his rusty, chipped bike and pedaled away mad at the world, but twenty dollars richer.

"You be buggin'!" Esco exclaimed as he pulled off.

"Tell that to Carlito, from *Carlito's Way,* Sunny from *A Bronx Tale,* Mitch from *Paid in Full* . . . Shall I go on?" Freeze retorted as he cracked open the envelope.

"Life ain't no movie," Esco rebutted as he ran through the red light. Patience was his biggest issue, which was why he refused to wait for the light to turn green.

Freeze didn't even notice. He was still trying to make a point. "Exactly, my nigga. Li'l nigga coulda smoked me, and you. You just neva know."

Esco couldn't argue with that. He had witnessed a lot.

Freeze continued, "Shit, look how many niggas we done put in the dirt when we was young."

"True," Esco confirmed, seeming mentally distant now. His mind traveled elsewhere. Something had settled in and disturbed him. His past had been dug up, and it resurfaced right in front of him in the most haunting way, but he kept it to himself for the moment. "So what the letter say?" he asked.

Freeze ignored the question and began to focus on reading, hoping that the letter he held in his hands wasn't anything like the last one when he was in juvenile prison. He still had it to this very day. It was that very letter that changed his entire life and what he blamed for how he turned out: heartless. Now, ten years later, here was a new one.

Youngblood,

I know it's been many years since we've been in contact. I'm not proud of myself about that. We all make mistakes. I've learned from mines. I know I'm still the last person you want to hear from, but you have to understand something. I thought I'd never see the light of day again. That's why I wrote that first letter. Being that you never responded, I can only imagine how you feel. But I will find out soon.

To get to the point, the reason that I'm writing you out of the blue is because, since you've been home, your name has been ringing bells all through the prison system. Most of the stories I hear I believe because it all stemmed from things I taught you when you was young. All the way down to the locations. I know you're doing real good for yourself. It took me a long time just to track you down.

I don't know any other way to ask other than straight up. I need your help. I know you've heard about our arresting officers getting killed. They admitted to planting evidence, and my death sentence is being overturned. I've been given a second chance, and I just need a good lawyer who can get me in quick for my appeal bond and immediate release. A paid lawyer. Any way you see fit to make my request become possible, I will be grateful, and I'll express just how much when I get released. I might be an old man, but I still put that work in.

*And I'll be forever in your debt as I am already.
I'll owe you my life. Please give this letter serious
consideration before making your decision.*
  Frenchie

Esco kept driving but stayed silent as he used his
peripheral vision to keep a close eye on Freeze. Freeze
rested the letter on his lap. He snorted and shook his
head in disbelief. Rubbing his chin, he found himself
drifting in deep thought.

This shit can't be real. As far as he was concerned,
Frenchie was as good as dead. He had long ago forgiven
him for the part he played in his father's death and his
mother's addiction to drugs, but he never thought there
was ever a possibility that he'd ever see Frenchie out in the
free world again. On the inside his emotions were running
wild but, on the surface, he was stone-faced, not wanting
Esco to bombard him with any questions. Esco was the
only one he ever told about his history with Frenchie, but
he left out the part about his parents. Not knowing how to
really feel or what he wanted to do about what he just read,
Freeze just stared down at the letter. He was still trying to
process the words on the paper. Then, without warning,
he abruptly crumpled up the letter into a hard ball, rolled
down the window, and threw it out, watching from the
side mirror as it rolled down the street in the opposite
direction. A few feet up the street, Freeze had a change of
heart.

"Stop the car!" he yelled.

"What?" Esco asked.

"You heard me!" Freeze said. "Stop the fuckin' car." His
tone was much more aggressive.

Esco slammed on the brakes. He watched as the passenger door swung open. Freeze disappeared in a flash.

Esco watched in the rearview mirror. Freeze was running down the middle of the street chasing the balled-up letter until he finally caught up to it. Seconds later he was hopping back into the X6. He shut the door without saying a word. He opened the paper, neatly refolded it, and tucked it in his back pocket. Shaking his head from side to side, Esco pulled back off as Freeze continued to remain silent.

No music played. As the moving vehicle floated up the avenue so did Freeze's mind. He traveled back in time to an incident he had remembered with Frenchie, when he was just ten years old, when the city was much wilder than it currently was.

After crack had taken over the streets in place of coke and heroin, things changed for the worse. The late eighties and early nineties set a bad example for all those coming up. It seemed like gangsters, hustlers, stick-up kids, pimps, and boosters ran the city. It wasn't easy to be from the inner-city ghettos, especially if you lived anywhere near Freemont Street, which was the wildest back then; and Frenchie was one of the reasons why, Freeze recalled.

It was a warm spring day. Freeze was coming home from school. He usually took the long way on purpose. Groups of kids his age and up were all around. He was by himself making his way holding both straps of his book bag as they came down his shoulders. He couldn't wait to get home and change into his basketball gym shorts and go to the local courts to showcase his developing skills. Freeze had made his way down the long backstreets dribbling his invisible basketball and imitating the fancy moves he would put on the nonexistent defenders who tried to guard him. It was a routine he practiced during most of the long walk home. It was the reason why he opted not to ride the bus.

Eventually, Freeze came to the beginning of his least favorite block, Freemont Street. And, to get where he was going, he had to walk the full length of it. First, the chipped-up sidewalks threw off the rhythm of his fancy footwork. Next, he hated passing through the countless amounts of junkies who popped in and out of the alleyways that somehow still managed to stay dark in the middle of the broad daylight. They always got in his way. And then there were the hookers who would try to use their filthy hands to pinch the cheeks of the cute little kid, him, and he would rudely spit on them and have to run. The only part of the route he did like was the hustlers who would pass him a dollar or two out of respect for his dad, or sometimes just for no reason.

On this particular day, aside from the traffic, the long path of Freemont wasn't that cluttered. Everyone seemed to be piled up at the corner of Las Vegas Boulevard. As he approached, he could see that both sides of the street were jam-packed. A lot of cars were parked up and down blasting the latest music over each other, mostly mix tapes. All of the hustlers and girls were out. But most of them were clumped up in one specific spot farther up the street in the same direction that Freeze was headed.

As he made his way, the crowd grew thicker with each step he took. Everyone seemed to be laughing at something. Freeze was too far away and too short to see, but was getting closer to the center of attention. He looked across the street and saw all eyes focusing on the same side he was on. They too were laughing. The hysteria didn't seem very genuine, though. It was either halfhearted or just plain fake. Most of them were over-doing it, as if they were trying to impress somebody.

As Freeze got closer, he could hear the constant roar of an engine, but he couldn't see the vehicle. He finally made his way to the first person he had to cut past to get through and be on his way.

Vroooooom, vroooooom, vroooooom, vroooooom.

The brand new Porsche 911 Turbo's engine roared as the gas pedal was repeatedly mashed. Each time it revved, the audience began to surround it and laugh even harder as if their stomachs were about to bust.

Vrooooom. Vrooooom. Vroooooooooom. The vehicle stayed parked in neutral gear.

"Again!" Freeze heard an aggressive voice yell as he finally maneuvered his way to the front of the sidewalk to see what was going on. He was too small. No one even seemed to notice him. Everyone was too focused on what was going on in front of them, prepared to share more laughter.

Vroooom, vroooooooom, vrooooooooooom.

The woman in the driver's seat followed the order with tears streaming down her face each time she stepped on the gas. Both of her hands remained on the steering wheel as she looked straight ahead.

"Again!" Freeze heard repeated.

Vrooooom. Vrooooooooooooooom.

This time the woman cried harder as she looked forward. Her sweaty palms gripped the steering wheel as she followed the absurd instructions while staring through the windshield.

As Freeze neared, through a tiny crack of people he could see that the female driver was really beautiful. She was looking his way. Through the small space, the two of them locked eyes. Although she appeared to be older than him, he could see that she was still young. Her long, beautiful hair was wildly undone and flaring out in tangled, sweaty strands. Her eyes were blackening from sleepless nights. Freeze watched as she wiped the tears from her eyes and snot from her nose. She pulled the wet strands of hair back behind her ears while keeping her eyes on the rearview mirror, watching the crowd in the back of the car. A tiny smile surfaced as she stomped down on the gas pedal on her own.

Vrooooooooom, vroooooooom.

The engine screamed to be put in gear but sat idle as she steadily continued while never easing up off of it.

Freeze finally had a clear view of what was taking place. He bullied his way toward the front of where the commotion was taking place. There, he saw Frenchie standing outside of the car with his pistol in his hand laughing along with everyone else who was looking in the direction of the back of the car. The crowd surrounded him.

"See here, this is what happens when you cross me. You pay. I make sure of that. It doesn't matter when I catch ya! Like this nigga here, who thought he could just rob one of my workers and get away with it. Obviously he ain't that smart. I know he put her up to it," Frenchie announced, referring to the young girl in the driver's seat. "Give it some more gas, bitch. He want you to supply his smoke habit. Let 'im have it," Frenchie commanded.

Everyone watched as an ass-naked Ronny was being stretched out with his chest flat on the ground. Four of Frenchie's workers each had their dead weight on either a leg or an arm of Ronny's. A fifth one, Tommy Gunz, held his head.

"Bite down on the fuckin' tail pipe! Hit the fuckin' pipe now, nigga!" Frenchie chuckled. His facial expression and tone could have been mistaken for humor, but he was as serious as a heart attack.

The exhaust pipe was halfway down Ronny's dry, burning throat. His lips were damn near melted on to the hot, thick metal. He would've rather it be the barrel of the cold chrome .38 Special that Frenchie was holding. But it wasn't. This was torture at the most extreme extent. Every time he was ready to black out, the person holding his head in place would smack him back awake. The carbon dioxide filled his lungs until the thick black smoke spilled out of his nostrils. He couldn't even cough. Being an expert crack smoker taught him how to trick the smoke to flow through his body and exit. It was the only reason he was alive for so long. What was happening was deadly. And it seemed like it would never end.

The engine kept roaring and, each time it did, the pain became unbearable. Ronny tried to hold on for as long as he could. He had been stripped ass naked in front of dozens of people, and it all came down to this. He promised himself that if he made it out of this predicament, he would change his life forever. As he ended the teary-eyed secret prayer, the engine finally seized.

Freeze couldn't believe what he was witnessing. He watched wide-eyed as Frenchie and his goons tortured Ronny with the help of his young prostitute.

Shamika took her foot off the gas pedal. She studied herself in the left side mirror this time and began to cry again. She couldn't take it any longer. Her life was once so perfect. She was a prom queen, the most beautiful girl in the school, voted most likely to succeed. It was all about her and her high school sweetheart, Melvin, who was killed in a motorcycle accident after graduation day. She never got the chance to tell him that she was pregnant with their child. It was too late. She slipped into a deep depression and never made it through college. She spent most of her pregnant days suffering from mental torment. After having the child on her own, she met "him," Ronny Blunson. He promised to change her life. He fulfilled it in the worst way.

In order to ease her pain, Ronny began to unselfishly share his drugs. It started with just cocaine. But, as his addictions mutated, so did hers. She would do anything for him. Once he realized that, he took full advantage. Every hustler wanted Shamika. Her habits had been kept confidential. They were dying for a piece of her. Ronny convinced her to do it for the first time. He told her that if she truly loved him, she would do it. After she went through with it once, he wouldn't take no for an answer ever again. He forced her to charge them. And then he felt that wasn't enough.

He began to beat her up whenever she wouldn't steal their drug packs. Sometimes the hustlers would catch her in the midst of her futile attempt and severely hurt her. Either way, she was between a hard place and a harder place. Ronny had promised that if she stole drugs from Tommy Gunz, who had the best product, it would be the last time. So she went on the mission. She sucked Tommy Gunz's dick so good that he never felt her hands enter his pockets, relieving him of his money and drugs, leaving him the burden of explaining to Frenchie why he didn't have his money, which was life-threatening for Tommy.

As Tommy held Ronny's mouth to the tail pipe, Shamika's mind started racing a hundred miles a second. Thoughts of Ronny and all that he made her do caused her to go cold again. The new tears dried up as she stared herself in her own eyes. Her foot went back down on the pedal. Her foot stayed on the pedal this time. She could hear the laughs over the steady roar of the engine. She looked in the rearview mirror and could see the five standing men ducking low. She looked to her right and could see Frenchie clutching his pistol out in the open. And then she locked eyes again with the confused young boy gripping his book bag, staring through the window at her. He was the only one who wasn't laughing. He didn't find anything funny at all. His face was pure, stone solid. She lowered her head and shot Freeze a glance that he would never forget. Her eyes seemed to be crying out for help to Freeze. She then pulled the seat belt strap across her chest, fastened it, and then: scurrrrrrrrrrrrrrrrrr smackkkkkk!

Shamika had slammed down on the clutch while releasing the emergency hand brake and she stomped down on the gas, pulling away from Ronny's bloody mouth at top speed causing his aching jaw to drop hard to the pavement.

The spectators gasped. The laughter stopped. Eyes bulged out of their heads as they had watched the tires spin out of control before the Porsche pulled into the middle of the street. Freeze watched, as Shamika had lost control of the wheel and flown into the opposite lane of oncoming traffic. She tried to cut the wheel back over, but it was too late. She was hit from the side. The Porsche flipped one full time and landed back onto all four tires. It came dangerously close to sideswiping a woman who had been watching the incident from a safe distance. The roof was crushed. Smoke rose from the hood. The other car had ended up on the opposite sidewalk in a complete wreck. Spectators began to scatter out of fear of being questioned by the police once they arrived.

Shamika was unconscious. Her body leaned forward, with her head leaking blood on the steering wheel as it rested there, blowing the horn nonstop.

The massive crowd dispersed. Some people scattered into the streets. Others stood frozen at the joke that turned into a deadly accident. Screams and cries could be heard by fleeing pedestrians as bullets whizzed through the air. Ducking heads could literally hear bul-

lets hitting and ricocheting off of walls and light poles as they came dangerously close to those seeking cover.

Freeze's eyes followed Frenchie as he ran into the middle of the street, seeming to be the most concerned. Tucking his gun in the front of his waistline, he approached the driver's side of the Porsche.

"Oh, shit!" Shamika yelled as she studied the smashed windshield.

"You a'ight?" Frenchie asked.

Shamika didn't hear him at first. The sound of the steady horn drowned everything else out, but she finally woke up and tried to shake it off. The horn stopped as she lifted her head. For the first two full minutes, she didn't remember what had happened during the past hour. She finally got the strength to shift her head and lean back against the headrest while trying to catch her breath. She was still dizzy. Her vision was blurry. Everything was spinning. Finally, a voice began to register.

"You a'ight? Can you hear me? Lemme know something! Can you move?"

She heard the string of questions and slowly turned her head to her left, still not comprehending or processing information well. She just turned toward the voice. There seemed to be at least six different people asking the same questions. She tried to focus in, still unable to respond. And then it seemed to be four, and then two, and then, as the spinning slowed even more, there was just one.

"Can you hear me? You okay?" Frenchie asked again through the shattered driver's side window. It took everything that Shamika had left to pull herself together enough to answer.

"Uhhhh, yes. I guess so," she struggled to gasp, surprised by her concern. She was almost ready to smile at the thought of her sentiment.

Frenchie grew cold and snapped, "Wrong answer, you nothin'-ass li'l bitch! That's a ninety thousand dollar car you just wrecked!" he yelled while drawing the .38 back out from his waist.

Frenchie cocked the hammer back and put it directly to Shamika's chest. In front of dozens of witnesses, he didn't hesitate. He relentlessly pulled the trigger in rapid succession. The first three shots slammed into Shamika's chest plate, giving her no time to react. Before she could even raise her hands to cover her injured chest, two more shots tore into her face. The point-blank range shattered her jaw bone and distorted her face instantly. Blood and brain matter sprayed the shattered windshield.

Blong! Blong! Blong! Each shot seemed to ring louder than the previous through Freeze as he witnessed the murder of Shamika. Even the rotation of the center barrel could be heard through the brief gasps of silence. Freeze, along with the rest of the crowd, flinched at each click. Most of them began to run for their lives. Only the ones who were with Frenchie stayed behind. The five workers kept Ronny's naked body pinned down on the ground. His face was bloody. His chest was embedded in the concrete. He was still coughing up the lung-soaking poison as he witnessed Shamika get murdered. He watched as Frenchie calmly walked back toward him, and he feared he was next.

Frenchie nonchalantly tucked the pistol back into his jeans. He wasn't concerned or scared of the repercussions at all. There weren't any cops to worry about back in those days. They were all on the payroll. The then-crooked Sin City was owned by gangsters. Ironically, it was the blatant public executions such as that one that kept the fear instilled in the community. Back then, nobody saw nothing. That's just the way it was. The streets policed themselves.

The murderous crash scene stayed exactly how it was as if help would never come. No police, no ambulance, no coroner, not even a tow truck to remove the car from the center of the street.

Frenchie looked down and focused on Ronny. "You see all of this trouble you caused out here today? That car was brand fuckin' new!"

Freeze drew his attention to Ronny, who began to panic. "Please, man. I swear, I . . ." He couldn't even finish pleading because he began to cough up blood.

"Look at him. He's fuckin' finished. Fuckin' pathetic," Frenchie snarled with disgust. He then looked up at Tommy Gunz, reached behind his back, and passed Tommy his gun. "Truthfully, this is your mess. You're lucky. Finish him off!"

Right then and there, Tommy knew he didn't have a choice. Frenchie was right. So he aimed down at the back of Ronny's shifting head as the other four men held him down. Ronny kept squirming, trying to beg, trying to pray, trying to live. None of the three was upheld.

Blong!

Freeze jumped as the sound of the weapon echoed in the air. When he looked, Ronny lay stretched out flat on the hot pavement.

"Now clean this mess up!" Frenchie ordered as the five men began to scramble.

He turned around and realized something he hadn't before. Freeze had never budged from his front-row view. Frenchie walked over to him, stood in front of him, and knelt down for them to meet face to face. "Everybody else ran. You stayed. You ain't scared, li'l nigga?"

Freeze shook his head no, gazing right past Frenchie and staring at the crushed Porsche.

"Oh, yeah?" Frenchie revealed a smile. "Just like your pops, stone cold."

Freeze shifted his eyes while clutching the straps on his shoulders as Frenchie spoke.

Frenchie rubbed his chin. "What you doin' out here? It's a hard world out here, shawty. Only the strong survive. You strong?" he asked.

Freeze shook his head up and down, still staring at the Porsche.

Frenchie smiled. "I like that. How old are you now?"

"Eleven," Freeze answered.

"Eleven," Frenchie repeated. "Well, this ain't no place for a kid. It's time for you to go home and forget about what you just saw here today." Frenchie rested his right hand on Freeze's shoulder. "If you ever need anything, you let me know, you hear me?"

Freeze nodded rapidly.

"Cool." Frenchie went into his pocket and came out with a crisp twenty dollar bill. "Go get you some pizza or something. And stay in school."

Freeze returned to the present. He let out a light snort as a half smile appeared on his face. He turned and looked over at Esco. "Yo, you know a good lawyer?" he asked Esco as they pulled into the same pizza place Freeze had gone to when Frenchie had given him the twenty dollars that day.

Chapter 8

Early the next morning, Agent Reddick entered the federal headquarters with a sluggish demeanor. He removed his dark sunglasses, tucked them under his FBI flight jacket and into his shirt pocket, and made his way to the elevator. As he passed the front desk, the guard sitting behind it hung up the phone. He called out to Agent Reddick.

"Hey, Reddick, Mobley wants ya ASAP."

Shaking his head from side to side, thinking, *this can't be good,* Reddick reduced his speed as he walked through the lobby and approached the elevator. During the short ride up, he did anything that seemed to mentally slow things down such as studying every part of the elevator, personally noting how it felt more like a time warp than a ride. The mechanical transition from floor to floor was so smooth, it felt like the great steal box never moved. The doors closed, and you were on one level of the building. They reopened, and you were on a whole other floor, one you didn't want to be on.

Agent Reddick reluctantly stepped out onto the carpet and made his way down to Chief Officer Mobley's office. The door was closed but, just as he was about to knock, it swung open.

"Get in here!" Mobley yelled, storming back behind his desk, flopping back down hard in his chair. His breathing revealed every bit of deep, burning frustration.

As Agent Reddick walked toward the desk, he avoided eye contact by looking out the huge wall-length window behind Mobley as the light spilled in. He sat in the thin leather seat and rested his right ankle on his knee trying to appear under control. Mobley wasn't buying it.

Mobley aggressively pointed his index finger at Agent Reddick the entire time he chewed him out. "I took McCarthy off the case 'cause I thought you was the man for the job. The one who would clean up his mess. But you let your rogue agent ego make matters worse for me, this case, this department, and this entire government. We're the fuckin' laughin' stock of law enforcement. Overnight rookie beat cops read the papers while they sit in doughnut shops, laughin' at us! Can you believe such a thing?" He let out a fake laugh as he slammed an open palm down on his desk. "They're laughing at us! Wow! Un-fuckin'-believable. Under your watch, every single lead we had went down the drain. We got shit, Reddick! Shit! Nothin'! Zip! Zilch! Zero! Nada! And any other synonym you can come up with."

He let out another sarcastic laugh while shaking his head. "Un-fuckin'-believable," he gasped as he reached down under his desk, pulled open the middle drawer, and retrieved the day's newspaper. He slammed it down on the desktop, facing Agent Reddick. The front page screamed at him. "This is what we got right here."

Agent Reddick's eyes were forced to gravitate to the bold headline: WITNESS UN-PROTECTION, DEATH AT FAMILY'S MEMORIAL SERVICE. It was in bold print. A shot of Office Douglass's body being hauled away from the front row followed the headline. A perfect shot of the two caskets were in the same frame.

Agent Reddick interlaced his fingers and locked his hands in his lap with nothing to say. It was a catch-22. His silence only irritated Mobley. But his voice would've done the exact same thing. So silence was the easier route. At least his words wouldn't be mocked and used against him.

Mobley continued, "In less than a week, Officer Blake, Agent Couiter, Benson, Lorretta, Cameron, and Officer Douglass were all deceased, murdered. And what do you have to show for it? Oh, that's right. Starrshma Fields. She's in custody, isn't she? On what kinda charges? She isn't facin' over one freakin' year. But she's in custody. Well, not anymore. We don't even have her. All of our leads are gone. What're we holdin' her on? Huh? Hopin' she'll confess to being the smartest criminal mastermind to ever exist? A fuckin' lesbian broad? And the federal government can't handle the likes of her? It's a fuckin' insult! And, guess what, that ain't even the best part. No. I saved that for last. There's the real bombshell here. We gotta let the bitch go. Walk right outta the fuckin' federal detention center! Humph! You haven't head the latest on her, huh? Well, I'll let you hear it for ya'self. Hang tight."

Mobley picked up the receiver of the desktop conference phone. He dialed the number and put it on speaker phone. Agent Reddick heard the other phone ringing. The call was immediately connected.

"Warden Lucas here."

"Lucas. Chief Officer Mobley here. I understand you're trying to reach me." He had already been prepped by a private source.

"Yes. Listen. I'm gonna be up front with you, Mobley. The bottom line is you haven't got anything on Ms. Fields. Please, it's in both of your best interests to release her."

"Well, we need more time," Mobley explained.

"I understand your position. Please, I'm going to ask you to understand mine. In half a week, we've had a young nineteen-year-old woman butchered under her order. Really butchered. I took the liberty of faxing over the photos to your department."

Mobley silently pulled the pictures out of the same drawer that the newspaper was in and handed them over to Agent Reddick to view for himself, which he did. His cringed facial expression revealed the gruesomeness he felt inside.

Warden Lucan continued, "And, of course as I'm sure you're used to, we have no leads. No witnesses. Not even the victim herself will give us anything."

"Well, how do you know it related to my detainee?" Mobley tested.

"Simple. Apparently, Ms. Fields's got a soft side after all. The day after her cellmate received information on a superseding indictment due to the victim's testimony, this happened. Trust me, her cellmate has nowhere near this type of power. That brings me to my next issue: a double homicide. In prison! My prison."

"From what I understand, they overdosed. And they were known drug abusers," Mobley probed.

"Correct. And they had been using while incarcerated. I admit that. But somehow, it wasn't until they had an altercation with Ms. Fields that this happened. Also, the next day, I must say, she enforced repercussions pretty quick. And, of course, there's no way to indict Ms. Fields on this but, once again, I'm sure you're familiar with that feeling. That brings me to my next issue. One of my officers was raped. He was sodomized with plungers and broomsticks by several of the female inmates. Of course, I'm sure it all sounds familiar to you. Sadly, here's the bad part. We can't prosecute. First of all, once again, as usual, there's no evidence linking this directly to Ms. Fields. However, the suspects are her codefendants. They'll never talk. In fact, they're not even denying the crime.

"See, here's the dilemma. Apparently, Office Williams had been sexually active and even abusive with many of the female inmates for quite some time. Truthfully, we knew of it, but it was under wraps. His father is well respected and holds high rank. If we choose to prosecute his son, the political backfire will be irreparable. Many of the female inmates are lined up to either testify or provide sworn affidavits against us if we choose to go after the girls involved. So it's in our best interest to transfer Office Williams to an all men's facility when he recovers. We can't even fire him. We need both sides to feel as if they won. Ironically, in doing so, we lose both sides."

"So, what now?" Mobley asked.

"Here's the point. I will detain Ms. Fields for only one more week. Just until her next bail hearing. I am prepared to bail her out myself or boldly let her go free. Whichever comes first. I want her as far away from my world as possible. I'll stick to the usual drug kingpins and scam artists. Or even the old, organized crime members such as the Mafia. What you have cursed me with here is something new and beyond my control. Do you play poker, Chief Mobley?"

Mobley's face wrinkled up with confusion. "I do," he confirmed.

"Good. That means you know how to fold. One week, Mobley. One week!"

The line disconnected.

Mobley mean-mugged Agent Reddick. "I thought I could count on you to clean up McCarthy's mess, not make one bigger than the BP oil spill. I'm removing you from the OCD. I gotta find McCarthy.

"What?" Agent Reddick yelled, jumping from his seat.

Mobley leaned back in his chair. "I gotta! There's no other choice. No other solution. McCarthy's got somethin' you'll never have. You wouldn't even get close."

"What's that?" Agent Reddick snapped.

"Someone on the inside."

Chapter 9

To make things easier, Teya moved into Starr's former cell with Kathy. Kathy was distraught. She had been crying her heart out ever since Starr was hauled back away to the Special Housing Unit (SHU). The prison claimed it was for Starr's own safety, but it really was for everyone else's but hers. Under these conditions, they were back to being able to monitor her every move. Legally, they couldn't deny her the privileges of visitation and phone use, but at least they got to keep track of who she was communicating with.

Starr lay stretched out with hands folded behind her head in the tiny six-by-nine solitary confinement cell after unsuccessfully trying to reach Diamond to let her know she had been moved. Since being back in custody, she had to deal with Diamond's phone always going straight to voicemail whenever she called, despite the fact that it was for good reason. She just hoped she'd catch her in between breaks in the trial. It was the only time of the day she was allowed to call.

As much as Starr wasn't happy about it, she understood. Every day, she watched the news or picked up the newspaper and she was reminded of how big a trial it was for Diamond. Because of it, the two of them barely had any communication. But, when one door closed, another one opened, Starr believed. It had been Monica who had been answering her phone calls and being her eyes and ears on the streets while she was on lockdown. She had been the perfect substitution and slowly was beginning to become the main attraction. Starr realized she had acquired feelings Monica during the time she had been incarcerated. Seeing her became the highlight of Starr's day.

Thanks to Monica, Starr did not have to survive off of the jail's food. Most of the food trays that came went right back out through the slot untouched. Starr refused to eat the majority of what they tried to feed her. She only ate the fruit or dessert and drank the milk or juice. If it weren't for Monica's steady visits, Starr would've starved to death. The only time she got a chance to eat was when she was out on the visit. Days had passed, and not one of them went by without her seeing Monica.

And, just to make sure Starr ate well, Monica would stay the full eight hours that was allowed. Sometimes, the two would seem to have run out of stuff to talk about. They would just sit there staring into each other's eyes while holding hands. Other times, the eight hours didn't seem like nearly enough. Each day seemed to be more intense than the one before. They both would lie awake at night anxious to see each other the next day.

Monica was completely on point. The many people who sat in the visiting room didn't even seem to exist as Starr and Monica embraced. The sweet-tasting kiss was extended. Sparks of desire and passion fueled a flame that ignited within both of their souls. The lust that was trapped in their bodies took over their minds, clouding their better judgment. They both had secret plans to cross each other. But, once they were in the same vicinity, the chemistry couldn't be neglected or ignored. They were supposed to be inseparable by design. Though Starr was much older, it just seemed so divine. They shared a part of each other, a deep connection that went way beyond scratching the surface. When they stared into the depth of each other's eyes, they were one and the same. It was as if the love was there before they had ever met. And in a way, it was.

Clear as day, Starr could vividly remember the very first time that she laid eyes on Monica. It was a full six months before making Prime her target and initiating her to become a Double G.

That night, Starr made one of her usual grand entrances into Club Panties. As she and her entourage were clearing through the dance floor, Monica turned around with half of a drink left in her hand and an overaggressive look for a young woman who was beautiful. Starr was in the center of her crew and watched, as frustrated Monica boldly strutted after Felicia, then one of Starr's most trusted friends in the Double Gs organization.

She was in the front of the line. Felicia was startled by the sudden breach. She quickly turned around and reached into her leather jacket, gripping her right-holstered pistol while snapping, as the rest of the Double Gs paused in their tracks. Even Starr smiled like a proud mother, enjoying the good old estrogen-fueled showdown.

"Don't be touchin' me, bitch! Get fucked up in here!" Felicia shouted over the music.

Monica wasn't scared for one second. She ignored the fact that she was highly outnumbered. She was by herself, but she acted as if she had entire army of her own. She snapped back, "Well, then you need to watch exactly where the fuck you're goin' 'cause you just bumped me on your way in and I don't appreciate it. You spilled half my drink, but I'm letting that slide 'cause you ain't know any betta!" Monica snarled, waving her extended index finger all in Felicia's face, embarrassing her.

Felicia had no choice other than to pull out her gun and point it at Monica's stomach, which went unnoticed to most of the people around; or they just pretended not to see anything, which was a number one rule in Club Panties: mind your business.

"How 'bout I pop a hole in ya liver and release the liquor you already did drink tonight, bitch?" Felicia growled.

Monica looked down at the pistol as she lowered her hand from Felicia's serious face. She placed her hand on her hip as she shifted her weight to her right foot and smiled. She took her left hand and splashed the rest of her drink in Felicia's eyes. "How 'bout you just wear the rest of the drink? How 'bout that, bitch!"

Felicia instantly dropped the pistol to the floor and flopped on her knees as the liquor burned her eyes. She had on her contacts. The fresh solution didn't mix well with the alcohol. She couldn't see a thing. If she would've started shooting, she probably would've hit everybody but Monica, who had swiftly slid out of the way after taking such a daring chance. Timing was everything.

The rest of the Double Gs rushed toward Monica as she bent down and picked up Felicia's gun. Monica popped back up pointing it at them, slowing them down into a complete pause as Starr made her way to the front before things got out of hand, while Bubbles helped Felicia back to her feet. Starr raised her right hand in the air to keep the rest of the Double Gs in back of her at bay. She walked up to Monica, smiling while reaching out for the gun. She didn't wait for Monica to hand it over to her. She gripped the top of it with her palm and slowly switched possession while holding a strong gaze as if she were hypnotizing Monica into submission. Once Starr had the gun, she passed it back to Felicia and then turned to the bartender.

"Give her an open bar tab for the rest of the night!"
she shouted before she turned back to Monica. "Have
a nice night. C'mon, girls." Just like that, that flock of
women disappeared into the thick crowd. Felicia was
the only one who didn't fall in line. But after hearing the
command of Starr's voice, she followed suit. She made
eye contact with Monica as she passed her. The two shot
daggers at each other.

(Phase one was complete. Unbeknownst to Starr,
Monica's plan had worked: get noticed.)

When Starr got upstairs to her office, she went straight
to her laptop and pulled up the security footage. She
searched the entire dance floor for Monica but couldn't
find her. She was gone.

Starr spent all of that first week allowing Monica to
cross her mind. She had felt the connection from the
very beginning.

The next Friday night quickly cycled around. As Starr
and her entourage entered, she skillfully used her eyes
to scan the bar and dance floor. There were no signs of
Monica. She went upstairs to her office and turned on
the computer. She tapped into the surveillance footage
of the front entrance and watched it for most of the
night. She studied every woman who came in and left.
Monica never showed. Starr figured that maybe Monica
was just one of the ones to attend for a single experience.
Starr could tell she was somewhat young, and she
rationalized to herself that maybe Monica was in her
experimental stage. The truth was that Monica was in
secret training.

The Friday after the last seemed to come around
even quicker than the one before. Starr and her team
showed up earlier than usual after making rounds of
greeting the VIP regulars. Starr made her way to her
office, locked the door, and walked to her computer to

watch the screen for everyone who entered. At first, she came across a couple of Monica lookalikes who stopped Starr's heartbeat and breath all in one. But, after Starr pulled up the frame and zoomed in on the faces, they were marked off as accidental imposters.

After an hour and a half of watching beautiful women spill in and out of her club, Starr had given up. Right when she placed her palm high over the flat computer screen to shut it, there Monica was, entering by herself.

Starr tracked Monica's every move, using all of the ground-level cameras. She watched her register her mink at the coat check, and she zoomed in as she sat at the bar. That's when Starr picked up the phone and called downstairs.

Bubbles worked as the bartender that night. She returned in front of Monica with her original order—two shots of Rémy Red—and also a bottle of Cristal with a small card attached to the napkin the extra empty glass was set on.

"Umm, excuse me. I didn't order this." Monica's voice heightened over the music.

Bubbles returned a secretly seductive grin. "It's on the house." She raised the empty glass to draw Monica's attention down to the card left on the napkin. "Enjoy. Oh, the card stays here. Memorize it and leave it. Come back next week for further instructions. Have a nice night." Bubbles stepped off.

Monica looked down at the card and studied it. On one side was simply the name of a drink, so it seemed. The reverse side explained it all in tiny typed words.

*   You are being scouted as a possible recruit for something very powerful. If you are not interested, then don't read any further. Simply fold this card in half and set it in the empty glass. If you are*

interested, memorize the coded drink on the other side. Next Friday, you will go to Club Panties's VIP level and order this specific drink every week until you are given your target and mission. Once you are given those, there is no turning back. This is your one and only opportunity.

Since that day, Starr secretly observed Monica's progression with the help of Felicia, who had also grown to love, trust, and respect Monica.

The visiting room was packed. Starr's attention became distracted by a baby crying. Both she and Monica set their attention on the incarcerated mother tending to her one-year-old daughter who was just brought to visit by the father.

"Children," Monica flatly stated.

"Yeah," Starr agreed as they gazed at the loving affection being given. They both reflected on their own motherless childhoods and tried to remember that same exact feeling of love before they were abandoned. Somehow, they both went down separate roads, and now here they were, in front of each other.

"You should be my baby momma," Monica joked, lightening up the mood.

Starr giggled at the thought. "Yeah, right. I'm the older one. You should be mines."

"Age don't matter," Monica retorted.

"Oh, yeah? Seniority comes into play when it's time to get up in the middle of the night and heat up a damn bottle."

"I'm sure we'd be up anyway," Monica seductively replied as she kicked off her heel and rubbed her soft foot up and down Starr's leg to reinforce the sexual innuendo.

Starr's face gained a shade of complexion as she blushed. Monica felt it was the perfect time to switch the topic when Starr clearly had her guard down.

"Anyway, so, tell me how you got into all of this. I'm not talkin' 'bout the very beginning. I know we're not supposed to speak on it, but you can trust me. If it helps, leave names out. I'm curious how you rose to the top so quickly and inherited this all."

Starr lowered her voice in a stern tone. "Monica, you know the rules. The rules were established long before me. I take them seriously," she stated while staring Monica in her eyes. She was really trying to avoid fulfilling the request. She felt that she had spilled too much to Monica already. Most of it was just ghost stories. Some of it was true. Still, even a little of the truth was way too much. But Monica was just undeniable, and persistent.

"Pleeeeeeease?" Monica begged while batting her long eyelashes.

Starr reluctantly submitted. She was about to share what she hadn't with anyone else ever before, not even Diamond. She leaned her breasts over the table and lowered her head but kept the eye contact as her tone descended into a softly private one to make sure that no one else could come within earshot. She slowly began.

"Back when I was in college, I had my first real girlfriend. She was beautiful. I was so in love with her throughout my entire freshman year. She loved me too. She was a junior. Real popular. All of the girls liked her, and all of the boys wanted her. Somehow, she managed to stay single until I came along. It was an instant connection. One that couldn't be denied. Sorta like ours. Our backgrounds were so similar. I grew up without a mother; so did she. In fact, we shared so many of the same childhood experiences. Anyway, we became inseparable. We did everything together. Eat, sleep, bathe, study. If it were possible, we would've attended the same classes. But there was just one slight difference that would soon change. She was extra social. A real partygoer. That's just how college life is. But it was more than just the regular dorm parties. She attended all of the local hotspots in Atlanta.

"When the first semester ended, I asked her to stay in Las Vegas with me. She had always wanted to go there. So we got a high-rise loft and leased it on a month-to-month basis because we wouldn't be out of school for long. It was a dream come true for her. She jumped right into the fast lane as if she had been there all of her life. I still wasn't really into partying, so she started going out on her own. Someone introduced her to Club Panties. There, she found a set of new friends. Ones much older. They embraced her and gave her everything she wanted. They spoiled her to death. She would meet them every weekend. Each time, she would try to drag me along, but I never would go.

"One Friday night, she came home early seeming kinda spooked. She wouldn't fill me in on all of the details. She just claimed that her new group of friends asked her to do somethin' kinda strange. I tried to get it out of her, but she just kept sayin' it was top secret. But she assured me that everything was okay. She even said that she would do what they asked, but still, she never said what it was. So when she went to sleep, I dug through her purse. I snooped around until I found the card."

"The one with the drink order?" Monica asked with her full attention invested.

"Yup. So I woke her ass up. She was pissed. However, she did explain that her new friends were a group of older women. And, not only that, they claimed that being that I was her girlfriend, they wanted to meet me too. Strangely, they knew almost everything about me already, and we'd never met. They knew all about us both. I couldn't believe it. So I became curious. I had to see for myself. But I had to wait until Lastarya carried over her secret order. She never revealed what it was to me. She just said she hated that it involved a man. That's when I got worried.

"It was all set up for the next night. She gets all dolled up. I mean, really dolled up. The works. It's like, she can't even look at me. She gave me a long kiss before she left. I waited up for hours. I finally fell asleep. When I woke up the next morning, she still hadn't returned. I began to get worried. The next night comes. She still didn't show. The entire weekend passed. It was like she just vanished. I called around to everywhere she could've possible been. I thought of calling the police to report her missing, but I really hate police, so I left them out of it.

"I was sick. I cried for four more days straight. The next Friday night had come around. I hadn't been out of the apartment all week. The only thing I had to go on was the card I kept that I had never returned to her purse. That was another reason I didn't go to the police, because if it was true that these people knew everything about us, then they had to be connected. So I wasn't putting myself out there, knowing they wouldn't do anything but open up a random case file they'd never look into. I did my own investigation.

"That next Friday night, I put on my best dress, heels, a li'l touch'a makeup, and I headed to Club Panties myself. I had no idea of what to look for. The card was the key and also my best clue: the drink order. Obviously, she was supposed to approach the bartender, so that's what I did. I went straight to the bar. There were three women to choose from. A young white one; I ruled her out. A slightly older black one; she was a good possibility. And then there was a middle-aged exotic-looking woman. She seemed to be mixed. She was beautiful and focused. The other two were flirting with male customers, but not her. She attentively catered to only the women. So, the first chance I got to catch her attention, I summoned her over. When she got to me, I caught the strangest feeling. But, I was so nervous. Especially from the way she was looking at me. She must've sensed it, and she smiled to make me feel at ease as she asked me for my order. My mind drew a blank. I tried to remember the code. I couldn't. So, I fumbled around in my purse until I found the card. I pulled it out and began to read from it. She lost her breath and quickly snatched it from me as she looked around with caution. 'What are you doin' with this, Starr?'

"I was shocked to hear her call me by my name. Me and this woman had never met. 'How do you know my name? Where's Lastarya?' I asked. She stuffed the card in her cleavage and stared at me with this intense glaze. She lowered her voice. 'Don't ask questions. Stay here. I'll be right back,' she ordered. I watched her walk away to the other end of the bar counter. She picked up the phone and stuck a finger into her open ear to hear over the music. She shook her head while speaking, and then she'd look back down the bar at me. She quickly disappeared into the back. In just a few minutes, she returned with a drink and a small pouch. She slid them both to me, leaned in, and said, 'This is what you asked for. Don't screw it up and you'll have all of the answers you'll ever need. But screw it up and you'll have all the answers about the afterlife.' She stood back up straight, smiling as if she hadn't just made the most blatantly chilling threat I'd ever heard in my entire life. But I wasn't nervous anymore.

"I excused myself and went to the ladies' room. I sat in the first stall and removed the small spy camera and the phone. Back then, the phones weren't all high-tech like they are now. They didn't have cameras and video recorders built in them. Not even texting. Just e-mail. When I turned on the phone, it went straight to an e-mail. There was a message I had to open. It explained who I was to look for and what I was to do. And just my luck, he was there that night.

"Originally, I was only given a physical description and a name I don't want to reveal to you. You probably don't know him anyway, but still. Moving on, the information I was given wasn't close enough, so I had to play it cool like I already knew him. I rolled through the club, tapping people who seemed to be a part of the 'in crowd,' asking if they'd seen him. Everybody knew him. I was steered all of the way upstairs to the VIP level. Being that I was a fresh, pretty face, I was let right in with no problem. I noticed him the second I saw him. He was much older than me. Luckily, he was surrounded by a group of men instead of women, which would've made it extra hard for me.

"I went straight to the bar and ordered a drink. I sat there barely sipping it and waiting for just the right moment. I began to think that it would never come. When he finally got up to go to the bathroom, I made my move. As you know, the ladies' room is directly across from the men's. So I timed it perfectly. When he was coming back out, I pretended to be drunk, and I stumbled into his arms. This muthafucka looked like he wasn't gonna catch me at first."

They both laughed.

"But he did. He looked at me like I was some drunk, dizzy bitch as he stood me back on my feet. That's when he got a better look at me. I could tell he was stunned. I saw the lust in his eyes as I ignored him while strutting away from him. He followed, calling me back. I had to play hard to get because I knew men of his caliber turned down groupies. They want the ones who they think think they're a challenge. It's like I had to reverse the reverse psychology on him."

The last statement lost Monica, but she was still following the overall story as Starr continued, refusing to slow down and wait for her to catch up.

"So, anyway, he stopped me as I approached the bar and kicked the usual game. Blah, blah, blah; I'll skip past the weak shit. I acted all stuck-up like I wasn't tryin'a hear him at first. And then I let him think that he finally wore me down. He gave me the keys to his car and told me to pull it around the front. Apparently, he had some real sort of solidified status. I can't front, he was well-respected. He was far from scared of me stealing his car or anything like that for that matter. I began to have second thoughts, wondering what I was beginning to get myself into. But every time I had doubts, I began to think of Lastarya. I had to find out what happened to her.

"I did what I had to do. I went outside and searched for his black LS 450, got in, and pulled around to the front. He had the nerve to have me out there waiting for a half hour sittin' in his car listenin' to his old-ass music. I was pissed, especially at the fact that when he finally did come out, he had two hoochies with him. One on each arm. They both gave him a kiss on the cheek before he got in the passenger's seat. He looked at me with this weird-ass grin on his face. He was real old school. And he was cautious, very cautious. So I had to stay on point. For all I knew, he sent his goons to ambush me at the hotel. I began to wonder if that's what happened to Lastarya. Like I said, I needed to know. I was responsible for her. I brought her to Las Vegas.

"So I followed the directions he gave me. He led me straight to the Ramada Inn. Other than that, we hardly spoke. I guess he just figured he'd pull off a quick hit 'n' run, and that would be that. The whole time I was driving, I was thinking about what the e-mail orders were. I didn't have a clue of how I was gonna pull off such a thing. Especially on a man like him. I realized why Lastarya was acting so strange, and why she couldn't tell me what she was ordered to do. She knew I would never let her leave.

"Anyway, I'm driving, trying to figure out my strategy. I began to feel his hand run up and down my thigh. Ugh! I was grossed out. But, I didn't show it. Shortly after that, I was in the parking lot in the back of the hotel. He had the nerve to have a room on the third floor already. He probably been traffickin' different sleezies back and forth for who knows how long. Oh, no! I had somethin' for his ass. Filthy men. Too arrogant and downright nasty.

"Soon as we got in the room, he jumped dead on me, girl. He tried to stick his tongue in my mouth. I had to find a way to slow his fast ass down. So I pushed him away and backed him up against the bed until he was laid flat on his back. He started unbuttoning his shirt and unfastening his belt, as I stood on the bed over him, givin' him a nice clear view up under my dress. Girl, he pulls a gun from the back of his waist and laid it on the nightstand. I could tell he was studying my face to see my reaction, but I stayed sexy and pretended to ignore it. I closed my eyes, licked my lips, and started slow dancing right over his face. I was driving his old ass so crazy. I guess he couldn't take it anymore. He reached up and grabbed my waist. I wasn't ready for it. The room spun around, and I realized I had been flipped on my back. He was hovering over me. He was strong. He was breathing hard. He kept trying to kiss me, but I kept turning my head away."

While Starr was telling the story, she and Monica had been holding hands the entire time. As Starr continued, Monica felt Starr's pulse rising, and her soft palms began to moisten with sweat as she mentally relived the moment. But they never broke eye contact.

"I was trapped under him. It wasn't like I could just get up and leave. I could tell by the way he would smile every time I fought not to kiss him that my evasiveness was only turning him on. He squeezed down on my wrists and knelt between my legs, pinning me down. I didn't like it. I started to regret it all. It was taking me back to a dark place where I didn't want to be and thought I'd never go again. So, I calmed down and stopped struggling to get free. I allowed him to kiss me until he loosened up his grips on my wrists. I wrapped my arms around his neck as he kissed me and then I started pushing his head down my body. I let him stop at my breasts for a few minutes and then I pushed him down to my stomach. He started using his fingers to play with my pussy through my panties, so I pushed his face down there. He started eating me out while I palmed the back of his head. He really like that shit. So, I wrapped my legs around his neck, locking him in as he held on to my thighs. He just kept sucking on me."

Monica watched Starr's pupils begin to dilate as her sweaty palms began to dry up and go cold.

"The more he licked me, the angrier I got from his touch. I started to hate him. I wanted to kill him. I wanted to kill him for touching me."

Just like back then, when it was happening, and even now, Starr began to have vivid flashbacks of the night her foster father tried to rape her. She despised men and hadn't allowed herself to be touched by one since. She only desired the sensitivity of a woman. So what had happened on that particular night brought out the worst in her. Her frigid clench on Monica's hand tightened.

"So, while he was down there violating me, I squeezed my thighs around his neck as hard as I could while I reached for his gun. I smacked him so hard over his head with it that it flew out of my hand and slid across the room. If I hadn't knocked him out, I would've been in some serious trouble. I looked down and saw the top of his head split wide open, but it wasn't bleeding yet. The gash was just white but getting redder by the second.

"I crawled backward on the bed to pull myself from under him. He was out cold. Face flat. I had to move fast while he was still unconscious. I quickly undressed him until he was completely naked and then I ripped the telephone cord out of the wall and used it to hogtie him in the middle of the bed. I made sure he couldn't move. And then I used his own boxers to gag him. He was still out cold. I picked up my purse and got the camera out. I snapped a few shots, but it wasn't enough. I decided to get really creative.

"I sensed how much of a gangsta he and everybody else thought he was so I had an idea. I picked up the gun. It was a chrome .44. I ejected the clip and removed six of the bullets and popped the clip back in just in case he woke up and broke loose. I would've shot him dead. I stood behind him shaking the loose bullets in my hand, smiling. One by one, I stuck a bullet in the tip of his asshole and took a picture of me shoving it in his rectum. The second one woke him right up. He was screaming through the gag. I took pictures of that, too. The violation. It left tears in his eyes. Here we were, I didn't even know him. Never heard of him. But he was paying for the sins of all men. I was so glad he was finally awake. I shoved all four of the remaining bullets into him with one hand while taking pictures with the other. His screams began to get so loud. And then the worst happened. I underestimated how strong he was. I heard a snapping sound. He had broken loose. I reached for the gun, but he kicked it off the edge of the bed while pulling the cord off of him. I started to go for it but said, 'Fuck it!' I grabbed my shit and ran for my life."

"So what happened after that?" Monica asked, captivated by such a story.

"To him? I'm not sure. There's different versions of the story. I never seen or heard from him again. I had also taken the keys to his car. I got pulled over not knowing he had another gun under the seat. That gun was used in previous murders. I was almost locked up for life. That's how I met Diamond. I was her first case. She rescued me."

Starr released Monica's hands and set hers on her lap. She leaned back and looked up in the air, saddened. "Turns out Lastarya ended up really having sex with the target. She caught feelings and tried to save him. They ran off together. But they didn't get far. Within the next two weeks, they were both hunted down and executed."

It took everything in Monica not to make any reaction. The last thing she wanted to do was alarm Starr and draw any suspicion. She knew Starr had the ability to sense and pick up on things if she studied a person long enough. A sense of nervousness invaded her body. She continued to match Starr's stare to avoid any suspicion, but it wasn't easy. It felt as if Starr could see right through her.

She couldn't believe how much the ending of the story about Starr's past lover related to her own real-life situation. Outside of the obvious of what would happen to her if they found out she was a fed, she knew if Starr or anyone in the Double Gs organization discovered she was dealing with Prime, she was as good as dead.

Monica listened attentively as Starr brought her Double Gs journey to an end. She was glad both the story and the visit were coming to a close. Any longer and Monica believed she would've passed out from anxiety or wound up confessing right there on the spot.

It wasn't until the visit had ended and Monica was out of the federal holding facility that Monica's heart rate decreased and she could breathe. She knew her secret involvement with Prime could get her killed and destroy everything she had been working so hard on. Since McCarthy had been dealing with his daughter's illness and hadn't really been in contact with her, she found herself slipping deeper and deeper. Normally his directions and instructions would be the guidance she needed to stay focused and stay the course while trying to infiltrate the organization from the inside. But as the days progressed, Monica became a confused woman with feelings for the woman she supposed to take down and the man who was a hardened criminal.

Monica shook her head. *I can't keep living like this. This shit has to end,* she concluded as she scurried over to her car.

Chapter 10

There was a light knock at Chief Officer Mobley's large oak wood door. "Come in," Mobley yelled with acceptance. As the door swung open and closed, Mobley reclined in his seat. "Tom. Good to see you. Have a seat."

Agent McCarthy sat across from Mobley, watching the bright sun begin to set behind him. The world seemed so delicate and peaceful on their side of the glass. His thoughts were interrupted by Mobley leaning forward and speaking in a stern tone while locking in eye contact and pointing to him with his index finger.

"Tom. I need you to know that you can do this. We had our differences, but we're still on the same team. I'm gonna ask you this one time: are you up to this?"

Agent McCarthy thought about all that was going on with his family. His daughter. His wife. And then he thought of all the other families of the most recent victims: the Douglass family, the Craven family, and all of the others. "I'm up to it."

Mobley reclined in his chair, staring at Agent McCarthy with blatant scrutiny while he drummed his fingertips across the edge of his desk as if he were typing two hundred words a minute on an invisible keypad. He suddenly stopped. "All right. I took the liberty of putting together a special task squad to serve at your disposal, the best of the best when it comes to the OCD. You have full discretion. But don't fuck me on this. Agent Reddick screwed a lotta shit up. We have nothing, Tom. Shit. Zip.

Zero. And guess what? The broad's free tammara. Not
bailed out. Free. All charges dropped. We got nothin' ta
hold her on."

Agent McCarthy showed no signs of being surprised.
He knew that the only reason he was being pulled back
in was because of his secret agent on the inside. Still, he
listened as Mobley continued.

"This case scares the heck outta me. I've neva seen
nothin' like it. Nothin'! And you know me, I've been
around. For God's sakes, I seen Kennedy get his brains
blown out right in front'a me. The freakin' president. I
thought nothin' would come as a shock ever again. I was
there during the Oklahoma bombing. The freakin' van
drove right past me days earlier. I personally brought the
DC snipers in. I oversaw the entire investigation. Fuckin'
John Gotti Sr. had a $500,000 hit on me when I became
head of the OCD. So tell me, Tom, afta all'a that, what the
fuck's this we're up against now? I go through the files an'
all I see is a buncha professional women. I go through the
case, I see cold-blooded murderers, anybody in their way.
I'd fear for the president if he wrongs these women in any
type'a way. Tom, you're the fuckin' key."

Chapter 11

The visit with Monica was over. Starr was back in her solitary cell wondering if she had revealed too much to Monica. Although she shared the bulk of her introduction to the Double Gs, she made sure she had left out some of the key incidents that had occurred. She lay on her bunk and locked herself into the rest of her history.

That day she left the courthouse after getting bailed out, the phone in her bag rang for the first time. She had forgotten all about it. She dug into her purse and reluctantly answered. "Hello?"

"Nice work. A little sloppy, but you'll get the hang of it," a vaguely familiar voice proclaimed.

"The hell I will!" Starr snapped. "Never the fuck again. I did what I did. Now I want some answers!" she demanded as she strutted down the white steps. The early afternoon sun was causing her to squint as she held the phone to her ear.

"Study your left. When you see a car pull up to the curb, get into it. From there, you'll have all the answers you'll ever need for the rest of your life." The articulate, stern older female voice hung up.

Starr placed her left hand over her eyebrow and extended five fingers as if she were saluting a soldier. It provided shade for her to see the snow white wide-body Benz S600 sparkling as it pulled over, stopping directly in front of her path. The windows were tinted. She cautiously looked both ways as if she were about to cross the busy street, before strutting to the right side back door as the female chauffeur made her way around to let Starr in. She was only half surprised to see Mirage in back, the bartender from Club Panties who had slipped her the pouch. Starr sat next to her, and they both crossed their legs in the far opposite direction of each other. Mirage seemed to have a chip on her shoulder for some unknown reason. She rolled her eyes up in the air as she reached her right palm out to Starr.

"Phone and camera, please," she demanded with attitude as if she despised Starr. She stared up at the sunroof as she waited.

Starr folded her arms as she refused. "No. Not until I get some answers."

"Chy-ald, pell-ease." Mirage slowly pronounced every exaggerated syllable while still holding her open palm in Starr's direction.

Starr forced a heavy sigh as she unfolded her arms and dug into her purse. She came up with both items and slammed them down into Mirage's hand. Mirage set the camera on her lap and then proceeded to take the phone apart. After inspecting every inch of it, she put it back together and turned it on while studying the screen. She dialed a random number and listened to the way it rang. When a stranger answered, she hung up. "It's not bugged," she whispered to herself. She set it on her lap and picked up the camera. She spoke into the air while staring at it. "Ain't you lucky they weren't smart enough to get this film developed," she indirectly stated to Starr as the car pulled back off. She stuck the thin camera into her bra and pressed a button on her door to roll down the electronic window. She snapped the flip phone in half, disconnected the battery, and threw it all into the middle of the street. The car behind it ran over it.

Starr turned her body halfway around to look out the back window as it happened. "She'll get you a new one," Mirage stated looking straight ahead.

Mirage was upset, and most would conclude that she had every right to be. She was part of the second half of the first generation Double Gs, and she had never once met Queen Fem in person. In fact, no one other than the original founding members and Starr had. Mirage was convinced that one day she would, but it hadn't happened yet. It was beginning to seem as if it never would.

It had been over twelve years, and Mirage had watched Queen Fem's identity get buried deeper and deeper. Those who got close to her mysteriously disappeared. Queen Fem became a phantom. Many began to wonder if she ever existed. Most believed that she was just a fictitious character created by many of the original members. Maybe all of them were Queen Fem combined. To everyone else, all Queen Fem was, was a voice. An authoritative one. Whatever she softly demanded in her light tone and sophisticated speech was done. And it was the same voice every time. The same one that came through every member's phone during unpredictable times. That was Queen Fem. Her voice was the sound of calm fear and consequence without remorse. Nobody wanted to test her, defy her, disgrace her, fail her, or look for her. But if she ever called, you would come running.

Mirage's strange orders had been made very simple: bail Starr out. Make sure she kept her mouth shut first. Retrieve the camera and phone, and bring her to this specific location where she would switch vehicles.

How does this little, young bitch who hasn't put in any real work get to meet her? It's bad enough that her girlfriend fucked up and got dealt with. And then this bitch gets sloppy, and then arrested. She sure ain't the highest card in the deck. *Mirage's thoughts screamed the sound of her own voice throughout her head. She was first suspicious when Queen Fem ordered her to go after Lastarya in the first place. She wondered how Queen Fem knew Lastarya was there. And why she knew so much about a young girl who wasn't from Las Vegas and then sent Mirage to go get her. That wasn't the regular method of their operation.*

It started with a drink. It was sent to Lastarya as she mingled her way around the dance floor. The cocktail waitress tapped her on the shoulder, whispered into her ear, and pointed to Mirage, who was standing behind the bar. Lastarya held the glass in the air and thanked her from long distance. Within the next half hour, Lastarya found herself at the bar ordering another drink. She wanted the same one she had just had because she never tasted anything like it, not knowing it was the mix of the Double Gs' coded drink order. She sucked it right up.

Mirage purposely serviced Lastarya, making her feel comfortable, welcome, and singled out. Although Mirage was much older, the two made stretched amounts of small talk before Mirage took her break. She escorted Lastarya through the club to a private VIP section to meet a few of her friends, who were also older. They all embraced Lastarya, making her feel special. Lastarya was quite impressed with the high-class group of women. They were all professional. There were at least six of them. They each descended from different nationalities but bonded as one. The energy seemed to flow so purely. The unbalanced age difference became only an afterthought when trying to place times on the charming stories that were being spread around. It was fun.

Lastarya met the same group of women for four full weekends in a row. Then, on one particular night, the ladies were acting a little strange to Lastarya. She

*couldn't make out half of the things they were saying,
as if they were speaking in coded plain English. Mirage
hadn't made her way over from working the bar yet.
One of the ladies suggested that Lastarya go order
drinks, even though they were being served by cocktail
waitresses. They made sure that Lastarya had the
coded drink flawlessly memorized before they sent her
to the bar. She was only to give the order to Mirage,
and that's exactly what she did. And all she came back
with was a spooked face and a small card that she kept
twirling around in her fingers before she finally stuck it
into her purse. The rest of the women just stared at her.
Their bright smiles, only a façade, slowly escaped their
beautiful faces. Seriousness kicked in. They began to let
Lastarya in on the most detailed intimate information
about her and her lover, Starr. Not to scare her, just
to open her eyes. But there was no turning back. The
card was in her possession. The ladies had exposed
themselves. There were only two options on the table:
ride or die. Lastarya ended up temporarily creating a
third: run.*

*The Benz slowly pulled off of the highway and rode
the shoulder of the curved exit. It drove straight down
the main road of the luxurious scenic route small town
unfamiliar to Starr. After passing many roadside hotels,
restaurants, car lots, and gas stations, the vehicle finally
pulled over at an empty lot of an office building under
renovation. It parked alongside an all-black Rolls-Royce
Phantom with deep black tints. Starr didn't know what
to do. Mirage did. "Get out," she snarled.*

Starr wished for nothing more than to escape
Mirage's unfriendly presence. She huffed heavily and
stormed out of the Benz, slamming the door and staring
at the Phantom. The Benz pulled off. The older female
chauffeur of the Phantom stepped out, strolled to the

J. M. Benjamin

back with a professional smile, and opened the door for Starr.

Starr entered the leather-wrapped interior. She sat with her back to the tinted divider, facing the rear windshield, staring the ghostly legend in her eyes.

And that was how it all originally started.

By the time Starr woke from her travel back in time, she was only minutes away from being a free woman.

Chapter 12

For those who don't know, being released from confinement isn't always such a refreshing feeling. Depending on how much time you've done, it becomes a great challenge. For starters, a state prisoner is forced to live way up in the mountains, where there are no normal traces of the society he or she once knew. Day in and night out, all you are aware of are great masses of land and the high terrain of mountains, deep woods, and dirt roads. No in-betweens. Steel fences, stone walls, and high gun towers. And that's just on the outside.

The inside is a world inside of another world, which is all set apart from the real world. Human nature is to adapt. The reality changes. The more you are confined to these new living conditions, the more it becomes home. It's such a slow process. After ten years or more, it seems virtually irreversible. Some people would rather not be released. To be thrown back into the real world in a single day becomes unfathomable. When time and technology has worked against you so for long, you develop a fear that's translated into hate for it. You despise the change, the constant reminders that you've been left behind. How long would it take to readjust? Why bother? Some choose to catch a new charge just to stay. Others would rather die. Most would rather take their chances on the outside.

With nothing but forty dollars and a bus ticket, Frenchie was released in nothing but a sweat suit, with all of his legal work. It was nearly an eight-hour ride back

into a society that he hadn't known in well over a decade.
He was more nervous than happy. A lot had changed.
Some things hadn't. He had done a lot of dirt. A lot of
lives had been altered, affected, or erased on his account.
To jump right back into the fire seemed senseless. Surely,
his implanted fear had worn off. There was a whole new
breed out there. He got a taste of the constant evolution
every time one of the young inmates came through the
facility. They never lasted long. Most of the time, bets
were placed against the length of their survival.

Gradually, the scenery began to change by the hour.
First, it was all mountains and dirt roads. And then, it
was long rows of cornfields and farmhouses. And
then it was cattle and horse ranches. And then the roads
became paved with cement. They turned into smooth
highways. The old, wooden houses became stone or
brick-layered. They were spaced out by the acres. The
neighborly distance got closer and closer until the only
thing in between was a small yard, fenced off by a low
fence or gate. And then there were gas stations, malls,
towers, car lots, restaurants, amusement parks, skyscrapers, exotics cars flying in and out of the lanes.

Life had gone on. And it didn't care that Frenchie was
back. It wouldn't give him time to readjust or adapt or
even try to blend in as if he hadn't been gone forever in
a world where a decade is like a century. No. The world
wanted its answer right now. The choice must be made.
Are you returning as a tax-paying citizen with a job? Or,
are you rejoining the underworld? Those who tried to
balance both failed the quickest. Those who had a real
plan had time. Frenchie's plan was to let society not
dictate, but decide. They would make the choice. *How
receptive will the streets be? A welcoming party? Or a
lynch mob?* he wondered.

Only one thing was clear to Frenchie: if he happened to be tested, he had no problem going back. So, he felt he had nothing to lose. And, as the long ride finally came to an end, Frenchie got his answer. Society had made the choice for him already.

There seemed to be hundreds of pedestrians on both sides of the street. People were everywhere, ignoring each other as they were passing by. As Frenchie stepped out onto the sidewalk, he sparked a Newport and inhaled the fresh taste of menthol. As the smoke swirled around his closed mouth's tongue, he saw what he was looking for. There he was in the flesh: Freeze leaning against the back door of the fire engine red Rolls-Royce Phantom. Frenchie hesitantly walked up to him, stomped his cigarette out, and the two embraced in a hug.

Chapter 13

It had been awhile since she had been in a casino but, just like riding a bike, it comes right back to you once you hop back in the seat, and that's exactly how Edge was feeling. Prior to being set up and going to prison, she practically lived in the casinos. Whenever she wasn't with Diamond, you could find her in Bally's or any of the other Caesars properties in Las Vegas. Taking the twenty grand Diamond had given to her at Johnnie's pizzeria, Edge bought in for half of it at one of the casino's blackjack tables, and she was already betting the table max of $500 per hand. She had already turned the ten grand into fifteen in less than fifteen minutes.

The dealer slid Edge and two other players their cards face up. The player on her left was buzzed and had a two of hearts. Edge shook her head because she already knew she was going to go twenty-one or bust. With the exception of the first time she played, the woman busted on every hand. The player on her right was more her speed. She was an older lady, easily her grandma's age based on the hard wrinkles that folded on her face and the sag in her lightly puffed cheeks. Her dark brown bob-cut wig tried to help her appear young, but Edge knew better. She glanced at her ten of spades. Not the way she played her game, but she knew she had to make the card work for her. The house dealer had a four of diamonds, and Grandma had a six of clubs.

Their eyes locked and she licked her lips. Edge winked at her. When her eyes met the attendant, she noticed the slight head shake of disapproval followed by a discreet smile.

"Trying to have them both I see," the dealer made small talk after she dealt the second set of cards. The drunken woman had a three of clubs. Edge was served a four of clubs, which pissed her off even more. The house had an ace of diamonds, and Grandma had a queen of hearts.

"I can if I want them," Edge bragged through clenched teeth.

"Hit me!" the buzzed woman commanded.

Edge hated that she controlled the board but she knew, with her hand, she'd join her. "Hit me," Edge replied subtly and took a sip of her doctored club soda.

"Hit me." Grandma took the risk.

The drunk woman had the best advantage with only five. Since the ace was already declared an eleven, the house had fifteen, and Grandma was holding sixteen. Edge counted on fourteen and being in the next best position.

The drunk woman was dealt the ace of hearts, Edge was served the two of clubs, Grandma busted with the king of diamonds, and the house held steady with the three of spades.

"Damn, ma," Edge whispered. She hated to see Grandma go because, next to her, she was the only sane one.

"Hit me!" The drunk woman was confident in her sixteen not going over. Edge didn't feel good about the hand. The house held with a soft seventeen and she knew that the chances of getting a five or less were slim. But the money was good if she continued.

"Hit me." Edge continued the game.

The drunk woman was dealt the jack of hearts, busting her at twenty-six. Luck spared Edge with the four of hearts, giving her another victory.

The attendant pushed her winning tokens to her hand. Edge tipped the dealer a twenty-five dollar chip and then said, "Color me up," requesting to turn her green twenty-five dollar chips and her black one hundred dollar chips into gray $5,000 chips. She stood up and took the tokens and put them in her right pocket. She'd won a few dollars short of ten Gs, and it was time to cash out. She decided it was time to quit while she was ahead.

As she made her way to the cashier's cage, her cell phone buzzed on the side of her hip. It was a text message from Diamond. It was an invitation to come hang out with her and some of her friends. Edge thought for a moment before replying. When she got to the cage, she pulled her casino chips out and set them up on the countertop. While the cashier quickly counted the chips, Edge pulled her phone back out and replied, "Thanks but no thanks."

"$19,060. How would you like that?" the cashier chimed.

Edge shoved her phone back in the clip and looked up at her. She was met with a warm smile and lustful eyes. She stared at the pretty Latina cashier. Ray Charles could see that the girl was flirting with her.

Edge looked around before she replied, "You can give me all hundreds please, and your number while you're at it."

Moments later, she exited Bally's Casino with an additional nearly $10,000 and something, or rather someone, to do later. It had been a long time since she had money or touched a woman sexually. Since she couldn't have Diamond, she figured the cashier would compensate.

Chapter 14

Navigating his way on Interstate 10 toward his condo, Prime had that look in his eye as he massaged Monica's inner left thigh. Monica began getting hot and bothered.

She squirmed in the front seat of his Range as his hand slid farther up her jeans. She couldn't wait to get to his place and show him just how much she missed him. Whenever she was alone, she thought about him. She didn't know if it was because she was carrying his child, but lately, she felt a strong connection to him. He had occupied her mind more than her job and job assignment. The more time she spent with him, the more she found herself having stronger feelings for him. *Why do things have to be the way they are?* she sat in the passenger seat and wondered in deep thought.

They were almost at Prime's house before any words were spoken. "Monica?"

"Hmm, baby?"

"Are you really serious about having this baby?"

Why would he ask me a question like that? Monica wondered. She hoped he wasn't having second thoughts. "Of course I am, baby. I never would have said anything if I hadn't been serious. I only intend to do this once. Why, are you having doubts?" she wanted to know.

"My bad, baby, you just make me so happy." The mood had seemed to become a bit somber. Monica had to fix that quickly.

"Prime, you make me very, very happy."

"Mmm, yeah. I feel you, girl." He turned into the parking lot of his condo and pulled into his designated parking spot, jumped out of the car, and ran around to her side of the car. Grabbing her by the hand, he helped her out of the car, and then picked her up and carried her to his front door.

"Prime, what are you doing?" Monica was laughing loudly and uncontrollably. She saw a couple of neighbors peeking out their doors and windows. She couldn't care less about what they thought at that moment.

"I'm practicing carrying my future wife over the threshold," Prime announced. He knew the statement would get her attention.

The look on Monica's face was priceless. Her heart nearly skipped a beat from his words. *Future wife?* She played the words back in her head. *Marriage?*

"Baby, put me down. I'm starting to feel a little dizzy."

"Oh, my bad, baby."

"Don't apologize. What you did was very romantic. You are a very loving and affectionate man, and I love that about you." She stroked his hair and rubbed the side of his face. "Future wife?" she repeated.

"Yeah. Did I cross the line with that?" Prime asked, knowing he hadn't.

"Oh, no," Monica immediately shot back. "It's just I didn't think . . ."

"Babe, you're carrying my firstborn. That shit is deep. Why wouldn't I want to be with the mother of my child." It was more of a statement than a question. Prime unlocked the front door of his condo and let in Monica, who was beaming.

Monica blushed. She felt like a high school girl meeting her school crush for the first time. "That makes sense." She smiled.

Prime closed the door behind them and moved in closer to Monica. He kissed her passionately, grabbing the bottom of her shirt. He lifted her shirt up over her head. Once that was off, he loosened her bra with one hand, exposing her breasts, as he struggled to remove her jeans with the other. They were too tight, but she wore them because she knew that he loved her in them. Monica didn't think she'd ever be able to wear them again.

Assisting him, she unzipped her jeans, and grabbed his hands and placed them on her plump ass. "Pull them off. Pull them off now," she cooed. Monica turned around and whispered into his ear, "You have brought the sex goddess out in me." Monica yearned for him to seek her wetness and bury his face into it. It wasn't long before he fed her desires.

"Umm, baby. Ooh, bay." Monica was fiening for his powerful manhood to penetrate her, slow and deep. She started removing his pants with her foot.

He looked up from what he was doing with a mischievous grin on his face and grabbed his massive dick. Monica nicknamed his big dick Captain Hook because it curved toward her every time it got hard. "Is this what you're looking for?"

"You know that's what I'm looking for." Monica lay on her back, spread her legs, and reached down and held her soaked vaginal lips open so that there wouldn't be any confusion about exactly where she wanted and needed him to go. "I want you inside of me. Now."

He bent down and kissed the lips below her hips once more before giving her what she needed—him—inside her, bringing the heat and the passion that she so desired. "Mmm, Prime."

"How you want it, momma?" He stroked her deeper and harder as he slowed down. "Like this, baby?"

Tightening her heated vagina around his thick manhood was her only reply. She loved the way he felt inside her as she felt her body tensing up before releasing another orgasm. She dug her nails into his back as she completely let go.

"Yeah, baby, let it go." He looked at her sated and satisfied face and began pumping his dick into her, faster, like he was on a mission. "Yeah, Monica, I love you, girl. Uh mmm, oh, girl!" He shook furiously before landing beside her on the plush carpet and kissing her as he drifted off to sleep.

"Baby, let's go lie down in the bed."

"Oh, yeah, hmm. Okay."

As they lay on the bed, Prime pulled her closer to him, and she relished the warmth of his arms. Monica cooed as he cradled her.

Prime looked down at her. *Gullible-ass bitch,* he thought as he stroked her hair. Monica started playing with his manhood. She looked up into his eyes. Prime matched her inviting eyes and smiled.

Enjoy this shit while it lasts, he thought as Monica crawled down the bed and slowly kissed the head of his dick and inched her warm mouth down his rock-hard pole.

Chapter 15

The most difficult thing to do during any form of imprisonment is sleep. So, at first, Starr wasn't happy to be awakened in the subzero-temperature solitary cell by the annoying sound of a hard flashlight tapping the window at 5:30 a.m. She rolled over and squinted at the door. There was no one out there. All she heard was, "Fields! Pack up! You're outta here!" He mumbled, "Thank God," in a lower voice when he felt he was far enough away for her not to hear. She did.

There wasn't any need to waste the court's time with another bail hearing. They decided it was best to keep the magistrate's good faith by showing more respect for the federal court of law. After all, it was the magistrate who signed all of the warrants. These days the only people who got arrested without warrants were low-level drug dealers who publicly exposed themselves on open street corners. That was the local police department's brand of catch, nothing for a federal agent in a suit and tie to waste time with.

Starr was handled in a very poor manner while being processed out and discharged. Not that she cared in the least. It all made her smile and act even more polite. A forty-five-minute procedure, at the most, ended up taking three whole hours.

Dressed up in the same clothes she had changed into at the courthouse, Starr exited the federal detention center, closed her eyes, and took in a deep inhalation of the polluted, smog-filled air of freedom. The early sun was shining bright but was blocked by the tall skyscrapers. The street was busy with cars, buses, and yellow cabs. The annoying horns honking due to backed-up traffic now seemed to be something special. Different sets of sirens could be heard racing in opposite directions. The sounds of a construction crew drilling into the pavement could be heard from the city block. It was the curse of the traffic congestion.

Starr opened her eyes wide and took a few steps forward to get farther away from the building. She stepped into a thin stream of direct sunlight that slipped through the narrow space between two towers across the street. There were no signs of Diamond anywhere. *Oh, yeah, the trial,* she thought as the recollection hit her. Even if there weren't any trial going on, Starr did not expect to see Diamond upon her release. Ever since the raiding of the club and her first arrest, there was tension between the two.

Throughout all of the early morning madness, a deep, dark charcoal gray Mercedes McLaren pulled up and parked in front of Starr. The passenger door electronically lifted upward, exposing Diamond's whole body as they smiled at each other. Diamond never ceased to amaze her. Starr shook her head in shame as she strutted toward the sparkling beauty. Once she sat down, the door slowly lowered and sealed itself closed.

"You didn't think I'd let some other bitch get the chance to play my position?" Diamond asked dryly as soon as Starr hopped in.

Starr knew she was referring to Monica. Not feeding her, she replied, "I didn't give it much thought."

Diamond cut her eyes over at Starr. She had already anticipated a sly or nonchalant remark from her. She was accustomed to it. When it came to evading or downplaying something, there was no one better at it than Starr, Diamond believed. She knew now was not the time or the place, so she changed the subject.

"I don't have much time. I have to get back to the courthouse in two hours. So, where do you wanna go first?" Diamond asked as she lifted her Chanel shades up to her forehead.

Starr pondered the question. "You can just take me to grab something to wear and then drop me off at my place," Starr replied. "By the way, nice car," she added.

Diamond smiled. "I'm glad you like it. It's yours."

Chapter 16

McCarthy awoke in the exact same spot where he passed out. He had a serious hangover, his temples were throbbing, and the inside of his mouth tasted like sour milk. After all had been confirmed that the female in the triple homicide was his female undercover agent, who had been killed out in Henderson at her home he had purchased with government-seized money some years back, he found himself at a local bar drinking his sorrows away. He pushed himself off the floor and realized he had something in his hand.

When he looked, he saw it was a business card that read: FOR BUSINESS OR FOR PLEASURE. It had her private phone extension on it. He was totally clueless how he came into possession of the card. Then, things slowly began coming back to him. The attractive dirty blonde from last night. He ripped the card up in tiny little pieces and flushed them down the toilet. It was bad enough he had to explain to his wife why he had come in so late; the last thing he wanted was for her to think it was behind another woman. Lucky for him, Linda McCarthy had already left for the day.

It wasn't until McCarthy was in the shower with the hot water pounding into his body that the fog in his brain cleared up. The clock ticked. McCarthy was running late, so he skipped breakfast and headed straight to work.

While he was in the locker room changing his clothes, Mobley snuck up on him. "How's the case coming along, McCarthy?"

Hiding the fact that his boss startled him, McCarthy replied, "It's coming along pretty well. I'm checking all possible leads."

Mobley stared at himself in the full-length mirror, looking extra dapper in a dark brown silk shirt, matching tailor-made slacks, and brown soft-bottom shoes, putting his neat afro into place. "Yeah, it turns out that one of the men who got killed, his mother is real close friends with the mayor. So that's why they're making such a big fuss about this case. I assured him that I had my best agents on it and the case would get solved. And I've always been a man of my word. And I want to keep it like that. Understood?" Mobley stated, brushing some invisible speck of dust off his immaculate wardrobe.

"Of course," McCarthy answered.

Mobley stared at McCarthy through the mirror. "A little late today, huh?"

"Yeah, I had a little too much to drink last night. It caught up with me this morning," McCarthy explained.

"Happens to the best of us." Mobley shrugged, then finished, "Don't let me down, McCarthy." He exited the locker room just as quietly as he entered.

McCarthy walked to his desk and saw that Reddick had his ass planted on it, talking on the phone. He listened to his end of the conversation. "Yeah, mm-hmm. Okay, so he wasn't lying. Yeah, lucky for him. Too bad. I really wanted his ass. Yeah, tell me about it. Well, okay. Thanks anyways, bye-bye," Reddick snapped, slamming the phone down. He focused his black, angry eyes on McCarthy.

"What was that all about?" he asked.

"Well, that was the PO of my last lead. Gonna go check him out. My final shot, 'cause all the other alibis checked out. If this doesn't pan out, it looks like I'm back to square one. Since the plane incident, I've been looking like an idiot. These fucking dykes are a pain in my freaking ass," Reddick admitted. "It seems like every time we get close, the path goes cold."

McCarthy nodded. He had felt the same way since investigating the Double Gs. "I totally understand where you're coming from," McCarthy offered.

Reddick grimaced. "I'm sure you do. You've been chasing after this gang longer than anyone."

"Longer than I expected to," McCarthy shot back.

"I know what you mean. Longest case I ever worked on had me obsessed for nearly two freaking years, about six years ago. A racketeering case that led me all the way over to the East Coast. But I solved that motherfucker," Reddick gloated.

"Looking forward to being able to say the same about this one," McCarthy replied enviously.

"You will," Reddick replied. "If anybody can take these chicks down, it's you."

"Thanks for the vote of confidence. But after the Douglass situation and the triple homicide, I'm not sure." McCarthy's tone sounded like that of a man defeated.

"So, you think those murders out in Henderson are connected to them?" Reddick wanted to know.

McCarthy hesitated before answering. Only he and whoever else she told knew she was an undercover agent. He had recruited her many years ago and deliberately denied her moving forward in the academy because of the special assignment she had lost her life while pursuing. He knew he could lose his job if it ever got out that he had done such a thing. He played it safe with his answer. "I'm almost positive," was all he said.

"Wow. Would've never even tied the two together. I guess having someone on the inside really comes in handy," Reddick stated slyly.

If you only knew. "It has its ups and downs," McCarthy responded.

"Well, one of us has to bring these women down. If you want, you can ride with me to meet up with the parole officer. You know what they say: two heads are better than one."

"Sure, why not," McCarthy accepted.

The blaring sound of his desk phone interrupted their exchange. McCarthy leaned over toward his desk. Reddick moved out of his way. "McCarthy speaking." McCarthy listened in silence until the caller was done. Reddick studied his facial expression and knew it wasn't good.

"Appreciate the heads-up," McCarthy chimed before slamming the phone back down on the receiver.

"What's up?" Reddick wasted no time asking.

"Starrshma Fields has been released." McCarthy grimaced.

Chapter 17

It had been awhile since she had been to the club. The Double Gs put together a get-together in honor of her freedom and return to the streets. *It's going to be good to see Bubbles, the twins, and 'em,* she thought. *And my baby, too.* She continued to drift in thought as an image of Diamond appeared in her mind.

She snapped out of her brief daze and continued to thumb through her wardrobe. Pondering which way to go, Starr decided to dress down for the evening. She pulled out something simple: a black pair of fitted jeans, a black Mass Fit sports top, and one of her customized Double Gs black jean jackets with gold embroidered letters on the back. She intended it to be a chill night tonight for her and she wanted to look like that was exactly what she was doing.

She knew all eyes would be on her and her squad. Going to the club brought back memories of when she and the Double Gs would walk through and receive instant love, respect, and hate, all at the same time. Especially when they were rolling deep up in their own spot.

Starr shook her head in disgust. The thought of the incident that transpired at Club Panties put a bad taste in Starr's mouth. She still couldn't believe they had managed to get so close to them, her. *I should've listened to Queen Fem,* Starr admitted, referring to the warnings her mentor continued to reveal and express to her. It seemed as if the raid at the club not only disrupted the normal operation of the Double Gs organization, but also her own personal life.

She couldn't help but blame that night for why she and Diamond had unspoken beef. It wasn't until that night when the feds busted in on her and Monica that a strain had been put on her relationship with Diamond. Nothing and no one had ever come between the two of them, until then. Outside of what she and Felicia once had, Starr had never even considered another Double Gs member outside of Diamond. Some of the other Double Gs may have hinted or tried to entice Starr, but none ever drew her interest or attention. She couldn't deny there was something about Monica that she connected with. *She was there for me too when I needed someone to be.*

She quickly pushed her thoughts to the side. She knew she had no business thinking about Monica like that. Once she was ready to go, she walked toward the end of her driveway. She looked left then right. Cars drove past bumping the latest hip-hop and R&B music. None were the ride she was waiting for. Moments later, a convoy of jet-black Escalades and motorcycles pulled alongside the curb. When the last luxury SUV came to a complete stop, Starr hopped in and it sped off.

Diamond occupied the back. For the first few minutes, they rode in silence. Once they were on the highway, floating, Diamond broke the ice. "So, you still playing around with that bitch, huh?"

"Babe, don't start. Let's talk about something else." Starr was not in the mood. She was fresh out, and the last thing she wanted was to beef with Diamond on a night she should be chilling.

It was no secret Diamond didn't particularly care for Monica.

"Oh, you not in the mood?" The sarcasm was undeniable in Diamond's tone. "Well, since you wanna change the subject, I was gonna wait, but now is as good as a time as any," Diamond announced. "Felicia was a cop."

"What?" Starr nearly caught whiplash the way she turned and faced Diamond. The look on her face displayed how surprised she was by Diamond's words.

Diamond said it so nonchalantly that it almost came across as a joke, but Starr knew she'd never play about something like that. Especially not about someone who was so close to them and high up on the chain.

"How? What the . . . Why am I just hearing this and where the fuck is she now?" Starr could hardly get her words out or finish a sentence. Her mind went into instant overdrive. Her mood changed from chill to deadly in a New York minute.

Diamond, on the other hand, was cool, calm, and collected. "No worries. It's been handled," she informed Starr.

Confusion revealed itself across Starr's face. She had an idea what Diamond meant when she said it had been handled, but she didn't understand how, when no one had consulted with her about the matter. There were only two people in the entire organization who could authorize or sanction a hit on a Double Gs member: her and Queen Fem.

"What do you mean, it's handled?" Starr wanted to know.

"I mean, I took care of it. Personally," Diamond lied. She already knew what Starr was thinking. She had already anticipated and prepared herself for Starr's reaction. It was bad enough she had Felicia killed without getting clearance first, but if Starr found out it was done by an outsider, and her ex at that, both she and Edge would be in the dirt before the sun came up.

"I know I wasn't supposed to make a move until I ran it past you, but you weren't here, and I had to make a judgment call," Diamond added. Her tone switched to the one she knew would appeal to Starr's soft spot. "I got proof, just so you know," Diamond added. "Video footage. At the club."

Video footage? At the club? Starr repeated Diamond's words to herself. The mention of it caused her to raise an eyebrow. She noticed Diamond didn't say when specifically she had obtained the video footage of Felicia, and she didn't want to ask. But it made her wonder if Diamond had seen any other video footage at the club, specifically footage of her and Monica the night she freaked her at the club in her office before the raid. *Is that why she's been so distant and acting funny toward me?* Starr pondered. "Are you sure it's been handled?" Starr asked.

"I'm positive," Diamond replied.

Starr eyed her. "I'm sure you did what you had to do," she then said. "We'll talk about it later."

Diamond just nodded. She was glad Starr had let it go for the time being. She was not in the mood to be grilled and interrogated.

The ride to the club made the other side of Vegas look like it was on the outskirts of Beverly Hills. The side of town it was on was nice and clean. It was one of Las Vegas's newest nightlife tourist attractions. It sat just in the right place for business people to pace the sidewalks with briefcases in their hands during the daytime. The women looked like they were either coming from professional clubs or they had stepped off a runway in Paris.

The flyers had been sent out, especially around the vicinity of Club Cloud 9. It was announced that Club Panties had been renovated and was back in full effect, better than ever. And to further enforce the extra hyped buzz, the rumor was put out that this was also Starr's first night as a free woman again. They had incarcerated her back to back on bogus charges they couldn't make stick. They tried to gain evidence that would tie her into the murders of agents and a few local dealers and respected figures in the city, with no success. They tried to tie her to the bank job, again with no success. Their only chance at detaining her any longer than they had was to connect her to the gruesome act against the correctional officer, but they failed at that attempt as well. There was never such a major-impact group of reasons to party so hard on a Friday night.

But the Double Gs weren't the only ones who had reason to celebrate and party.

Freeze's freshly detailed fire engine red Phantom pulled up to the entrance of Club Panties and illegally parked in front of the long line. The street was packed. Both sides. Club Panties was shining brighter than ever. The extended rows of the finest women were standing in place. The top ballers from all over stunted hard doing everything within their bankroll to impress them or catch their attention. Exotic vehicles were everywhere. Some sat right in the middle of the street's lanes. Men were popping bottles of champagne and bouncing from side to side. Music blasted from every angle. Somehow, it all blended perfectly. The best weed smoke was in the air. High doses of Ecstasy and bottled water flowed through veins. Some people were numb off cocaine. Others were high off life. But only one person was in awe of it all.

Frenchie sat in the driver's side back seat of the Phantom staring out the window with a clear view of Club Cloud 9. He had never seen so many women. They all seemed to be flawless, just like the calendar girls, video vixens, and porno magazine stars he was used to for the past decade. Nothing tangible. But now it felt like if he just pointed at any specific one, they would come running. He had waited for this moment for so very long.

It was a moment that was never supposed to come. A moment that he had shut out of his dreams the second he received a life sentence. He used to wake up in his health code violation of a cell, mad at the world. The same dream he used to curse came true. He began to think about the many he had left behind with nothing to look forward to but that dream, which was now his reality.

Before night had fallen, Frenchie had been shopping all day, thanks to Freeze. Freeze had a lot of business to take care of but left him in the company of Lisa, the high-yellow complexioned, long-haired, petite chauffeur. She chose the stores and the wardrobe for Frenchie. Everything was top-of-the-line designer threads. And when they were done, he took her to fill the closets of his fully furnished high-rise condo. Time had flown. He had only a little time to get dressed before he was to meet Freeze and his crew at Club Panties for his welcome home bash. Freeze tried to lock down the entire third level, but there were two crews he couldn't pay to get shut out: Prime and his peoples, and the Double Gs. Sammy, who owned Club Treasure across the street from Club Panties, wasn't going to commit such a suicidal business move. He knew both parties would be out for such a big night.

Esco pulled up and parked the X6 behind the Phantom. Freeze hopped out the passenger side, and they both strolled down the street to meet Frenchie. Frenchie let himself out after he finally located the door handle. He kept forgetting where it was all day. It was nothing more than a button.

The moment they made eye contact, the past resurfaced. Frenchie couldn't place Esco's face. Esco's features had changed drastically after growing up. But Esco could never forget Frenchie. Frenchie altered his life. No more basketball. The hoop dreams died with his mother. He never even returned to school. He lived off the streets, purse snatching, boosting, breaking in cars, stealing them. It wasn't long before the police caught up with him and sent him to juvenile prison where he would later meet Freeze, who came in a year after. Esco had never revealed to Freeze or anyone else about witnessing the murder of his mother.

Frenchie didn't even seem to remember. He stuck his hand out and greeted Esco as if they were now a family. Esco shook hands and pulled him into a false embrace, not sure if the time of revenge was near or would ever come. Once they released, Freeze stepped up. As he and Frenchie hugged, the ground began to shake.

Above all of the loud, blended music, the rapidly approaching thunderous roars could be heard from a mile away. They could be felt. Frenchie watched the men and women scramble to clear the streets in a matter of seconds. Before he could ask what was happening, the answer came straight at him. The three of them were the only ones still standing in the streets.

The grand entrance was a little different this time. First, two twin R6s came flying down at top speed as if they were racing. They shot down the street and, at the same time, the helmetless female passengers on the back stood up and fully extended their arms, performing a stunt called the Jesus Christ. A loud, strong round of applause erupted as the two bikes passed the bystanders. The passengers managed to drop back down into the seat and grip the waists of the drivers before the bikes skidded into a 180-degree turn and wheelied their way back up the street before dropping the front wheels back down to the ground and stopping on a dime between the fronts of both clubs. They were revving their engines and then, all of a sudden, the front wheels shot right back up, pointing at the sky as the bike stayed in place, while all four women simultaneously hopped off. The two bikes stood rested on their back license plate tail guards. The girls stood on each side of them and looked ahead, up the hill, as the roar got closer.

Two more R6s came flying down the strip heading straight toward the underside of the two bikes that were standing up. The public audience was frozen as they watched the bikes pull in closer together in the middle of the street riding side by side. The two also helmetless, daring female passengers switched moving bikes at top speed. And then on top of that, they sat down just in time before both bikes squeezed through the two standing bikes. The four girls standing beside them never flinched. A louder round of applause filled the air.

Frenchie had never seen anything like it. He chose to act just as unimpressed as the men he was standing in the street with. They were leaning against the Phantom with their arms folded, wearing sour facial expressions.

Before Frenchie could digest and process what was happening, six more motorcycles shot down the street, shooting between the standing bikes. They all made a U-turn after the previous two and faced back the way they came. And then he saw the Escalades.

Starr tried Monica's number one last time as the two Escalades pulled up and parked directly side by side in front of each one of the standing bikes.

"You've reached—"

Starr disconnected the call, cutting the voicemail short.

The four bikers who stood on the sides of the standing motorcycles each strutted to the two back doors of both Escalades. Double Gs spilled out of the first one while Starr stepped out of the back one. Heads nodded, fists pumped chests out of respect and love, and whistles blew from the crowd, while beady eyes and blank stares filled the faces of others as Starr floated toward the club. As they neared, cheers were screamed as if some rock stars had just stepped out on stage at a concert. Everybody had heard about the feds picking Starr back up and arresting her for a second time. Her presence confirmed that she had, once again, slipped through their fingers. That was well-respected in the streets, so Starr wasn't surprised by the love or hate. She knew those in the crowd who loved her were the ones who she made sure she was fed. She waved at the crowd as if she were the queen of England.

The cheers grew even louder. Men were standing on top of their cars. Some were blowing their horns. Women were flashing their breasts. For a minute, it seemed as if confetti would fall from the sky. When Starr first emerged from the back right side of the second Escalade, she could feel the crowd's energy. She could see the hate and love. She caught brief eye contact with Freeze, Frenchie, and Esco. Her smile dropped from her face as she turned her back on them and walked around the front of the Escalade, through the high beams, and onto the sidewalk. The crowd in front of her parted, giving her and her team more than enough space to enter Club Panties. When they were completely through, the crowd closed in again, and the party in the streets resumed after the Escalades and motorcycles disappeared. It wasn't like old times. It was better.

The job done on the Cloud 9 interior was impeccable. Starr vividly remembered the way it had been turned upside down the last time she seen it. Not only was it all redone, it was upgraded. The plush carpet was thicker. The lights were brighter. The aquariums were bigger. The wood grain finishing was extra polished. The sound system was crisper, and the liquor stocked was the absolute finest.

Starr greeted all of those she came across on the way upstairs to her office. She opened the door with Diamond standing right behind her. The mink covering was back up on the walls. The best tropical fish floated to the left of her, providing a transparent view of the lower level. Everything was in order. A laptop sat in the center of her desk. The couch was to her right. It all felt great again.

"This didn't cost me a penny?" Starr turned to ask Diamond.

"Nope. Courtesy of Sammy. Guess he's finally realized his business is nothin' without ours. I hear Cloud 9 kicked his ass," she proclaimed.

"Get this entire place swept for wire transmitters of any sort," Starr ordered as she spun around. "There's one more thing I want to check. C'mon, D."

Starr led Diamond down to the sublevel tunnel. The Double Gs meeting room was the first stop. The chairs were stacked in a neat row. She smiled with approval as they went back out. They went back to the end of the hall and opened the door. The Double Gs round table was in one full, solid piece again. Everything had been redone. It was all perfect. Starr turned to face Diamond. "They did a really good job." Starr smiled.

"I thought you'd like it," Diamond replied.

"I love it. Let's go party," Starr announced. She led the way back upstairs to the main floor.

As Diamond and Starr walked through the main floor of the club, the first thing they noticed was that all eyes were indeed on them. A sea of faces stared at them. Starr smiled on the inside at the faces that appeared as if they had just seen a ghost.

Yeah, it's me, bitches, Starr wanted to say. Instead, she kept it moving as if she hadn't even noticed the attention she and Diamond were receiving. A bunch of pictures of celebrities lined the narrow hallway that led to the main floor of the club. The hall was colored in multiple colors by children who had visited the club. As they got closer to the main floor, the blaring music got louder and louder. "Look over there." A grinning Diamond nudged Starr.

When she looked where Diamond was pointing, Starr lit up like flashlight. A slew of Double Gs had an entire section on lock. They all held up bottles in Starr's direction. "Welcome to the new and improved Cloud 9, formerly known as Club Panties," the deejay announced. "Don't want this to be your last trip here. This is the hottest spot in Vegas. Hope it's an exciting experience that you want to share with your friends." He continued on the mic between song verses. "And shout-out to my homegirl, Starr. I see you. We missed you," the deejay added.

Starr drew her attention toward the deejay's direction and made eye contact with him. After giving him the head nod, she looked around at the mass of people. Just then a pretty brunette with breast implants appeared out of nowhere in front of her and Diamond. In each hand, she had a bottle of Belaire Rose.

"Hello, I'm Lacey," she introduced herself, with a Colgate smile plastered across her face. "I was told to escort y'all over to y'all section with the two more bottles," the pretty brunette bottle girl announced.

Starr's eyes went from Lacey over to the Double Gs section. Both Sparkles and Glitter were cheesing at her and Diamond when she glanced at the section.

"Lead the way," Starr accepted.

Moments later, Starr was pulling out a crisp Benjamin bill to tip the server and hugging her Double Gs sisters.

"Good to see you." Bubbles wrapped her arms around her boss's back and gave her the tightest hug she could manage.

"You too, sis," Starr said. She could see by the expressions on everybody's faces that her presence and guidance had been missed. She always knew the importance of her position, but it was moments such as this one that made her realize just how many women were affected by her choices and decisions as well as what happened to her. "I miss all of y'all," Starr chimed. Starr took a swig of the Belaire and smiled. When she lowered it, she saw that Lacey stood in front of her for a second time, holding a drink in her hand.

"She told me to pour you this," Lacey said, referring to Diamond.

"Oh, she did, did she?" Starr toyed with Lacey.

Lacey giggled like a schoolgirl.

"You didn't slip anything in it, did you?" Starr continued with her humor.

Lacey's eyes widened. "Oh, no, not at all. I'm not even that type of chick," Lacey made an attempt to clarify.

Starr chuckled. She peered over at Diamond. A half smirk appeared across Diamond's face. Starr returned to Lacey. She took the drink from her and took a sip. She could taste a small hint of cranberry mixed in with the Rémy. "Yeah, I like this," Starr approved of the drink. It was what Diamond had always made her to calm her. Starr slid her hand into her pocket again and came up with another hundred dollar bill. Lacey beamed more than the first time. An appreciative look appeared on her face when she saw the money. She knew she hadn't done nearly enough to earn her tip. But she accepted it respectfully.

"Thank you again." She smiled at Starr.

"Don't worry about it." Starr leaned in. "Just make sure my girl knows how to reach you outside of the club."

Lacey shook her head rapidly. "Oh, she does already," she informed Starr right before she excused herself.

"Sorry I'm late."

The voice behind her caught her by surprise and startled her a little. She could recognize it anywhere, despite the fact that she hadn't been hearing it regularly lately.

When she turned around and looked, her heart skipped a beat. Monica stood there with an inviting look on her face, looking lovely as ever.

"You look good," Monica offered, looking Starr up and down.

Starr's clit throbbed and pulsated from the compliment. Monica's sudden presence ignited her. Since she and Diamond hadn't been on the best of terms, Monica had been there to fill the void. Seeing her standing there, dressed in a different version of the Mass Fit apparel, caused her to crack a smile. But she immediately erased it. Feeling Diamond's eyes on her, she regained her composure. But the one-piece sports gear Monica was sporting made Starr want to get her alone and show her how much she really appreciated how she held her down. With lustful eyes, she took in every inch of Monica's curves, thanks to the fitness outfit. Monica looked like she had come straight from the gym to the club.

"Thanks." Starr continued to play it cool. "And I wanted to thank you again," she added. "You seemed to be the only one truly there for me when it counted," she declared. She wanted to stroke the left side of Monica's face, but instead, she offered an appreciative smile. "Everyone else was so caught up. Nobody else even sent me a single letter. But you, you were there for me every day."

"Don't mention it." Monica smiled back.

Starr nodded. "Nice job by the way."

Monica knew she was referring to the funeral assassination. It was actually Prime who had taken care of it for her, but there was no way she was going to let Starr know. Instead, she took the credit for it like she and Prime discussed. Monica played her part to a T.

"I'm here for you. Just keep letting me prove myself," she whispered. She leaned forward so only Starr could hear her, only to pull back abruptly.

Without having to look over her shoulder, judging by Monica's facial expression Starr knew Diamond was near. Diamond slid up behind Starr and slipped her arms between hers and hugged her from behind. She kissed Starr on the right side of her neck.

"Am I interrupting something?" Diamond asked.

Starr quickly backed away from Monica. "No, not at all," Starr calmly replied. "It's good to see you," she then directed to Monica. The two walked into a hug, an abrupt embrace.

Diamond never even acknowledged Monica's presence. She reached for Starr's hand and pulled it behind her. "C'mon. The real party's over there. There's plenty of time to be the lover girl you are."

"D, don't—"

"No, don't you," Diamond cut Starr short. "Let's just enjoy your freedom," she added as she led the way.

Starr nodded and smirked as she followed. She knew she was going to have to have a sit-down with Diamond, but tonight was not that night.

Monica slowly trailed behind, feeling uninvited.

"You ready to party tonight?" Diamond asked, cutting her eyes over at Monica.

Starr let out a light chuckled and nodded. *This day was bound to come,* thought Starr. The last thing she wanted was for Monica and Diamond to get into it, but she knew that if they did she'd have to remain neutral. Regardless of how she felt about Monica, seniority ruled, and Diamond had status in the Double Gs organization. Starr glanced over at Monica. Her eyes said more than what Starr hoped would come out of her mouth. *Be smart,* Starr thought, hoping Monica held her tongue.

Stupid bitch, your time coming to an end, Monica wanted to say but knew better than to so much as blink the wrong way. There was no doubt in her mind that

Starr still loved Diamond, no matter how she felt about her. If anything were to jump off, she was sure that Starr would not stand in the way and the rest of the Double Gs would take Diamond's side. She did a quick survey of the VIP section. All eyes and ears were tuned in to the small exchange among the three of them. So rather than create a lose-lose situation for herself, she smile politely and waved at Diamond. Diamond didn't return the gesture. She rolled her eyes and returned her focus to Starr.

"You sure you ready?

Starr knew what Diamond was doing. The tension between her and Monica was unmistakable. Diamond had never been the jealous or petty type, but tonight she was both. Starr was surprised at her behavior, though. It was not like her to display so much public affection, or to be extra, especially when they were out with the Double Gs. But Starr understood and blamed herself. Though she loved being in Diamond's embrace, she hated the fact that they were still not on the best speaking terms. True, they were still together, although some thought they weren't, but after all that had been happening, Starr realized she wanted so much more for her and Diamond. She looked at the woman who was the same five foot six stature and wanted to believe the two of them could have a respectable future together.

"I'm always ready."

"Good." Without warning, Diamond pulled Starr away from Monica and guided her over to where Bubbles and the twins were. She didn't let Starr finish whatever it was Monica and Starr were conversing about.

"Why you do that?" Starr asked.

"Fuck her," Diamond said calmly. "We're here to have a good time and be with family," she reminded Starr. "You lucky I didn't smack fire outta her mouth," she added.

Bubbles caught the last few words and knew who and what Diamond was referring to. She shook her head. "Sis, chill. Let that go." A light chuckle accompanied her words.

"Just for tonight," Diamond replied.

"That's a start." Bubbles's chuckle turned into laughter. "So, what's up, bossy lady?" Bubbles punched Starr in the arm playfully. "How you feelin'?"

"It's good to be back out and on the scene," Starr admitted. "It's important everybody know that we still out here, and we untouchable," Starr snarled. She could feel her normal boss juices starting to awaken. It was as if she had turned from Dr. Jekyll to Ms. Hyde. Out of nowhere, she felt the urge to want to ball out and stunt on dudes in the club, who were trying to do the same. Feeling that the city may have been thinking they were getting weak or falling off, Starr caught the attention of Lacey and waved her over.

"You need something?" Lacey asked.

Starr dug her hand in her pocket and came out with a monstrous wad of cash full of hundreds. She counted out twenty-five bills and handed them to Lacey. "Bring me twenty-five hundred in singles."

Lacey's eyes widened. "All singles?"

Starr never looked up. Instead, she counted out another twenty-five bills. "Matter fact, make that five," she corrected, handing Lacey an additional $2,500.

"That's how you feeling?" Diamond grinned.

"Damn right." Starr smiled.

They'd come to the club to celebrate the face of the Double Gs, and that's exactly what they were doing. "Bring me five too," Diamond requested.

"Y'all ain't gonna be making me look like I'm a broke bitch," Bubbles chimed. "Bring me some too." Bubbles reached into her back pants pocket and pulled out a stack that appeared to be half of the one Starr and Diamond had pulled out. She gave Lacey twenty one-hundred dollar bills.

"Aw, shit, it's about to be lit!" Glitter boomed.

She and Sparkle had already started pulling their money out. Before Starr knew it, every Double G in the area requested singles. Before the night ended, nearly one hundred bottles of champagne and assorted liquor were run through, and over twenty Gs were tossed in the air, despite the obvious, which was that it wasn't even a strip club.

After the night had wound down, Diamond invited a few of the Double Gs to one of their honeycomb hideouts for an after-party. Among them were Bubbles, Sparkles, and Glitter along with Starr and Diamond, to freak a few chicks from the club, including Lacey. Diamond had recruited her personally for her and Starr. She knew how much Starr enjoyed the pleasures of a thick white girl in all the right places. Out of spite, she started to invite Monica, to show her how she meant nothing to Starr, but decided against it, not sure whether that was the case. Thirty minutes later, they were all engrossed in some sort of sexual activity.

Diamond cooed as she lay next to Starr on the plush living room couch. They both were receiving some bomb oral from Lacey, while Sparkle and Glitter were preoccupied with one of the other girls and Bubbles freaked another. It had been a long time since the two had indulged in a ménage à trois together. It was Diamond's peace offering and welcome home gift to Starr. She knew how much Starr enjoyed threesomes.

Starr gazed at her. To be a short bitch, Diamond held her own, and that quality was always attractive in Starr's eyes. Her natural blond curls smelled like cotton candy from the state fair and hosted twists that looked like her favorite sweet, black licorice that she bought from Aldi. Starr peered over at Diamond, whose pecan tan skin glistened as she watched Lacey switch from her to Diamond's love box. Starr couldn't help but admire her beauty. Her legs were sculpted firm like a bodybuilder's, and her feet were well maintained and suckable. She loved the way Diamond's smooth hands guided Lacey up and down as she slightly thrust her waist in her face.

Starr leaned over and kissed Diamond. The kiss ignited a familiar feeling within her, one she had missed. In all the years she and Diamond had been dealing with one another, this was the longest they had gone without any sexual contact. Starr tried not to think about it. She shook the feelings off, not wanting to kill the mood to the well-orchestrated welcome home party/orgy.

Diamond stared back. In a way, she felt guilty knowing in the back of her mind that she had been giving Starr the cold shoulder. The truth was, she missed her. But the Monica incident still left a bad taste in her mouth. That night she watched the videotape of Starr and Monica the day the club got raided nearly rocked her, but she was able to keep it together. She still wasn't sure whether she was going to reveal to Starr that she had seen the footage. She glanced at Starr's six foot two frame and 185 pounds of mocha coffee goodness. *Damn, I love this bitch,* Diamond concluded.

Diamond loved hard and fought harder, and she couldn't see herself going through life without Starr being in it, and as more than just her boss. She needed one good friend who loved her and accepted her for who she was and, for her, Starr was it. After her encounter with Edge, old feelings had resurfaced, but she realized that although she still loved Edge, she was in love with Starr, despite her cheating on her with Monica. Tonight wasn't about love or being in love, though. It was strictly about having fun and enjoying the release of her boss and lover. Diamond peered over and down at Starr, who was tickling her nipples with her hand and mouth as Lacey attacked her clit.

Off to the right, Sparkles and Glitter double-teamed a thick chick, while Bubbles had another sprawled out on the living floor.

"Naw, bitch." Glitter gripped the waist of the big, light-skinned chick she and Sparkles had who was trying to get away, as she continued to smack and pound her with the strap-on dildo like tomorrow was Armageddon. "Naw, you ain't going nowhere. You gonna take this," Glitter stated.

Sparkle got a thrill out of hearing the girl moan and groan with pleasure while being pressed against the window by her sister. She toyed with the girl's voluptuous breasts as her sister continued to ram the plastic dick in and out of her.

Glitter stopped smashing the big girl and backed away. "Sis, I think we should switch places so you can get it in."

"That's what's up," Sparkle answered as she stroked the strap-on she was wearing.

Glitter spun the girl around and bent her over in front of her sister. She pushed the girl's face between Sparkle's inner thighs, wanting to get a few licks in before her hole got pummeled by that monster dildo.

"Can I get some?" Bubbles asked as she downed the watermelon-flavored Four Loco with her right hand and massaged her strap-on with her left.

"If you put your tongue on this, I'll get on all fours and let you breed me like a bitch," the other female they had brought back to the bachelorette pad announced. She got on all fours and arched her back. Bubbles granted her wish.

Diamond and Starr wanted to see the show. Bubbles always talked about how she would make different chicks cream left and right from the slightest touch of her tongue and how good she could perform with a strap-on. And she had never lied. By the time she sucked on the girl's clit from the back and entered her with the strap-on, Bubbles's skills had the girl begging to stop because she couldn't take the multiples anymore. Starr, Diamond, Sparkles, and Glitter, along with the two other females, all stopped to watch Bubbles put in work. It was indeed a welcome home party Starr would never forget. It almost made her forget the hellhole she had just been released from. After her last round with Diamond, Starr showered and drifted off into a deep sleep.

The cocking sound and the feel of a barrel pressed to the side of her head immediately caused Starr's eyes to shoot open. "Bitch, is you serious?"

Diamond hovered over her with a pistol in her grip.

"What the fuck is the matter with you?" Starr mumbled.

A look of rage appeared on Diamond's face. "You! That's what's the matter," Diamond spat. "You been saying that Monica bitch's name all night, tossing and turning saying you loved her and shit!" Diamond shouted.

Starr couldn't believe her ears, not because she was being accused of dreaming about Monica, but because she had been talking in her sleep. "Dreams are just that: dreams. They don't mean shit," Starr shouted.

"Oh, really now? Bitch, you was moaning in your sleep, tugging at your pussy like you was fucking, too!" Diamond barked.

"Diamond, you bugging." Starr was unfazed by the gun Diamond now had pointed in her face. "I'ma give you one minute to get that fucking gun outta my face," she warned.

Diamond looked down at Starr. "I can't do this anymore," Diamond bellowed before she abruptly stormed out of the room.

Starr jolted out of bed after her.

"Tired of this fucking shit!" Diamond chanted.

Starr grabbed hold of her arm, but Diamond jerked it away. Grabbing both arms this time, she pinned Diamond to the wall.

"Don't fucking touch me! Don't fucking touch me!"

"Baby, listen to me!" Starr spoke.

"No, you listen," Diamond shot back. "You calling some other bitch's name during love when it should be mine! Why the fuck is she on your mind when I'm the one you claiming to love? Huh, Starrshma?" Diamond barked.

Shaking her head, Starr replied, "What do you want me to do? Tell me."

"I want you to prove you love me!" Diamond chimed.

"How? Tell me what I have to do, and I'll fucking do it, okay?" Starr burst out.

"I want you to kill that bitch," Diamond said with authority.

Starr frowned and drew back. Desperation was on her face. "What did you say?" Starr murmured.

"You heard me. The only way to get her off your mind is to take that bitch out. She's no more use to the Double Gs," Diamond responded.

"What are you saying? You want me to choose?" Starr stated.

"It's either her or me."

Starr grunted. Diamond's request confirmed to Starr that she knew how serious things had gotten between her and Monica. She knew Diamond all too well. If she saw the tape, then Diamond had been building a personal secret case against both Monica and her. Starr also believed this was the sentence Diamond wanted handed down for her actions behind her back with Monica.

Without a doubt, outside of Queen Fem, Diamond was the only woman in existence who could request such a thing and have Starr honor it, no matter the case. Diamond had proven both her loyalty and love on more than one occasion to her and Starr couldn't deny her.

"Okay, Dee. You win. I'll take care of it." Starr grimaced.

Diamond walked over to Starr and kissed her on the lips. "Thank you."

Chapter 18

McCarthy and Reddick introduced themselves and shook the parole officer's hand, explaining their situation to him quickly.

"I'm glad to be of assistance. I guess I'll just give you the facts and you can take it from there," Parole Officer Roberts began. "At approximately two-sixteen in the morning, a Benard Parker and Samuel Baxter were admitted into Clark County Hospital. It appeared at first glance that they had been on the losing end of a fist fight. But my kid Parker's nose had been broken, and his jaw in two places. He swallowed three of his teeth and had several deep lacerations that required stitches. Baxter made out a little better, I guess you could say. He got clubbed in the head with a blunt object that we're assuming is a gun. He has a nasty gash in the back of his head and a huge knot. More than just a hairline fracture, that's for sure. A major concussion and he keeps slipping in and out of consciousness. We all just naturally assumed they got jumped. Local street kids going to war with each other, you know how it is. But come to find out the usual victimizers became the victims, and it appears that they had been robbed."

"And how did you find this out? Parker and Baxter gave you this info?" McCarthy asked.

"Fuck no! Parker's ass is sitting in the county jail as we speak. I violated his ass!" the parole officer announced with authority. "He wasn't supposed to be in that kind of neighborhood or atmosphere, and he violated his curfew.

While he was in the hospital I gave him a piss test, and it came back hotter than a prostitute's panties on an August day," Roberts said, erupting in laughter. His pale face turned pink as he slapped his thigh.

McCarthy thought the man's laugh was very aggravating. It reminded him of that guy's laugh from the *Revenge of the Nerds* movies.

McCarthy and Reddick stared at each other, then back at Roberts, not seeing what the joke was. The PO noticed that he was the only one laughing, so he stopped, regained his composure, and continued, "Baxter is also in custody. We found thirty-three bags of heroin in the front of his long johns. Neither one of them are cooperating with us. This is really no surprise to us. Plus my kid's jaw is broken and wired shut so you can already imagine he's being pretty closemouthed about the whole situation." The large man exploded in another fit of laughter. His extra-tight Dockers slacks looked as if they were about to bust open at any second.

"Closemouthed about the situation," Roberts repeated as tears squeezed out of his eyes. "I love it. Aww, man, I love it," he finished, wiping his eyes.

Reddick looked as if he was ready to slap the shit out of him. "So if they didn't give you the information, then who did?" Reddick asked, trying to keep his temper and attitude in check.

"Uh, huh? Oh, okay, well, here's where things get a little interesting. Parker and Baxter didn't come to the hospital by themselves. They were escorted actually by a third man, who refused to give his name up. It was apparent that he knew Parker and Baxter, but he told the nurses that he was driving along and saw them getting jumped by a group of men, so he pulled up, causing the men to flee. He was the ordinary good, law-abiding citizen and dropped off two complete strangers at the hospital. Yeah, fuckin' right, is what I say. He was right there at the robbery too. He just somehow managed not to get himself all jacked up. By refusing to give his name, he let us know that he's just as shady as the two men he dropped off. He damn near fled the scene, but not before a security guard copied the license plate down. Come to find out, the car belongs to a female by the name of Shonte Stevens. We go question her, and she was a little bit more helpful than her buddy, but not too much." He paused to collect his thoughts.

"She didn't give up the name of the guy driving her car, but we found out that they were all victims of a home invasion and where that invasion took place. Off of Freemont. Rough area. Lot of drugs, lot of gangs, lot of guns. You wouldn't want to raise your dog there, never mind your kids, but I don't have to tell you guys something you already know," he said, ready to break into another laugh until he noticed both sets of eyes focused on him that didn't look amused at all. So he swallowed his giggles, cleared his throat, and continued. "But she still gave us a hard time. She refused to identify the man who was driving her car. She wouldn't tell us who else was in the house, wouldn't give us the exact location or the address. Even refused to admit it was a drug-related robbery. But we knew better. A neighborhood like that, I bet you anything drugs were involved."

As McCarthy listened to the parole officer talk, he quickly came to the conclusion that Roberts wanted to be a police officer. He probably tried to become one but failed at the academy, so he decided to become a parole officer instead. McCarthy noticed how he included himself in with the Clark County police by saying words like "we" and "us." Roberts looked like the type to just sit home and watch back-to-back episodes of *Cops*. He kind of felt sorry for the man with the snug-fitting pants and geeky laugh.

"Probably could've gotten more out of her, but she was rambling about us not doing anything about it and how her little cousin and the kid's father were just killed in some other home invasion a couple days and we still haven't solved that. As if people don't get killed in Las Vegas on a regular basis." Roberts snorted in a laughing manner.

"Did she say where that took place and whether it was connected to the beatings and robbery?"

"Nope. That's all she said. Frankly, I think she was just blowing smoke to get out of cooperating. When the local cop I went with to question her asked if she would be willing to give a statement and testify, I didn't hear her through all the carrying on and cursing she was doing in between. It was really difficult to understand her," Roberts replied nonchalantly.

Reddick shot Roberts a look of disgust that went unnoticed by the parole officer. "Do you have a description of the guy who dropped the two victims off?" McCarthy asked.

"Yeah, between six foot two and six four, probably weighing between 220 and 240 pounds. A big fella. Really couldn't see his face because he wore a hat pulled down low, but he was light skinned and had a goatee."

"You get an address on the girl?"

"Sure did." Roberts beamed.

"You mind getting it for us? Me and my partner would like to have a word or two with her," Reddick jumped in. His patience with the parole officer was wearing thin.

"Not a problem," Roberts stated, happy to be of assistance and involved with a somewhat big case. It made him feel important, like he was somebody. He disappeared into his cubicle within seconds to retrieve the address.

"So what do you think?" Reddick asked McCarthy, standing nearby.

"It's hard to tell right now. The physical description of the driver didn't help. We have to find out who else was in that house before we start assuming," McCarthy replied. "I do want to find out about the woman's cousin, though. Didn't want to say it in front of *Top Flight Security* Roberts." McCarthy let out a light chuckle.

Reddick joined him. "That guy was the epitome of trying too hard. But what are you thinking?"

"Not sure yet. It could be something, but then again it might be nothing," McCarthy truthfully answered.

Just then Roberts reappeared holding a small piece of paper in his hand. He handed it to McCarthy. "Yeah, I'm going that way. I could show you two how to get there."

"That's quite all right, sir. My partner and I will be fine, thank you. I'll be in the car, McCarthy," Reddick replied briskly in a no-nonsense tone before walking off.

McCarthy could see the disappointment in Robert's face. He had served his purpose and was no longer needed. So McCarthy decided to stroke the man's ego a little bit. "Thanks a lot, Officer Roberts. Your help is very much appreciated; and if this lead helps my partner and me crack the case, you will definitely get an honorary mention for playing a major role in helping us solve it."

Roberts visibly puffed up and beamed like a child receiving a compliment from an adult. "Well, yeah, like I said, I knew something was up from the get-go," he bragged.

McCarthy made his way outside, while at the same time checking out all the women who passed by.

"That guy was fucking annoying." Reddick wasted no time expressing how he felt about the parole officer.

"Yeah, but if what he gave us pans out to be something, then he'd be a good annoying." McCarthy looked at the glass as half full.

"Touché," Reddick agreed. He backed out of the Clark County probation department and peeled out.

Twenty-five minutes later, McCarthy and Reddick were pulling up in front of the address provided to them on West Ogden Avenue. As they pulled up, both agents noticed how the once nice suburban area looked run-down and abused.

McCarthy rang the doorbell and, several seconds later, they heard a little kid's voice question, "Who is it?"

McCarthy was about to answer when a female voice shouted, "Move, Omar! Get'cha little ass out of my way! That's ya problem now, you're too damn grown." The door swung open, and a very attractive, light-skinned young woman faced Reddick and McCarthy. She instantly pegged the agents for what they were: cops.

"I thought I told y'all to leave me alone. I told y'all everything I know," she said, annoyed.

"We're sorry to disturb you, Ms. Stevens. I'm Agent McCarthy, and this is my partner Agent Reddick, and we're from the Federal Bureau Of Investigation." He pulled out his gold shield to support his claim.

She did a quick scan of the badge. By now, Reddick was standing in the background with his badge out as well.

"We need to speak to you," McCarthy informed the young lady.

She frowned, a puzzled expression on her face. "The feds? What y'all need to speak to me about?" Shonte asked.

"May we come in?" Reddick asked.

"Yeah, but y'all got to cover those up. I got an eight-year-old son," she commented, nodding to the agents' guns. McCarthy and Reddick immediately zipped their coats up, hiding their firearms. They were soon escorted inside of the house.

McCarthy couldn't help but notice Shonte's body. Her breasts were stuffed in a tight tank top and looked ready to bust out at any second. And she had her smooth yellow thighs on display with a tiny pair of shorts that barely covered her ass, which was big, like her titties. Her son rushed over to Reddick.

His mom noticed too. "Boy, that ain't your daddy," Shonte said, grinning.

"Well, aren't you an absolutely adorable, handsome young man," Reddick replied, hugging the young boy. He turned to his mother. "He's going to be a heartbreaker when he gets older," he continued.

"Like father, like son," Shonte said with a saddened expression. "Omar, go in your room and play ya games. Mommy has to talk, okay?"

Omar glanced at Reddick once more then took off running to go entertain himself.

"So how can I help y'all?" she asked directly, sitting on the couch and folding her legs underneath her.

"Well, we heard you were a victim of a home invasion robbery. Now we're really not too interested in the specifics, like the drugs that were in the house, or your little drug-dealing buddies you're covering for. We just need to know who else was in the house with you that night. That's it," Reddick said.

"I told the other cops everything I know already, so I really think you're wasting your time," she replied with a casual, nonchalant air about her.

Reddick kept his piercing gaze locked on the younger woman. "No, you didn't, Ms. Stevens. You told them what you wanted them to know. But you didn't tell them everything. Like I said, my partner and I aren't interested in your drug-dealing friends. That's the local authorities' problem, not ours. You can keep on loving the hooligans and hoodlums. Believe me, sister girl,

I've been where you are at right now. And hopefully
you'll learn sooner instead of later, and hopefully you
don't have to learn the hard way. But I'm not here to
preach to you, either. Me and my partner here are only
interested in the people responsible for the incident.
We just need you to confirm."

McCarthy sat back and admired Reddick's technique,
acting as if he already knew who was in that house that
night, but really having no idea at all. It was an age-old
cop trick, but it still worked to this day. It was a shot
in the dark, but it worked wonders on Shonte, who
momentarily lost her game face and stared at Reddick. It
seemed as if she was shocked that Reddick could know
about Koko. In seconds, she regained her composure,
and the game face returned, but by then it was too late;
the damage had already been done.

McCarthy felt like they hit the jackpot.

"Why you think I know something? I told you before I
don't—" Shonte said with a wary expression on her face.
Before she could finish her sentence, Reddick cut her
short.

"Please let us ask the questions, Ms. Stevens. What we
need for you to do is tell us everything you can about the
night," Reddick instructed.

Shonte's wary look turned into an angry one. She
didn't like the tone in which Reddick was speaking to
her. "Look, I answered all I'm going to fucking answer,"
she spat. "I don't appreciate you coming up in my house
grilling and chastising me like I'm some damn child or
a criminal. With all the motherfuckas out there gettin'
away with murder and shit, I'm sure you can go out there
and do your job and catch you some real criminals to
interrogate." She tore into Reddick like hot slugs.

McCarthy contemplated stepping in and saving
Reddick, but instead, he sat back in amusement. He

could tell by her facial expression as she spoke that Reddick had gone too far and crossed the line when he interrupted Shonte. He had a feeling she wouldn't take too kindly to it. He wished he could've pulled out his phone and taken a picture of Reddick's face as Shonte continued. "I haven't done anything wrong, and I pay my damn taxes to the government. But you motherfuckas wanna come up in my shit like I'm the bad guy," she ranted. "What y'all need to do is go out there and find the sons of bitches who killed my cousin and baby father instead of worrying about some niggas who got their asses beat."

Her last remarks caught McCarthy's attention. He had gotten so caught up in the exchange between Reddick and Shonte that he had forgotten about a theory that had crossed his mind earlier when the parole officer was conveying to them what Shonte had claimed to him. That was his cue to chime in. Knowing he had to do some damage control since Reddick had gotten her riled up, McCarthy went into his "good cop" mode.

"Ms. Stevens, my condolences to you and your family," he began.

Shonte directed her attention to McCarthy. She grimaced and nodded. "Thanks." Her response was abrupt and dry.

Seeing that she was receptive, he continued. "I won't even pretend to begin that I know what you're going through, but I can only imagine. Seeing your little boy back there, the thought of him without a father is very disheartening. I have a little girl myself, who's in the hospital as we speak, fighting for her life, and there's nothing I can do to help or save her." McCarthy couldn't believe he had just disclosed that to her. Just hearing his own words about his daughter nearly caused him to choke up. He fought back the emotions that were trying to surface. Although he was trying to make a connection with her to get her to open up to him, at that moment, McCarthy realized just how hard it was for him dealing with his daughter's medical condition.

Sniffling, he continued. "But if the roles were reversed, I know my little girl would be devastated and heartbroken if she ever lost me."

Shonte sat misty-eyed as McCarthy spoke. Even Reddick, who sat across from Shonte, had to hold back his emotions as he listened to McCarthy.

"Now, there's no other place I'd rather be than by my little girl's bedside right now but, instead, I'm out here trying to solve a case bigger than you can probably even imagine, because I took an oath to protect and serve. And my baby girl knows and understands that. I don't know if you told your boy, and as a mother, that's your choice to decide how and when, but it's our job to seek justice and, if it's in our power, bring those responsible for such crimes to justice. I won't sit here and sell you any dreams or offer any false hopes, but I have a strong feeling that you may have some information that can not only help with our investigation but also help catch the people responsible for the robbery and assault on your boyfriend and his friends and killing your cousin and kid's father. Now, if you can tell me anything about their deaths or the home invasion, I'd greatly appreciate it."

Before he finished, Shonte was already in tears. The news about his daughter had hit home for her. She too had lost her daughter, to what they call SIDS—sudden infant death syndrome—just a year prior to having her son Omar. Wiping her face with the back of her hand, Shonte cleared her throat. "I brought her to the house," she admitted.

Both McCarthy and Reddick's eyes widened.

"I met her at a club down on Freemont, and we began talking. She told me she was from California and just relocated out here to get a fresh start. Said she had recently gotten out of an abusive relationship and was looking to try something different." She looked from Reddick to McCarthy before she continued. "We started seeing each other. Low-key, though, because I have . . . well, I had a dude."

"Did you tell her that your boyfriend sold drugs?" McCarthy's question made Shonte flinch, because she had tried her best to protect La France from the law even though, ever since the robbery, he didn't want anything to do with her anymore.

"Um, I'm not really sure. I think I might have, 'cause I wanted her to know I was involved with somebody from the door and that he was from the streets so there wouldn't be no misunderstanding. I had never cheated on La France." Shonte winced, realizing that she had just given up his name; but she continued. "I never cheated on him for the nine months we were together. Even though I'm almost positive he can't say the same thing. But once I laid eyes on Lacey, I just had to have her. She was that banging. I don't even fuck with bitches like that, especially no white ones. No offense." She was staring at McCarthy when she apologized.

"None taken." He smiled as she continued.

"Every once in a while when I'm feeling crazy; but Lacey was like a breath of fresh air for me. Sweet and sexy. Intelligent and hood at the same time and that combination drove me crazy. So I began creeping with her. But she insisted on meeting my man. At first, I was kind of scared, but I finally broke down and introduced them. Excuse my French, but La France almost bust a nut on himself when he saw her, and he don't even like white bitches either. He tried to get at her but—"

"But she refused to have sex with him, saying that you were who she wanted, right?" McCarthy pried, cutting Shonte off.

"Yeah, how'd you know that?" Shonte asked.

"Just a wild guess. Tell us about the robbery," McCarthy said.

Shonte began replaying the horrible night for the agents, telling them about how two bodacious masked women had made their way up into the house and pistol-whipped Ty and knocked out Irv but told them he was dead. And how they had stripped the men naked and used her and Lacey to help pull the robbery off.

"How much did they get, Shonte?" McCarthy asked.

Shonte hesitated at the question.

"Shonte, we're not interested in locking up you or any of your friends. Truthfully, we just want this Lacey chick."

McCarthy's insistence put a worried look on Shonte's face. "Why y'all want Lacey?"

"I'll answer that question after you answer mine. How much?"

"Well, they took all of our jewelry and whatever money we had on us. Plus they took some drugs and twenty Gs from my boo."

Shonte's answer made McCarthy's eyes stretch wide, and he stared over at Reddick, who mouthed, "Sweet mother of Jesus."

"Now, answer my question," she demanded of McCarthy. "Why y'all so interested in my peoples Lacey?"

McCarthy stared at Shonte for a few seconds as he considered her question, and he realized that there was no easy way to break it to the younger woman. She had been played, used like a pawn in a chess game. So he just came out with the truth.

"First off, she's not your peoples. Far from it. Lacey set up you and your boo to get robbed. Now, before you start denying it, just think logically for a second. You meet this beautiful girl at the bar. She appears out of nowhere. You two hit it off. Well, at least that's the impression she gave you. If you hadn't have been involved with your little drug-dealing friend, she wouldn't have given you the time of day. She was way more interested in him and his money than you. That's why she insisted on meeting him, 'cause it was him she was after all along. How long had you known her before the robbery took place?"

"A little over two weeks," she answered. She didn't want to believe what McCarthy was saying about Lacey, but she thought hard about what McCarthy was saying.

"She probably spent as much time as possible with you, painting all kinds of pictures. All lies. The truth is, she was most likely acting out orders given to her by a cold-hearted female with no conscience and no soul, just like the two masked women you spoke about." McCarthy waited to see how Shonte was taking what he said before he continued. "There's a powerful lesbian criminal organization secretly running around Las Vegas called the Double Gs. Ever heard of them?"

Shonte shook her head no.

"Well, what you just told me fits the MO of the organization and we're trying to put a stop to them before anyone else gets hurt," McCarthy informed her.

"Let me guess, the woman Lacey gained your trust and used you, and now she's nowhere to be found. Am I right?" Reddick asked.

Shonte nodded weakly. Since the robbery, she had been searching for Lacey daily, hitting all of the bars, to no avail. It's as if she had disappeared. She took in all the new information slowly but surely.

"See, what my partner and I believe is that the whole robbery was a setup and the two female robbers were Double Gs. Did they rough her up a little bit while robbing the place?"

"Yeah, one of them slapped the shit out of Lacey," she answered, surprised at how McCarthy's guesses were so on point.

"All acting, just so you guys would never suspect that she was in on it. The slap was probably real. But definitely worth it. A twenty thousand dollar backhand slap. Hell, I've been slapped for free, so I can imagine for twenty big ones. Are you following what I'm saying, Ms. Stevens?"

Again Shonte nodded, finally realizing that Lacey had played her. It was she who showed Lacey La France's stash in the first place. Shonte thought about the event, how the women had stripped them naked and had the money and jewelry, all that they'd demanded, but they still felt La France was holding out on them, as if they knew there was another stash somewhere.

Shonte wanted to cry. McCarthy could sense this. He quickly rose and walked over to Shonte. "Listen, you can't blame yourself. You're a good girl. You come from a good family and you were raised right, I can tell. How were you supposed to know that she was plotting against you? Just like you said, she was a breath of fresh air, so you thought. It's not your fault that she turned out to be a breath of rotten, polluted air. You got a good heart, but it just so happens that there are a lot of people who prey on people with good hearts like yours. And Lacey is one of 'em. You're not their first victim, but with your help, we might be able to make you the last one. Please tell us everything there is to tell about her. Any little thing might help."

Shonte got up and began pacing back and forth. She began to give a description of Lacey. They learned that she had a tattoo right above her crotch that spelled out her name. Shonte told McCarthy and Reddick everything that Lacey had told her, but all three of them knew that it was mostly all lies.

"I'm glad I was able to shed some more light on things, but I don't see what this has to do with my cousin and baby daddy," Shonte stated with a distorted expression plastered on her face.

"Did you introduce her to your cousin or you son's father?" McCarthy switched to the question he had been waiting to ask. It had been weighing heavy on his mind since he had gotten there.

"No, not at all," Shonte replied abruptly. "That's why I was wondering, how does all of this have anything to do with my baby daddy and cousin?" she questioned.

"That's what I was trying to figure out, Ms. Stevens. Thought you could help us with that," McCarthy replied.

"I told you everything I know." Shonte sniffled. "My boyfriend and my baby daddy or my cousin didn't even mess with each other or travel in the same circle like that."

The disappointment was all over McCarthy's face. His gut was telling him that there was some type of connection between the robbery and the murders, which included his deceased female agent, and he believed that connection was the Double Gs.

"Please don't take this the wrong way, but was your child's father a drug dealer also?"

Shonte rolled her eyes. "Even if he was, Agent McCarthy, like I said, he and La France traveled in two different circles." Her tone had confirmed that she was offended by the question, even though she knew McCarthy, unlike his partner, didn't mean to offend her. Shonte knew she owed it to her little cousin, for all the love he had shown her and her son when she was struggling, to be forthcoming with information if it meant bringing their killer to justice. She already had an idea why they were killed or at least who may have been the cause, but she had not offered that piece of information as of yet, especially when it had nothing to do with any gay gangster chicks.

"La France and 'em got robbed out in North Las Vegas. My cousin and baby daddy got killed in a whole 'nother town out in Henderson at some bitch's crib one of them was probably fucking, who you need to be talking to."

Shonte hardly got to finish before McCarthy chimed in. Hearing the words "Henderson" and "bitch's crib" immediately caught McCarthy's attention. His heart nearly jumped out of his chest. *It's gotta be.*

"I'm sorry, Ms. Stevens, if you don't mind, what are the names of your cousin and son's father?" It was a question McCarthy had just realized he had never asked.

Shonte eyed him for a second. She wondered what names she should provide, their birth names or street ones. *Hell, they're the feds. They can easily find out anyway,* she concluded.

"Christian Reeves and Sean Wesson," she answered.

McCarthy wasn't surprised when the names didn't ring a bell. It had been a long time since he had his ear to the streets of Las Vegas and knew all of the major and key male players in the game. His focus had been strictly on the Double Gs, who he thought to be the most significant and biggest criminals in Clark County. But he was convinced that the two names Shonte Stevens had just provided were connected to his investigation of the Double Gs.

Were they two of Starrshma Fields's puppets? If so, how did she find out my agent was undercover? As careful as she was all of these years, how was her cover blown? How didn't she see this coming? And who killed these two fellas after they killed my agent? McCarthy had a ton of questions floating through his mind that he was determined to find answers to. He played the two names back in his head repeatedly until something clicked.

Shit, he felt like a rookie for not thinking about it the moment Shonte mentioned the names. He remembered that he'd received an e-mail, which he had glanced at only once, with the names of the other two victims they found in his agent's home. He reached into his inside suit jacket and came back out with his iPhone 6s.

McCarthy unlocked his phone and went into his government-issued e-mail account. Doing a quick scroll down, he tapped his screen and opened the e-mail from the locals in Henderson, Nevada. His armpits began to moisten from anticipation as his eyes quickly read through the e-mail. "Son of a bitch," McCarthy uttered under his breath, but not low enough not to be heard.

Reddick's eyes shifted over to him, while Shonte sat up erect. "What is it?" a hopeful Shonte asked.

Reddick wanted to ask the same question, but he knew he'd find out soon enough from McCarthy.

McCarthy cursed himself for reacting to the e-mail openly in front of Shonte. Despite the fact that she was more than helpful with the information she had provided him and Reddick, some things were simply on a need-to-know basis, and police business. He closed his phone and placed it back inside his suit jacket.

"I'm sorry," he offered apologetically, for getting Shonte Stevens alarmed. "I thought I had something, but I didn't." His tone was flat. "But when I do, you have my word, you will be one of the first to know."

Shonte gave McCarthy a hard stare. She couldn't tell whether he was lying, but she didn't believe him. She now felt like a fool for trusting him with information that could possibly get her and her son killed if found out. She rolled her eyes at McCarthy. *All these motherfuckin' pigs are the same,* she concluded. "If you say so," Shonte dryly replied.

"You have my word, Ms. Stevens."

"Is that all?" Shonte was ready for the two agents to leave her home.

McCarthy grimaced and stood up. Reddick followed suit. "Yes. Thank you again."

Silence was all he received in return. Realizing he had worn out his welcome, McCarthy spun and turned toward the front door.

"Ma'am." Reddick nodded before doing the same.

Shonte sucked her teeth and rolled her eyes at him. She slammed the door forcefully behind them to express her attitude toward them.

Seconds later, McCarthy and Reddick were back in their unmarked car. "So, you wanna clue me in?" Reddick wasted no time asking. There was no doubt in his mind that whatever McCarthy had discovered in his phone was valuable to their investigation.

"Pull off from here first," McCarthy suggested. Once they were back on the main road, McCarthy began to fill Reddick in. "The day Douglass was murdered, I was up at the hospital with my daughter, watching the news about the triple homicide out in Henderson."

A twisted look appeared on Reddick's face. "Don't remind me," he said. He was still pissed behind the fact that the officer turned informant was killed on his watch.

"Well, that day it came across the screen about two males and one female being executed in a possible gang-related incident. The fact that they mentioned it was gang related caught my attention, so I reached out to the locals. The investigating officer was kind enough to send me over everything he had on the case and the victims. The males were from Las Vegas." McCarthy had Reddick's full attention.

"There wasn't much on the female, nothing at all really," McCarthy lied. He knew there was no way he could be totally honest with Reddick about who the female was without opening up Pandora's box, so he was careful with his words. "But one of the males had at least a few run-ins with our locals, and the other was a convicted felon. They sent me over their mug shots and rap sheets. But I never took the time out to really look into it. Until now," McCarthy claimed.

Reddick's eyes constantly shifted from the road to McCarthy. "And?"

"And, the two victim's names were—"

"Let me guess: Christian Reeves and Sean Wesson," Reddick finished his sentence.

"Exactly," McCarthy confirmed. "Better known as Clips and Smoke," McCarthy said, providing their street monikers. "Ever heard of either of the two?"

Reddick pondered the question as he exited the highway. "Can't say I have," he then answered.

"Yeah, me neither," McCarthy admitted. "But, there's no doubt in my mind that Starrshma Fields was behind this," he revealed.

Reddick hooked a right onto Las Vegas boulevard, headed toward the federal building. "How can you be so sure?" he asked McCarthy.

McCarthy grimaced. "Because the female, Felicia Richards, was a Double G."

Chapter 19

Blaring the latest Young Thug track, twenty-five-year-old Lacey Smith pulled out of her job's parking lot. *Good riddance, motherfuckers.* As she backed out, she cursed the headache of a club she had told herself she'd never return to. To confirm it, she tore up her last paycheck, not wanting any more part of the establishment. She had done some degrading and regrettable things to survive.

A disgusted look appeared on Lacey's face at the thought of some of the things she had been subjected to and done in order to make ends meet. Old white men propositioned her on a regular basis, wanting to dip their pink, shriveled, tiny dicks in her sweet vanilla pudding. Lacey would just grit her teeth and deal with it. On occasion, she had to do what she had to do, though. For nine dollars an hour plus tips, she put on a phony smile, laughed at wack-ass jokes, and ignore the rude sexual comments made toward her. Her weekly checks were needed; bills had to be paid. She couldn't wait for the day when she could quit and tell the whole office to kiss her fat, natural white ass. She even daydreamed about getting her two bosses robbed. Since meeting Diamond, she had pictured the look on their pale faces when they laid eyes on some of the Double Gs like Glitter and Sparkle with big guns shoved in them. But she believed those days were officially over as of today.

She viewed it as a blessing in disguise, meeting Diamond at the club. She had learned about and heard of her and the Double Gs in passing, but when Diamond had approached her and explained what it would require to become one of them, Lacey believed it was an opportunity of a lifetime. She was looking forward to the meeting she had that night with Starr and the Double Gs. She knew the setup she successfully helped pull off would lead to her membership into the Double Gs, which was what she'd hoped would be the case. She felt a little bad because she really liked Shonte but, for the most part, she knew what she did had to be done. It was made clear that it had to be done the way it was instructed, or else it would be frivolous to do it when it didn't come with membership if done incorrectly.

After hearing and seeing a little of what the Double Gs were about the night during Starr's welcome home and the orgy after-party, Lacey was all in. She particularly loved the fact that the Double Gs were an exclusive organization and had a strong sisterhood, so she believed. She was grown and could do whatever she wanted with her life, and Lacey planned on living it.

Right now she had enough money to pay off the rest of her student loans and credit card bills and drop another chunk of change on a nice livable crib better than the room she was renting out of a sleazy motel while working the club. That was all thanks to the Double Gs. But she wanted everything fully paid off and some money on the side to play with. She already wanted to pull off some more jobs.

Lacey always had a thing for women, preferably plus-size women of all colors, so meeting the Double Gs was like putting her in urban heaven. Every single one of them was a tasteful sight to her. Being a Caucasian woman growing up in the slums of Las Vegas had inspired her taste for women and crime. All her life she had dealt with gangster dudes and chicks. That had always been her most major turn-on. She thought back to how while the robbery was going down she was supposed to be acting like a victim. That scene had turned her on, and she fought to suppress her attraction to it, but her nipples became hard enough to cut diamonds, and her pussy got wet enough to sink the *Titanic*.

Lacey damn near came on the spot several times right in the middle of the robbery. That violent, gangsta shit always worked wonders on her. But she was getting older and growing up. She wanted more out of life, and she was determined to get it. Whether it took her acting by herself or with a crew, whether it took illegal or legal means to get it, it was going to be what it was going to be, she'd concluded. She strongly believed that the Double Gs would be the perfect women to do it with.

Pulling into the bar, Lacey texted Bubbles, who she was told was her contact person, to let her know that she was outside the bar waiting.

Bubbles grimaced at the text. She said good-bye to the light-skinned dancer with the fat, soft ass who had been playing Bubbles close ever since she got a glimpse of all the hundred dollars bills she had on her. It was hard for Bubbles to walk away from that soft ass grinding on her. She knew she could've taken the dancer somewhere and thrashed her right quick. But Bubbles knew she had no time for that. Starr didn't play when it came to the Double Gs meetings and membership.

Bubbles stumbled out of the bar and hopped in the car with Lacey.

"I hope you weren't waiting long," Lacey apologetically said as soon as Bubbles got in.

"Nah, you straight. I was low-key already coming here even before I knew you were supposed to meet me here." Bubbles chuckled. "I been here about an hour and some change," she informed Lacey.

They drove in silence for a few seconds before Bubbles broke it. "The twins told us you did your thing that night, like a real G," Bubbles acknowledged.

"Thanks, but a bitch wished I could've been one of the ones robbing them niggas' punk asses," Lacey retorted, using the slang term loosely and freely despite the fact that she was white.

"I hear that," Bubbles said. "But don't worry, you'll get your chance," she assured her.

A few minutes later, they were pulling up to the address Diamond had texted Bubbles and exiting the vehicle. "Tonight's your night." Bubbles smiled. "Enjoy!" she added as she flung her arm around Lacey's neck and escorted her inside the secret location.

Chapter 20

It was a long shot, but McCarthy decided to visit the club where Shonte Stevens had said she'd met the woman known as Lacey. He invited Reddick to tag along, being that he had extended the same courtesy to him when he was following up on the lead that landed them at Shonte Steven's home.

Since he had come across the street names of the two men found dead in the house with his female agent, McCarthy had realized he had heard one of the names in particular. The name Clips started to ring a bell in McCarthy's mind, but he didn't know why. He was almost certain he had come across the name previously, but he just couldn't remember where. He had a feeling that this was a major factor in the case, and if he could figure out where he heard that name, he'd be one step closer to solving the case.

"What's on your mind, McCarthy? Something's going on in that dome of yours. Spit it out," Reddick said, breaking his train of thought.

McCarthy snapped out of his daze. "That name. Clips. I heard that name before. It doesn't ring a bell with you?"

Reddick thought it over for several seconds. "Can't say that it does. You think the name means something?"

McCarthy nodded. "I'm almost positive. I just know it is." McCarthy banged his hand on the steering wheel, racking his brain, trying to remember where he had heard that name.

Reddick asked him a question, but he couldn't hear him. His mind had drifted off elsewhere again. *Think, Mac.* He pushed himself to remember why the name Clips continued to resonate in his mind.

Then, out of nowhere, it hit him. He recalled a conversation he had with Agent Richards about someone who was snooping around and may have been stalking her. The name given was Clips. Once the name became clear to him, McCarthy remembered the conversation as if it were yesterday. Especially the fact that he was one of the young top earners and shooters of a crew whose leader was one of the Double Gs' victims. Piece by piece, McCarthy could see the connection coming together. Then it hit him. Monica popped in his head, and he realized that she was connected to Clips's boss.

McCarthy accelerated to Lacey's, still ignoring Reddick's questions. He began punching and pounding on the steering wheel and dashboard as he blew his horn and weaved in and out of traffic. A shocked and confused Reddick looked on.

Five minutes later, they were pulling into the parking lot of Lacey's job, only to receive the unfortunate news that they had just missed Lacey by a couple of hours. They were hopeful until her manager followed up with the news that he doubted she'd return because she asked for her last paycheck.

After getting nowhere with questioning the manager and a few of the other bottle girls, McCarthy led the way up out of the club. A look of defeat appeared on Reddick's face as he trailed behind him. Once they were back in the unmarked car, McCarthy looked over at Reddick with a smirk on his face.

Reddick noticed him staring at him. "What has that shit-eating grin on your face?"

McCarthy chuckled. "Don't worry. We have another lead to follow."

Looking at him oddly, Reddick asked, "Who?"

"Give me a second." McCarthy held up a hand. He pulled out his cell phone and sent a quick text message out and then drew his attention back to Reddick.

"One of the biggest drug dealers in Las Vegas, the Prime Minister himself." McCarthy's smirk returned.

It was a name that Reddick was all too familiar with, the name of another organized crime leader in Clark County who seemed to be untouchable.

"Do tell," Reddick inquired as McCarthy rolled down his window and tossed the red light onto the top of his unmarked car and peeled off.

Chapter 21

Coming out the shower naked and putting on lotion in front of him had been Monica's way of seducing him. This was like a ritual with them; every time after they pulled a job off, they would both be extremely horny and would end up having some banging sex. The violence, money, and guns gave Monica a serious rush that always got her pussy soaking wet.

"It's okay, Prime. You did what you had to do. Besides, that rough gangsta shit turns me the fuck on, daddy. You know that." And Monica knew Prime loved when she called him daddy.

They began to kiss. Prime let his hands roam all over Monica's smooth body. He palmed her titties first, playing with her nipples, then palmed her ass. Monica moaned, loving how his big, rough hands sent sparks through her body. She quickly unbuckled his belt and slid her hands inside his boxers, gripping his dick, squeezing, touching, and rubbing it.

Prime pushed her back onto the bed and stripped, peeling the wife beater off first. Next went his jeans and finally the boxers. Monica let her eyes feast on the man in front of her, and then they came to rest on his manhood that was standing at full attention as if it were saluting her.

Monica pulled Prime toward her so he was standing directly in front of her and she began kissing on his chest and gently biting and licking his nipples. She kissed a trail down his stomach. When Monica got down to his magic stick, she began kissing on the head and swirling her tongue around it. Then she took him in deep and began hitting him off.

When they first started fucking around, Prime had schooled Monica on how he liked to be pleased. He said most men like their head just how they like their pussy: tight and wet. The wetter the better. Monica was a good student and a quick learner; she slobbered and slurped on Prime's dick until her spit was dripping off his sack. She lightly ran her fingernails up and down his body, making Prime shiver in pleasure. With her other hand, she played with her pussy, rubbing her clit and moaning like crazy. Prime slowly pumped in and out of her mouth, loving how she handled his dick. His head was back, his eyes were closed, and his mouth was open. "Umm, damn, girl. Mmm, yeah, just like that. Suck that shit, bitch," he mumbled.

Monica dipped her head a little lower and caught his balls in her mouth and began sucking on them while she stroked his dick with her hand. "Like that, daddy?" she asked.

"Just like that," Prime whispered.

Monica began sucking on the head, just the head, loving the look of pleasure Prime had on his face. Then she spit on his dick and began deep-throating it, fast and hard, tightening her jaws. She felt Prime's body tense, and she prepared herself. Monica knew that hot milk would soon be coming and she was going to swallow every drop just like Prime taught her to.

But Prime wasn't ready to bust yet. He pulled out of her mouth and got control of himself. "Face down, ass up," he ordered in a hoarse whisper.

Monica quickly assumed the position: face in the bed, back arched, knees spread, and ass in the air. Prime stared at Monica's wet, shaved pussy and put his face all in it, kissing and sucking on her wet pussy lips, then gently licking on her erect clit. Monica moaned in pleasure. As Prime ate the pussy, he gripped and smacked Monica's ass, inching his finger to her most sensitive hole.

As he slurped on her clit, he gently slid his finger into her ass, causing her to gasp and cry out, but not in pain.

"Oh, yes. Mmm hummm. Oooh, Prime, here it come. I'm about to . . ." Monica purred, on the verge of a serious orgasm. She ground herself on Prime's mouth and came. Prime slid his finger in her ass deeper. Monica was rubbing her clit, working on her second nut. She already felt the fluttery feeling again building up inside her belly. Just then Prime stopped, got up, and walked to the other side of the room, returning with the strap-on in his hand. He resumed tossing her while he rammed the strap-on inside of her pussy. Within seconds, Monica was cumming again.

Prime dangled the dildo in front of her, which was covered in her juices, and she immediately took it into her mouth, sucking on it. "Ya pussy taste good, don't it, girl?"

"Mm-hmm," Monica answered with her mouth full. Prime pushed himself into her wet, waiting pussy and began viciously assaulting it from the back, loving the way her ass jiggled each time he stroked.

Prime slid his finger back into her ass and began finger popping it. The pleasure of having all three of her holes filled at the same time was overwhelming, and Monica put her face in the pillow and screamed as she busted back-to-back nuts.

"Ooh, fuck. Harder. Harder, Prime!" Monica demanded, throwing her ass back at him, meeting Prime halfway. Prime smacked her ass cheeks as hard as he could as he plunged in and out of Monica. She couldn't take any more and fell forward on the bed. Prime stared down at her beautiful, sweaty body.

"We ain't finished yet."

She rolled over and looked in Prime's lustful eyes. Then she stared at his dick that was still harder than a mu'fucka. "Wait, hold up," Monica said and crawled over to the stack of money and recklessly spread the bills all over the bed. "A fantasy of mine. I always wanted to do this."

Monica lay on her back and lifted her legs, keeping them together. Prime gripped the backs of her thighs and leaned in, pushing her legs back farther, so her knees and chin were touching; then he proceeded to beat the pussy up.

"Like that, baby, like that?" Prime breathlessly asked as he pounded Monica.

"Yes. Oooh, shit, just like that," Monica gasped.

Prime noticed how noisy their lovemaking was. The bedsprings creaking, their bodies slapping together, the wet slurping noise Monica's pussy was making as Prime pumped, her moaning and screaming and him grunting like a wild animal: this was all music to Prime's ears. He felt the pressure building up in his balls.

"Cum in me, Prime. Please, cum all in me," Monica begged.

Prime planned on doing just that. He gritted his teeth and began long-dicking the shit out of Monica. When he felt it, Prime went balls-deep inside of her tight, wet walls and exploded. He collapsed on top of Monica, who gladly welcomed his body, wrapping her arms and legs around him. He had to admit, he enjoyed fucking Monica, but not enough not to play her the way he was. As a reminder, he kept at the forefront of his mind the fact that Monica made a failed attempt at setting him up. *Had that not been the case, things may have been different,* thought Prime.

They remained in this position for several minutes. Monica felt Prime's dick get soft inside of her. He rolled off of her and lay beside Monica, reaching for a Black & Mild.

"Did you tell her about us yet?" Prime asked.

Oh, boy, here we go, Monica thought as she watched Prime light up a gutted Mild. "No, I haven't told her yet."

"Why not?" Prime pressed her.

"Because now isn't the time."

"When are you gonna tell her, Monica?" Prime asked.

Uh-oh, he's using my whole name. "When the time is right, Prime. We got too much to worry about right now, like a baby."

"You are full of shit, you know that? Why do you keep putting it off? What'chu scared of?" Prime pretended to be upset.

Monica shot Prime a hard look. "Don't do that. Stop what'chu doing. I ain't scared of no-fuckin'-body and you know that."

Prime let out a heavy sigh as he inhaled the Mild. She was right, and they both knew it.

"The problem is that not only am I fucking you, which is at the top of the 'don't' list in the Double Gs organization, but I'm now in a love triangle with two rival crew leaders." Monica chuckled.

"Oh. Soo, you love this bitch?" Prime asked, his nostrils flaring slightly.

"Prime, stop."

"Yeah, you do," Prime answered for her. Based on Monica's responses, he could tell that he'd convinced her that he felt some type of way about her not telling Starr about them. He had been working on Monica for weeks now.

Monica rolled her eyes.

"You know what? The next time I see her I'm telling her about us, myself." Prime quickly hopped up and closed the distance between him and Monica. He gripped her arms and pulled her close, so his face was inches from hers.

Monica stared into Prime's dark eyes and saw anger and rage. The grip he had on her arms was starting to get painful. Prime lightened his grip and lowered his tone fast.

"You know what? Do whatever you wanna do." Prime gave up.

A frown appeared on Monica's face. She had been putting it off for a minute now, and she really didn't know if she should break away from the Double Gs, and particularly from Starr, especially after what happened to Felicia, which was a mystery. Monica knew she had to say something as a form of damage control. Clearing her throat, she cooed, "I'm gonna tell her, baby. Trust me, I am. But I'm the one who broke the rules, and the penalty for that is death."

Mission accomplished, thought Prime. Still, he kept his cool "You sure?" he asked with a straight face.

Monica slowly nodded. She looked up at Prime and saw the sincerity in his eyes. She was about to speak, but Prime cut her off with a hungry, urgent kiss. He pulled Monica into a powerful embrace, and his tongue pushed its way inside of her mouth, probing and searching. Monica felt her body reacting to the kiss. She felt Prime's manhood get hard and soon it was pressing against her stomach. Prime pushed her onto the bed, and Monica could tell by the look in his eyes that it was about to go down. She knew her hands were really about to be full. For one, this was Prime's second nut, so he was definitely going to last longer this time. And, two, he had a point to prove to her. This was his little way of apologizing: makeup sex for the minor beef they just had.

Prime stared down at Monica, slowly stroking himself with a devilish grin on his face. "Round two, Miss I'm a Grown-ass Woman."

Hours after their lovemaking session was over and done with, Monica sat in the bed, smoking a blunt of haze and thinking. Prime lay next to her, sound asleep. Monica stared at him and thought how cute and innocent he looked in his sleep. It made her think about how pretty or handsome their daughter or son would be. She admired his dark peach fuzz over his top lip and a wisp of chin hair. His face was like the rest of his body: well defined and chiseled.

Monica let out a heavy sigh as she stared at Prime. Sometimes it surprised her just how much she loved him and how fast it happened. Just couple months ago, she was a confused, bitter, anti-man, full-blown female with lesbian tendencies even though she was still young and tender.

Monica had decided that all men were liars and cheaters. She remembered her first boyfriend. She had met him in high school. Monica gave him two years of her life, making him wait patiently to have sex with her, four months to be exact, before she allowed him to pop her cherry. *That was a long time ago.*

The vibration of her cell phone returned Monica to the present. Looking down at it, she noticed she had just received an unwanted text message. It had been a minute since she had answered any messages from him. Without opening her phone, she read the text on her screen, then quickly cleared it.

She hadn't been checking in or providing any real-time updates on what had been going on with her mission. She was lost in what was commonly known as deep cover. She had lost sight of who she really was and her purpose for being there. The Double Gs lifestyle became real to her. All of it became so surreal. She had become her character. Even when it came down to her broken agreement regarding Prime. She knew she wouldn't be shown any mercy if her secret involvement was found out by the Double Gs or the agency. It seemed she was in bed with everyone relevant to her initial and intended mission—the Double Gs, Prime, and the FBI—and she didn't know how to get out of any of them without being thrown under the jail or buried six feet deep.

Never would she have thought she'd been in the predicament she was in, but sex had clouded her judgment with Starr and Prime, and she found herself back in bed and in the arms of them both repeatedly. And that was the part that was pushing her further away. She knew she was slipping and it was imperative that she get refocused, but she wasn't convinced that she really wanted to.

Another text message came across Monica's screen. She quickly read it. The second one caught her attention. She did her best not to make any reaction toward the message, careful not to alarm Prime. The first message to pop up had read, We need to talk. That's all he ever texted when he needed to get in contact with her or wanted an update. But the words You've been compromised disturbed her.

Her eyes shifted to Prime, who was now awake and staring at her while she was looking at her phone. "That's her?" Prime asked.

The question couldn't have come at a better time. She was already trying to think of an excuse to give to Prime for her next move. "Yes. I have to go, babe. We have an emergency meeting," she lied.

Prime nodded. He was ready for her to leave anyway. He too had something to tend to. "It's cool," he said nonchalantly.

Monica rose up off the bed and began to gather her things. The words, *"You've been compromised,"* continued to ring off in her head as she dressed.

"I'll see you soon," she told Prime once she'd gotten fully dressed.

After exchanging kisses with him, moments later Monica was putting distance between her and Prime's crib. Pulling out her phone, she read the alarming text again, wondering what her superior officer, McCarthy, meant by her being compromised. She was tempted to respond, but she had no clue what to say. Rather than reply, Monica tossed her phone into the passenger seat.

She remembered McCarthy telling her in the beginning that if he ever texted her that, then he was pulling her out. That was the last thing Monica wanted or felt she needed. She couldn't figure out how she had been compromised, but outside of responding to McCarthy, she knew the only other place she would be able to find out if it was true was if she went around her Double Gs family.

She glanced at her Michael Kors watch. "Shit," she cursed, realizing today was the day they introduced and held a get-together for the new Double Gs members.

She abruptly pulled over alongside the street's curb. She took her key out of her ignition and unlocked her glove compartment. Retrieving the .40-caliber and extra clip she kept in it, she then popped her trunk and exited her vehicle. She snatched up the P89 she had stashed in her trunk, and she climbed back into the driver's seat. *If McCarthy is right, I'm damn sure not going out without a fight,* she told herself as she threw her car back in drive.

Monica knew that if her cover had been blown, she'd be finding out soon enough, because all of the Double Gs were expected to be at the welcoming festivity; and she wanted to at least have a fighting chance.

Chapter 22

Frenchie rode shotgun while he and Freeze cruised the city, vibing out to a trap music CD. They were conversing about Frenchie's plans now that he was a free man.

"All I'm tryin'a fuck wit' really is that weed money. If it ain't green and leafy, it's beneath me. If it's white, it ain't right. I gotta change my game up some, that's all. I been researching the market out here since I been home. I just need a strong plug," Frenchie informed him. "Fuck all that hand-to-hand shit. I'm past that. I'm tryin'a sell weight to the niggas who hand-to-hand. I still know how to grind, feel me?"

"Damn, you been doing your homework on the weed business, huh?" Freeze asked.

"Hell yeah! Think back when you was young coming up. All niggas wanted to do was get money, fuck bitches, and get high. Shit ain't change. I don't care how long I been gone. Everybody and they mother is smoking. The only difference now is you got that exotic, name-brand shit. Haze, Pep, Sour Diesel, and all that other shit and that shit cost money as you know. It got these motherfuckas lookin' like fiends out here. They gotta have it," Frenchie explained.

Freeze knew that he spoke the truth because mostly everybody in his crew was a bona fide weedhead who smoked multiple blunts a day. "Well, you know I got the lane for that, but it's not really my thing," Freeze stated.

"Yeah, you like that dope game," Frenchie said, shooting Freeze a sideways glance.

"Yeah, that fast, scary paper," Freeze chimed in, and began laughing.

Freeze handled the big truck with ease, weaving in and out of traffic. Freeze noticed a lot of people squinting their eyes trying to see through the tinted windows and find out who was pushing the exclusive SUV. Other people knew that the truck belonged to Freeze.

As they floated through the city of Las Vegas, some local hustlers "yo'd" him, throwing up a fist of acknowledgment. Freeze would return the gesture by honking his horn. Frenchie laughed as he saw a group of young girls nearly break their necks, openly gawking at the truck as it passed by.

"I see this big mu'fucka gets a lot of attention."

"Yeah, that's why I barely drive it. I usually stay in one of my hoopties or a rental car. This shit attracts the wrong kind of attention. Too many eyes be on me when I come through in this shit. Plus, narcs be on my dick for real. Anyway, you home now. If that's what you wanna do, then I got you," Freeze assured Frenchie.

"I was sitting in that fuckin' jail for too long. I ain't trying to go back. I just wanna stack my bread from the bud and stay in my own fuckin' lane. But if you need me or if something pops up and it's sweet enough, worth my time, and worth the risk, then you know . . ." Frenchie didn't finish the statement. He was sure Freeze knew what he meant.

"Yo, I might have something for you. It's definitely some major paper involved, too."

Frenchie's interest grew. "Yeah, holla at me."

Freeze was already putting a plan together in his head as he spoke. "I be fuckin' with these Arizona cats, 'cause I'm trying to branch off to that E pill game. It's a lot of money in that shit and I been fuckin' with them for damn near two months now and they heavy. We might be able to put our heads together and make something happen," Freeze said. "Only thing is, it's these fucking dyke bitches in the way, fucking up the flow."

"The chicks from the club, right?" Frenchie asked.

"Yeah, them motherfuckas." The disdain for the Double Gs could be heard in Freeze's tone.

"Since when bitches start running shit in Vegas?" Frenchie wanted to know.

"Shit change, unc." Freeze shook his head. *Same way I felt until they caught me slipping,* Freeze wished he could have said, but he knew he never would, due to the blackmailing content they had hanging over his head. He reflected on the eventful day, remembering the evening and the words that had altered his life forever.

He thought it was all just a bad dream. The image of him being cuffed to the bedrail angered him all over again. The recollection of the burning sensation that had registered in the lower half of his body still had him randomly waking up in cold sweats. "Wha . . . What the fuck did y'all do to me?" he remembered asking the two thick twins, not really wanting to know the answer. He couldn't even remember if he was awake for it all, but the sharp pain shooting through his anus told the story of exactly what happened. And then he heard the unfamiliar voice enter his left ear.

"Hello, Mr. Frost. Or should I address you by your street moniker?" The voice let out a light chuckle. "Anyway, this is the leader of the Double Gs organization. Maybe you've heard of us, maybe you haven't, but we are a well-known resistance group of the underworld. And we are well protected. You have just been part of an initiation process by these two young ladies. They are now under our umbrella. We are responsible for them and their well-being. So, please, before you think about any type of retaliation, do your research on us

first. You will find that there are many just like you who have been targeted and then forced to become our allies if ever we need assistance of any kind. If you weren't considered to be a useful asset to our organization, then we wouldn't be having this conversation, because you'd be dead already.

"I am very aware of your power, and exactly what you are capable of. I also know your limits and, more importantly, your reach. And that's where we are up on you. You are restricted. Local. We are spread throughout the entire nation. We are everywhere you can think of or even imagine. And, everywhere we are, there are dozens like you who are forced to deal with us, even though they despise who we are, what we do, what we are about and, even more importantly, what we have done.

"Here's the deal. I have live footage of what just took place. It is stored away in a computer file along with hundreds of others. If you choose to retaliate or show resistance in any kind of way, shape, form, or fashion, you will be killed. But only after we finish stripping you of everything and every person you love or even cared about. And, on top of all that, the footage will be played at your funeral. Copies will be handed out to everyone throughout the entire Las Vegas area connected or associated with you. Your crew will spit on your name. Your legacy will be tarnished and reduced to dirt. And all you will be known for is being a has-been gangsta who got killed 'cause he fucked with the wrong bitches and got fucked!"

Those were the last words spoken before the phone went dead in his ear and the twins uncuffed him.

Freeze shook off the thoughts and returned to his conversation with Frenchie. After hearing Frenchie's question, Freeze's mind was made up. He knew if he ever wanted to feel whole again, he had to do something about those who had violated him and were holding him back. Before, it was Prime and his crew who stood in his way of progression, but since their last encounter, the Prime Minister was no longer a factor. In fact, both he and Prime had the same issue: the Double Gs.

"So, if I needed some work put in, you would be interested if the price was right?"

"Oh, most definitely," Frenchie confirmed. "But for you, price or no price I got you," he added.

"Appreciate it. But business is business. I actually wouldn't mind paying for this shit."

Frenchie nodded. "I feel you, nephew. Sounds like some personal shit."

More than you'll ever know, thought Freeze as he pulled up to Frenchie's destination. "Very," Freeze replied.

"Any nigga or niggas I know? I mean, I know I been off the scene for a minute."

"Nah, it's no dudes," Freeze corrected him. "It's some bitches. Twins to be exact," he explained.

"Oh, yeah?" Frenchie was surprised. Not that it had mattered. It wasn't like he had never killed a female before. "The ones you were just talkin' about?"

Freeze gave a confirming nod.

"Say no more. Holla at me when you ready so we can sit down and build, know what I'm saying?" Frenchie dapped Freeze up before hopping out of the truck.

As he pulled off, Freeze had already started to feel better about things. *Yeah, you bitches' days are numbered,* he concluded. *Fucking Double Gs.* The thought caused him to let out an insane laugh as he pulled back onto the main street.

Chapter 23

McCarthy and Reddick pulled up to the luxurious condo Prime owned in the outer part of the city. McCarthy had no way of knowing that he had just missed Monica by thirty minutes. A group of young men stood posted up in front of the gated home that Prime had added along with all of the security surveillance. They all were legally strapped with their weapon of choice. After being radioed, they slowly dispersed from in front of the gate right before it opened up.

"Fucking crackers," one of the men sang loudly before sprinting off.

"Assholes," Reddick mumbled under his breath as McCarthy pulled in.

The door of Perry Minister, known to the streets as the Prime Minister, lay ahead of the agents. The pungent odor of marijuana hung heavy in the air. They reached the door and just listened for a second before knocking. McCarthy heard footsteps approaching the door. He knew at that moment he and Reddick were being thoroughly inspected through the peephole.

"Who are you and how may we help you?" a male voice asked.

"Ahh, the FBI, and you can help by opening up this door and letting us in," Reddick answered. He held his shield up to the peephole and placed it in front of it.

"Yeah? And? What do you want?" the voice snapped.

"Bold motherfuckers!" Reddick uttered.

"I got this," McCarthy silenced him and then stepped in front of Reddick with his shield out. "We need to ask a Mr. Perry Minister a few questions. Is he here?" McCarthy asked.

There was silence on the other side of the door for a few seconds, and then locks could be heard clicking, and the door swung open. A young light-skinned male who appeared to be in his early twenties faced the agents. He had a scarf wrapped around his head and face like he was from Iraq, with an image of the Cuban revolutionary Che on his T-shirt. He reeked of marijuana like he had bathed in it.

"Are you gentlemen here to serve an indictment against Mr. Minister?" he asked, crossing his muscular arms over his chest and leaning against the doorway.

"No, we're not. We just need to ask him a few questions," McCarthy announced.

"Questions?" He boldly sized the detectives up, first giving McCarthy the once-over, then doing the same with Reddick. "And you guys say you the feds? What type of questions the feds need to ask Mr. Minister?"

Reddick flashed his badge. His frustration got the best of him. He spoke out of emotion. "Look, we just need to speak to Prime—Mr. Minister—for a few minutes, and we'll be out of you guys' way, and you can get back to doing whatever illegal activities you were doing prior to us popping up."

The young man chuckled. "Is there a problem?" he asked.

McCarthy intervened. "No problem at all," he replied to the young man, right before turning to Reddick. "Listen, I'm lead on this, let me handle this. No matter the circumstances, let's respect their home."

The words McCarthy delivered to him were hard pills for Reddick to swallow. He didn't like to be checked or told what to do, even if it was his superior; and that's what it felt like McCarthy was doing to him. But he respected McCarthy, both as an agent and a man, and he was able to see the bigger picture. He knew McCarthy was right. He nodded to McCarthy and then turned to the young man. "My apologies. There was no disrespect intended," Reddick rendered.

The young man nodded then spun around and shouted at the top of his lungs, "The feds are here to just ask a few questions."

Prime came swaggering into view. He had on a dingy wife beater, baggy jeans, and fuzzy red slippers. His beard was scruffy and rough. He had mean, hard eyes that were boring into the agents. He had a bottle of Belaire Rose in his right hand.

Reddick and McCarthy looked at each other. They both had the same feeling once they laid eyes on Prime.

"Mr. Minister," McCarthy began, "we're trying to gather some information on a"—McCarthy deferred to his phone as if he didn't have the names embedded in his head already—"Mr. Christian Reeves and a Mr. Sean Wesson." He locked eyes with Prime.

"I don't know what type of information you're looking for, but it has nothing to do with me because I've never heard those names in my life," Prime answered. And that was the truth. He hadn't known the two names mentioned.

McCarthy did the best he could to hide his look of shock. He was skillfully trained to detect whether a person was lying in certain instances, and Prime had passed. *It doesn't make sense.*

"Are we done, gentlemen?" Prime calmly asked. He could see the look of defeat on the agents' faces. Reddick's was more obvious than McCarthy's, but it was there nonetheless.

Reddick peered over at McCarthy. McCarthy felt like a fool as it came to him like a thief in the night. He chuckled to himself. *Idiot.* "My apology," McCarthy replied.

"No problem. You gentlemen have a good day." Prime flashed a phony smile.

"Oh, no, I wasn't apologizing for my question. I was apologizing for the delay and the misunderstanding of it. What I meant to say was we're gathering information on Smoke and Clips," McCarthy said all in one breath. Before he even mentioned Clips's name he already had a strong idea of what Prime's response would be.

"My answer is the same. I've never heard those names in my life," Prime repeated. Only this time it was abrupt and his words came out a little choppy. "Whatever information you're looking for, I can't help you. Sorry," he added. "Is that all?" Prime asked for the second time.

"Actually, no," McCarthy shot back. "I have a couple more questions, if you don't mind."

Prime chuckled. "Okay, gentlemen. Here's the deal. I'll be glad to answer any questions just as soon as I contact my attorney, Mr. Dom Cochran."

"Damn, everybody around here is so damn polite," Reddick sarcastically remarked.

"You gentlemen have a good day," Prime ended. "Mu, see these men out for me please."

Once again, Reddick was pissed and felt defeated while McCarthy remained calm. Prime had reacted just enough for him to determine that he was lying. There was no doubt in his mind that Prime knew more than he was telling. He just had to figure out a way to find out more. On the way out, he pulled out his cell phone and texted Monica again.

Chapter 24

Glasses clinked together while liquor bottles popped as Starr ended her toast. She silenced the crowd of Double Gs so she could move forward with the ceremony of their newest soon-to-be member, Lacey. Diamond stood alongside Lacey, since she was the one who had recruited her, while Bubbles, Glitter, and Sparkle were just feet away from Starr. Double Gs filled the room with bold, bodacious, beautiful, and intelligent women. They were wall to wall and lit, Double Gs style.

Monica sat at a safe distance at the bar on full alert as she sipped on a Long Island Iced Tea. She watched and listened from afar as Starr prepared to swear Lacey in.

"Lacey, place your right hand on your chest, listen, and repeat after me," Starr instructed. The secret location was filled with serious and stone-faced Double Gs who were attentive to Starr's words.

Lacey knew there was no turning back after this. She inhaled and then exhaled as Starr began.

"I am confident, I am bold, and I am beautiful. I am big both in heart and in flesh, and I am who I am because God designed me this way. I am a woman who makes no excuses for who and what I am and I refuse to let anyone pass judgment. Most importantly, I refuse to be oppressed by any living man and will stop at nothing to ensure that neither myself nor my sisters will ever be."

Lacey recited each line Starr delivered.

"No man shall ever or any longer degrade me, belittle me, or disrespect me, nor shall they lay a hand on me in any form or fashion with or without my consent. I am a Double G, which means I am double the trouble and I am a Gangsta Girl. I swear that if another violates or crosses me or my family, the consequences and penalties shall be severe. Double Gs is not a gang; it is a way of life. A life I pledge to live until I breathe my last breath!"

Once Starr had ended the Double Gs initiation pledge, Lacey stood in awe. She had never felt more alive in her life. A sense of belonging filled her body as she repeated Starr. She knew she had made the right choice.

"Do you accept this pledge?" Starr asked.

"I do," Lacey replied strongly.

Starr nodded. "Good. Welcome to the Double Gs family."

Diamond was the first to offer a welcoming hug. It was a happy and proud moment for Lacey. "Thanks, sis," she thanked Diamond.

The Double Gs women standing all around delivered a thunderous round of applause. Starr pumped her fist in the air and shouted, "Double Gs for life!"

As if on cue, the entire club followed suit and soon began to chant, "Double Gs for life."

"Double Gs for life," Lacey joined in as she was welcomed into the Double Gs organization.

"Double Gs for life," Monica cooed. But she wasn't sure just how long she had before that was no longer the case. McCarthy had spooked her, but it didn't seem as if there was anything out of the ordinary. Still, she remained on point.

Now that the ceremony was over, the night broke out into a full-blown party. The deejay threw on the infamous Baltimore Club mix, "Watch Out for the Big Girls," and almost brought the building down. Nearly every Double G was on their feet rocking to the their anthem track.

Even Monica couldn't help dancing to the club banger from her stool. Little by little, she began to relax. *I'm still a trained agent,* she reasoned with herself. *I would know if I were in imminent danger,* she concluded.

Her mind began to drift, and she felt as if she were floating. A touch on the shoulder snapped Monica out of la-la land. When she turned and looked, she was surprised to see Starr standing there. She squinted to confirm that her eyes weren't playing tricks on her.

"What brings you over here?" Monica asked. Her words came out a little slurred.

"You bring me over here. I came over here to see you."

"Oh, really?" Monica replied with a partial smirk. She took a long gaze at Starr. The longer she stared, the more her vision blurred.

"Are you okay?" Starr put her hand on Monica's shoulder again.

Monica's body felt numb to her touch. She felt as if she were floating. Just holding her head up became a strenuous uphill battle. Starr held a very concerned look on her face.

"You don't look too well. Let me get you outta here," Starr stated.

"No, I'm fine," Monica refused. She tipped over, heading for the floor. Before she could hit it, Starr caught her and stroked her hair. "I got you. I got you," Starr repeated.

Starr winked at the bartender who, in return, gave a quick appreciative nod. She looped her arm around Monica's waist and guided her away from the bar and out of the secret location.

Chapter 25

The following day, McCarthy and Reddick were back out in the streets following leads and doing pop-ups. They were able to track down La France's place of residency and figured it wouldn't hurt to pay him a visit. Now they stood in front of his place, ringing the doorbell bright and early. No one answered, so they knocked on the door and identified themselves when asked.

The door was flung open by a bald dark-skinned dude. He promptly informed them that person they were looking for was in the back parking lot, exercising. McCarthy and Reddick made their way to the back and found La France doing pull-ups on a thick pipe that protruded from one of the buildings.

"La France?" McCarthy asked.

La France glared at the two agents. His eyes were bloodshot and still had cold in the corners of them. "Who y'all?"

"Morning. I'm Agent McCarthy, and that there is Agent Reddick," he said. "Sorry to disturb you this early in the morning, but there've been several robberies and murders in the past few months. Can you account for some particular dates and give us some of your whereabouts?" McCarthy asked the man and handed him a list.

La France frowned. He was shocked that McCarthy and Reddick had the nerve to disturb him while he was working out. "Ya damn skippy," La France replied.

"No need for the attitude, buddy," Reddick chimed in. "I'm sure you had a long, tiresome night last night. Selling crack and robbing and shooting people has to be exhausting. But in order for you to get rid of us and get back to your morning workout that you most definitely need, you gotta give us some real good alibis," Reddick commented.

McCarthy tried to keep a straight face.

La France abruptly scratched his balls and yawned before he took the list and glanced at it. He promptly handed it back. "I originally got paroled out to Jersey. I got my parole switched out here when I met my woman."

"Oh. Ms. Stevens left that part out," Reddick antagonized him.

"What? You talk to that bi . . . my woman?" La France spat.

"Let's just say we're going to be checking—" Reddick never got a chance to finish his statement because La France went inside and slammed the door in the detectives' faces.

"Ignorant cocksucker," Reddick muttered.

"Back to the drawing board," McCarthy said as he made a sour face and headed back out to the unmarked car.

"I know you're not giving up on me, are you, Reddick?" McCarthy asked, pulling off.

"Of course not. But I am starting to get a little discouraged. I don't understand how these female criminals can keep eluding us. It's like every time it seems like we're closing in on 'em, we're actually one step behind 'em. Then they pick up the pace, and we're left eating their dust and clueless. I wouldn't be surprised if they were somewhere watching us and having a field day seeing us run around in circles making fools out of ourselves."

"We'll get them, Reddick. I promise you that. Luck's been on their side so far, but it's bound to run out. I'll admit that they're good at what they do. But so are we.

They're good, but we're better. We just gotta keep our eyes and ears open, because we both know the streets talk. We just gotta listen," McCarthy said.

He and Reddick both knew, just like any good agent, that the majority of criminal cases solved themselves and that, sooner or later, even the most skilled and careful criminal would make a mistake and slip up. Then they'd capitalize off their mistake.

"Yeah, well, I hope so, McCarthy, 'cause the Double Gs are really starting to piss me off," Reddick grumbled.

Chapter 26

Chains rattled against what sounded like a metal pipe; she was restrained. Monica's ongoing grunts and moans followed in correlation. She was stripped of her clothes. They lay dormant on the floor below. She was in the nude in a king-sized bed. Her wrist and ankles were restrained in rusty handcuffs. She couldn't believe her situation. She never gave it any thought that she could be drugged through her drink. She realized McCarthy's text about being compromised was true. If only she hadn't been thinking about her lust, she wouldn't be in this predicament, she told herself.

Monica's vision began to come into focus. She turned her head to the left toward a fogged window with a bit of light shining through. She couldn't tell if it was daytime or sunset. She then shifted her head to the right as a tiny red light and beep caught her attention. She noticed a camera on a tripod pointed directly at her. Her eyes widened. *Hell no.* She continued to struggle and fidget with the restraints with little to no change.

Suddenly she heard someone suck her teeth repeatedly. When she looked in the direction of the annoying sound, she saw Starr standing in front of her at the foot of the bed with a fuzzy robe on. "Don't try to fight. It hurts worse that way."

Monica shook her head as she made a failed attempt to break free. "Please," she pleaded.

Her cries were ignored. Starr moved backward toward Monica and took off the robe she was wearing. Her nude beautiful curvy hips and glutes hypnotized Monica. What caught her attention even more was the thin leather belt around her waist. When Starr turned around, she revealed the strap-on dildo she wore.

"I know what you did, you know what you did, and it's not tolerated in this organization," Starr mentioned.

"I know. It was a mistake. I'm human. We all make them. Please, let's not do this," Monica began to ramble. She wasn't even sure what part of the deception or betrayal Starr was referring to: dealing with Prime or being a federal agent.

Starr stepped closer, slowly, one foot in front of the other, over to the camera. She pressed the night vision button, causing the light to beam into Monica's eyes even more.

"Trust me, it has to be done. It just filled the void, but that shit ran out."

Monica winced. She closed her eyes and shut them tight. There was no way of getting out of it. She had been caught slipping, and now she had to pay the consequences.

Starr climbed on top of her and hovered her breasts over Monica's. Monica screamed in agony as Starr's body shifted upward and delivered a forceful and strong thrust with the strap-on dildo, penetrating Monica. She exited and rammed the dildo inside Monica's dry walls again. The same cries rang out, only louder this time. Starr began to stroke even harder. It was as if she was in a state of rage. Monica's eyes begin to flood with tears; her body became limp. Starr grunted as the strokes intensified.

"I love you, Starr," Monica managed to let out in a whimper.

The tone and words hit Starr like a pound of bricks to the face. She fought the emotions that tried to surface. Her eyes began to get glossy. She leaned over Monica and gently caressed her face with her hand. Monica opened her eyes.

"I love you too, Monica," Starr replied dryly. "I'm sorry."

They passionately kissed. Interlocking their lips, their tongues wrestled. The smooching escalated, growing more intense. Starr grabbed her bloody strap, tossing it off. She lay next to Monica and cradled her. "I'm sorry, Mo," Starr apologized again.

Here it was she was supposed to be killing Monica to prove to Diamond that she loved her and only her. Instead, she was lying next to the woman she really wanted to be with.

"Let's get you up and out of here." Starr rose up.

Starr wasn't sure whether she had done any damage or ruptured anything inside of Monica from how rough she had just been. The first thing she wanted to do was take Monica to one of the private physicians who were affiliated with the Double Gs. After that, she knew she'd have to have a sit-down with Diamond.

Chapter 27

Mere hours beforehand, the Nevada legislator Rick Sinclair had prepared for a night he would never forget. He stood firm, flatfooted, as he stroked a few strands of gray in his dark greased-back hair. He wore Gucci suits like a celebrity. He was known for being one to get things done. If strings were to be pulled or cards to be called, he was the man with leaks and videos out the ass of the FBI's screw-ups, and he was the eraser of them. He was a tall man with thin arms and a bit of a gut. He seemed like an almost impenetrable fortress. His only weakness was lust.

Not only did he have the power to get shit done in the city, but he also had a fetish for BBWs. He was a regular of underground sex clubs, and he possessed chokers, dildos, you name it. He also had such a sexual appetite that he never took on fewer than two women at a time, due to the horny goat weed pills on him at all times.

He opened a door that led him through the large white pillars of the town hall. He wedged an earpiece into his ear as he planted his hands on the pedestal. He stood before what looked like a few thousand people. *Show time,* he thought as he grabbed the mic.

"People of Nevada," he began, "this speech is geared toward the ongoing problem with its citizens being constantly victimized and falling prey to organized and unorganized crime. This is an attempt to communicate with the police department and you, the hardworking, taxpaying citizen, to take action to protect one's self."

The crowd of people clapped, while pictures were being snapped. Rick scanned the crowd, not for assurance, but for women. He bit down on his lower lip as he caught sight of two bodacious twins. They sat near the back row, touching and feeling on one another. Rick's elbow was nudged by an agent near him to snap him out of it.

"Our method has not, over the past few years, been useful," Rick said. He began to tug at his tight collar the longer he locked eyes with the twin sisters, who now began to kiss and discretely fondle each other's plump, juicy breasts. He could literally see from where he stood their nipples erect and protruding through their thin shirts. One twin sister leaned over and nibbled on the nipple as the other held her mouth open.

Rick began to sweat. His manhood stiffened. The only problem was when his speech was over and he left the podium, his hardened manhood would be seen by the thousands there and the millions watching him on television screens.

"I concur that gangs such as the Double Gs have been terrorizing the city for countless days. If you see or know something, it's simple: do something, take action. Some things happen because we let them happen. It's up to us law-abiding citizens to not just rely on law enforcement, but to make a citizen's arrest as well as inform the police," Rick lectured.

The crowd was pleased, clapping nonstop.

The twin chocolate thick women unwrapped a lollipop and stuck their pierced tongues out. They took on a full assault with their tongues on it, deep-throating it. Rick nearly lost his shit.

He leaned over to a security guard. "As soon as I move away from this podium, I'll need you to cover my front. And you better not fucking let up, understand?" Rick whispered.

The security guard nodded, instructing the others to form around Rick. Rick held up his wrist, his Rolex glowing, as he waved good-bye to the saps who attended the speech.

Rick ventured backstage; news reporters snapped pictures of him, flashes and beams blinded him. Holding his hand up against them wasn't enough. The security guards picked up their pace, guiding Rick at the same rate.

"Get me those twins. Doesn't matter the price," Rick lustfully stated.

"Coming right up, boss," the guard responded.

Meanwhile, Sparkle and Glitter stood off to the side. They had their instructions and were just waiting to carry them out. They had already executed the first part of their mission by making contact with their intended victim.

"You see the way his freak ass was eyeing us the whole time?" Glitter asked her sister.

"You know I did," Sparkle replied. "All them politician motherfuckas like that," she added.

The brief exchange became even more brief when the security guy approached them. "Ah, excuse me, ladies, but would you be interested in meeting with Mr. Sinclair? He's having a little get-together with a few invited guests, and he'd be honored if you two could accompany him."

"What's in it for us?" Glitter abruptly asked. She and Sparkle had been briefed on the fact that Rick Sinclair liked plus-size women and paid for sex.

The security guy didn't even blink. "I'm sure whatever it would take you'd be compensated for," he replied.

"When and where?" Sparkle asked.

"Now, if you follow me. And as for location, that's on a need-to-know basis, ma'am."

Both Glitter and Sparkled nodded understandingly. The security guy raised his left wrist and spoke into his cuff link. "Two coming your way," he announced and then turned to the sisters. "Right this way."

An hour later, Glitter and Sparkle entered a room where candles were lit and a bottle of the finest wine was chilled in an ice bucket. The first thing they noticed and expected was that other than them, the security, and Rick Sinclair, there were no other attendees.

The twins sashayed into the room where he was. Rick immediately jolted to the door in his red silk robe. He attempted to peek out of the window for the whereabouts of his men. The twins pressed their hands on his gray-haired chest at the same time.

"Don't worry about them. You're gonna need all your energy," one twin noted.

Rick grinned. "Works for me," he spat. He rubbed his hands together and licked his lips. He ventured over to his closet of BDSM master set consisting of whips, leather belts, penis constrictors, gag balls, you name it. The twins stepped near the closet.

"Safe word's 'twins.'" Rick grinned.

Sparkle giggled. Glitter wanted to smack the shit out of him for the corny cliché.

The twins stepped farther into the closest, spotting a glossy dildo in the back of the closet; they looked at each other. "What's with the strap-on? You like to party like that?" one of the twins asked.

"Depends on the mood, ha. Hell, anything goes with a pair of stallions like yourselves," Rick shot back.

The twins grinned. *This is gonna be interesting,* thought Glitter.

Rick snapped on his BDSM boots, put his gag ball in his mouth, and began spanking his own ass as the twins dropped the little clothing they wore and slipped into the leather lingerie. They both placed a Catwoman-like mask over their faces that included pointed ears. Rick stroked his manhood as he choked himself. His view was of the twins suiting up.

The twins looked at each other once more. "This one sick motherfucker," one whispered to the other.

Glitter went to work, grinding on his manhood.

"You, other bitch, this isn't a one-thot show! Get on this dick or gag me! But what you're not gonna do is stand around!" Rick barked. You could tell he was hyped up on some kind of adrenaline drug. It caused one of the twins to lower the dose of drugs they intended to slip him, as they didn't want the old geezer to keel over before they could use him.

"You take E?" Sparkle asked. She popped two real ones into her mouth and then came up with two different ones in the palm of her hand.

"Give me that!" Rick snatched the pills, quickly scarfing them down.

"Good boy." Sparkle smiled.

Rick Sinclair barked like a dog.

The twins tag-teamed him until the drugs kicked in. Sparkle ground her leather-covered snatch on his face. Glitter ground and rode cowgirl with her leather-covered sugar walls on his semi-hard manhood. She squeezed her thighs on his manhood. Rick moaned and groaned. Instead of becoming sedated, he seemed to become stronger. Sparkle and Glitter looked at each other. Sparkle's eyes widened as Rick nibbled through the leather at her moistened woman cave. She couldn't help but gloat, gently moving it back and forth.

Things took a turn for the worse when Rick began to foam at the mouth. Sparkle quickly popped up. Rick jolted up and threw Glitter to the ground. His eyes were bloodshot.

"What the fuck did you give to him?" Glitter spat.

"The blue pills that looked like ice." Sparkle gestured. Glitter was shocked.

"Those were not the sedatives; those were the new batch of E pills!" Glitter screamed.

Rick was now a violent zombie chasing the girls around the room with a rubber band tied to the base of his stiffened dick. Glitter tried to deliver a swift kick to his sack but failed. He grabbed her leg, power-driving her to the floor, then attempted to bite into her flesh.

Sparkle grabbed the ice pick from the ice bucket. Glitter held her hand up.

"Don't kill him! He's worth more alive than dead!" Glitter shouted.

"Well, what the fuck am I supposed to do?" Sparkle protested.

"Restrain this motherfucker like we intended to do!" Glitter suggested. Glitter fought for her life, but her strength was no match for the horny zombie man.

Sparkle opened the bag they dropped down near the door on their entrance. She fidgeted through the accessories and found nothing of use, just pistols and a video camera.

"Shit, we forgot the motherfucking cuffs!" Sparkle shouted.

Sparkle tackled Rick to the ground and repeatedly punched him in the face, but nothing seemed to injure him. Glitter crawled to the BDSM closet, military style. She grabbed a pair of pink furry handcuffs and a Taser.

"Give it up, bitch!" Rick chanted as he tugged at Sparkle's leg, attempting to chew on her foot. Sparkle swung her free hand, landing a blow to his midsection. Rick let go of her leg. Glitter began to choke him from behind with the chain of the pink handcuffs.

"Oh, yes, baby. I like where you're going with this!" Rick roared, as he slung Glitter to the floor. Before he could do any more, Sparkle Tasered him in the neck.

Spit and foam accumulated around his mouth as he plummeted to the floor.

"Twins." Rick spat the BDSM safe word as he slowly closed his eyes.

Chapter 28

Edge stood up in a hotel room. It wasn't a luxury room, but it wasn't trashy, either. It had fine wood cabinets and a fine California king–sized bed. The trim was gold. A stern look held on tight to Edge's face as she glanced through the window, with her eyes locked on a car that circled the block below her second-story hotel room. She moved away from the window. Below, the car that circled the block came to a halt. It was a black Dodge Dart with pitch-black windows.

Who the fuck is that? And how they hell they know where I am? Edge wondered as she continued to peer down at the vehicle.

Unbeknownst to her, the black Dodge Dart was packed with agents, all equipped with jackets with the FBI initials across their backs. They concealed SMGs under their seats. The driver was Agent McCarthy. At first, when he received the tip that led them to the hotel, he didn't take it seriously. But when he was told that a female capable of pulling off a triple homicide was connected to the Double Gs' attorney, the tip became more promising. He and Reddick had chased every other lead that had come across their laps, so one more wouldn't hurt, he figured.

When he ran an NCIC check on her and saw that she had just been released from prison after having her sentence overturned for murder, the lead piqued McCarthy's interest even more. But when he discovered that the arresting officers were Blake and Douglass, and the file said to proceed with caution, that made the lead even stronger for him. He rarely believed in coincidences, and he wasn't going to start now.

After rounding up a strong strike team, he along with the others sat outside her hotel. The tech agent sat in the passenger seat, and they both had headphones pressed firmly on their ears. They were connected to a fat, thigh-burning laptop that possessed a large black box, with a dial that McCarthy repeatedly turned.

"Hold up. I think it's picking up something," the tech stated. The device was a mechanism that listened for high and low pitches.

"Do the dishes."

The more they turned the device, the more voices and conversations it picked up.

"Dave, get that lube out, I'm dry!"

The agents chuckled. Agent McCarthy shushed them. He was serious about this. They had lost enough agents. There's was nothing to laugh about as far as he was concerned. Since the first news of a fallen fellow agent, it was a nonstop pursuit of the Double Gs for McCarthy. He couldn't care less if he died following them. Just the thought of them all being caught or killed brought joy to his eyes. He waited and listened as he steadily moved the dial.

Edge's cell phone vibrated on the side of her hip. Never taking her eyes off of the vehicle, she pulled it out and answered. "Hello?"

No one said anything. There was complete silence.

"Hello? Who this?" she asked.

This time someone responded. "Is this Edge?"

"Who the fuck is this?" Edge snapped.

"Somebody who wanna see you win. The feds are watching your spot, but they don't know which room you're in. You still got a chance if you get out now," the anonymous caller announced.

Edge hung up the phone. The fact that the caller knew somebody was outside of her crib was enough for Edge to take the call seriously. "Shit," she cursed. The words, *"You still got a chance if you get out now,"* rang out in Edge's mind.

Edge backed away from the window and dropped to the floor. She snuck her way into the room and snatched up her money and guns.

"We have the confirmation she's in there. We can storm the room now!" Agent McCarthy assured everyone.

"Not quite. We still need probable cause," the tech agent argued.

"She is a murderous, cunt-loving animal; that's cause enough right there," Agent Reddick barked.

"Hang on. You hear that?" the tech agent pointed the device in another direction.

"Hear what?" Reddick leaned in. "I don't hear squat. What the hell are you—"

Agent McCarthy shushed him midsentence. He heard something. The tech agent pointed the black box device toward another direction. They could barely hear through the static.

"Do you know who . . . You can't do this to me . . . legislator of Nevada!"

The voice was muffled. Every agent in the car was baffled. They looked at each other for a response.

"What the fuck was that?" Agent McCarthy spat.

The tech agent stuck his arms out of the window with the device in hand to get a second helping of the conversation. "Sounded like a distress call," he answered.

"Tell them . . . uble Gs did it, mu'fuck . . ." The device picked up the broken words of another speaker.

The agents were dumbfounded. Although he didn't hear it crystal clear, McCarthy would bet his life that whoever was talking was a Double Gs member. "How far away you think that conversation is?" Agent McCarthy asked.

"Could be one or two miles. It's somewhere in that area," the tech agent said.

"Well, what the fuck are we waiting for? Let's find them." Agent McCarthy commanded. He banged his fist on the dashboard. "Another time," Agent McCarthy said, looking up at Edge's hotel before he made a U-turn in the middle of the street.

Edge shimmied her way back into the living room. Carefully standing back up, she peered back out the window. To her surprise, the Dodge Dart was no longer parked where it once sat. Edge looked left, then right. Nothing.

What the hell is going on? she pondered.

Better safe than sorry, Edge grabbed up her duffle bag and exited her apartment. She cautiously made her way into the parking garage and hopped in her whip. She pulled out her phone and pulled up the one person she believed would know what was going on and why. She scrolled down to Diamond's number and sent her a text before pulling out of the garage.

The black Dodge Dart turned the corner after a pickup truck zoomed past. The truck managed to pass through a red light, though nearly colliding with another car. Although the Dodge Dart was filled with agents, their attention on possible trouble was far more important. The tech agent glanced up to a three-story historical hotel, where only the elite or wealthy resided.

"This has to be the spot," the tech man said.

"Well, this may be our big ticket. After this, maybe we could get the guns we've been asking for," an agent spat.

Agent McCarthy grabbed hold of his SMG submachine gun. He cocked it back and snapped on his Velcro holster alongside his bulletproof vest. "I wouldn't bank on it, but let's stay focused. A man's life is in jeopardy," Agent McCarthy said.

All agents were prepared, suited up, and booted up. All but the tech agent. "I'll sit here, stationary. We don't all need to die in there," the tech agent reasoned.

Reddick grabbed hold of him. "Bring your scared ass on. We need somebody to man the device through the halls when the shit hits the fan."

"You are gladly welcome to leave, and don't forget your tampons and high heels on the way down," another agent teased.

The tech agent flashed a fake smile and let out a light chuckle. "Come on, you guys, don't bust my balls here. I was only joking."

All of the other agents including McCarthy zeroed in on him.

"Pussy!" another agent spat.

"Okay, that's enough," McCarthy said. "Let's look alive and stay focused." The last thing he wanted was to lose an agent over carelessness or not being on point.

The agents all tightened up, including the tech agent. He drew his weapon, removed his safety, and cocked it.

Seconds later, like a hive of killer bees, they swarmed into the building. Customers, valet drivers, and chefs were startled by the size of their weapons as they coasted with them through the gold-trimmed white-and-black lobby. The floor was marble. Agent McCarthy glanced down and saw his reflection. The longer he stared, he didn't see a hero en route to save a victim, but a tortured man who climbed from the depths of hell with scars still on him. The man he was protecting was the devil who put him there in the first place, and he wondered if it was too late to turn around and say fuck it.

"McCarthy, you good? The geek's saying the signal's gearing toward up top. You need to hear it," Reddick said.

McCarthy nodded. Taking a deep breath, he strutted up the stairs alongside the other agents.

He led the way as four agents followed closely like a school of fish. They didn't know if they were the prey or the hunters. Every corner they turned sent chills down their body. The tech agent tagged along a yard away. He had a small .22 pistol in his right hand and the listening device in his other. His headphones were on tight as he aimed the sound device at room doors like a gat.

"Keep up, cumshot!" Reddick spat, careful not to notify who they were looking for.

"You're gonna get enough of calling me that shit. I swear I'll—" The tech agent's comments were cut short by voices he heard. The bed's mattress was bouncing.

"Spank me, daddy!" the device picked up, followed by moan after grunt.

The tech man turned in a 180-degree angle.

"Where's my money?" the voice spat.

The tech man gestured the agents to turn around. They all gathered around the door. The tech agent peeled his headphones off of his ears for the voice to be heard by the other agents.

"This is the final straw! I can't take this shit anymore! The legislator's fucking—"

That was all the agents needed to hear to spring into action. They all cocked their fresh clips filled with hollow-tip bullets back in their assault weapons and handguns. This was the moment of truth for them.

"You ready?" Reddick spat.

Someone fidgeted with the doorknob. The voice inside switched their tone.

"You hear that shit? Somebody's fucking with the knob," the tech agent revealed. The agents pressed their backs against the door hinges.

A flicker of light caught the corner of Agent McCarthy's eye. He slowly turned his head as a woman came out of nowhere. She held a bag of groceries. Her expensive wristwatch flashed. The moment she caught sight of Agent McCarthy, she took a step back, wide-eyed.

"Please don't scream," he said with a gesture of shushing her.

His request went ignored. She did the very opposite. She dropped her bag that held items made of glass, along with milk, eggs, and a few other items. None of it mattered as her bloodcurdling scream rang out. It was one that seemed it could wake a man from the grave. Her sudden cries triggered Reddick's survival instincts.

Boom. Boom. He turned around as fast as he could and let off two rounds. The hollow tips exploded in the woman's chest, spreading fragments over her body. Her knit sweater was soiled and stained with blood the second they went through her sterling-silver heart necklace.

The two shots sent her traveling back like a car in reverse as blood flowed from the two bullet entries. Reddick instantly felt sympathy for the innocent civilian woman.

"No, fuck, no! It was an accident I swear! I fucking swear!" Reddick spat.

The opposing agents kicked the door in. The voice behind it belonged to a black man, watching a replay of Rick's town hall speech. The impact of the door busted his nose.

"Yo, what the fuck did you do?" the man boomed.

Reddick's eyes were glossy. His skin and eyes matched in color: red. "Shut your mouth!" Reddick spat.

Agent McCarthy watched in disbelief, along with the rest of the agents.

"Nice going, wiseass. What the hell are we going to do now?" the tech man spat. He was the first to speak after an innocent woman was just murdered.

Reddick cuffed the resistant man. "Stop resisting!" Reddick barked.

"I didn't do nothing. Let me go!" the man barked back. He slid on the ground outside of the door and caught a glimpse of the dead woman. His eyes widened in horror.

"Nooooo! That's my fucking moms! You damn devils shot my moms!" the man cried.

The agents all looked at each other. They'd fucked up before, but never like this. Eyes from peepholes and the cracks of doors with locking golden chains barricading the entry caught it all from start to finish.

Agent McCarthy grimaced.

The tech agent turned the volume up on his headphones as they all took a long walk of shame. Reddick was still clutching the distressed man.

"Why don't you just let him go? Let him mourn," Agent McCarthy spat.

Reddick let him loose. He immediately rushed over to cradle his dead mother. Tears ran down his face like a river.

"You hear that? My team's here, so I suggest you two thots give up now!" the device picked up.

"Please, I didn't mean to say that, no, nooo! Okay, I'll give you whatever you want!" the voice continued, followed by female voices.

"You got that shit right."

The tech agent was dumbfounded. He stopped. The rest of the agents turned around, locking eyes with him. "I think it's—"

The tech agent's sentence was interrupted by Reddick. "Are you stupid? What the hell are you doing?" The sound of police sirens came from outside.

"That's the right voice. I know it is," the tech agent spoke, refusing to let the device go.

"Give it a rest already." Reddick snatched the device from the tech agent. "You want that fucking device? Go get it!" Reddick tossed the device into a corner at the end of the hall. The tech agent went chasing after it. He froze in his tracks when he laid his eyes on two guards dead with a single shot to both their heads.

"What the . . ." the tech agent mumbled. The door was slightly open.

The tech agent grabbed hold of his .22 pistol and gestured for the agents to join him. They all drew their weapons. Agent McCarthy was the first to reach the tech agent and took the lead, as the door swung open. What caught their eye was the Las Vegas, Nevada legislator trapped in a kinky death trap. Sparkle's and Glitter's tits were out, and their torsos were laced up with leather. Rick, on the other hand, his dick was bent like a bendy straw, and his face was battered. The entire scene brought a porn from hell to mind.

"Step away from the legislator!" Agent McCarthy barked.

"You better tell them motherfuckas to stand down!" Glitter ordered.

Rick nodded, agreeing to her command.

"You serious?" Agent McCarthy questioned.

"As a bent dick," Rick responded.

Reddick, tense, paced back and forth.

"Now that we're all acquainted, you pigs can be witnesses," Sparkle spoke.

"To what exactly?" Reddick spoke.

Glitter held a light smirk. "Two out of three things are about to happen. One: we're walking the fuck up outta here. Two: the bill you just passed, we need it un-passed, vetoed, whatever the flying fuck needs to be done," Glitter uttered in Rick Sinclair's ear.

Sparkle tossed a sheet over Rick's bent manhood.

Rick grabbed hold of a pen, signing the document to veto the printed choice. He then directed his attention to the agents in the room.

"I need every law enforcement officer in this goddamn room to lower their weapons, and that's an order!" Rick spat. Hesitant, every officer in the room lowered their weapons as Sparkle and Glitter closed up shop. They threw on the premium hotel-issued robes after shutting down the camera. And then just like that, they strolled out of the front door.

Agent McCarty couldn't believe his eyes. *What the hell just happened here?*

He stood clueless as a high-ranking political figure let two notorious gang members and possible killers walk scot-free in front of him. *I need some goddamn answers,* McCarthy concluded.

Chapter 29

Monica was swept with heavy thoughts as she packed and stuffed her only luggage. Starr had dropped her off to collect what few belongings she could gather. She made it clear that they were leaving Vegas for a little bit, and Monica didn't protest. As she packed, images of Prime and the life growing inside of her came to mind. The fact that Starr didn't kill her proved how strong of a love she had for her, but Monica was not so sure if she'd feel the same if she knew all of the facts.

Relax, girl. She'll still love you if you tell her you made a mistake falling for Prime and tell her truth about the baby, was what she frequently told herself to keep from running off from Starr. After her near-death experience with her, Monica knew she was capable of doing anything to her if she felt some type of way about something. As she ventured to the front door and tugged at the door-knob, she felt an opposing force tugging on the other side as well. Monica was baffled. She yanked at the doorknob again, and the force was released.

She poured into the hallway vigilant of what it could possibly be. Maybe she was just overthinking it. That was her first thought.

As she swayed farther down the hall, the elevator's ding went off. The doors ripped apart as a cart's wheels were heard rolling toward her. Monica didn't pay it any mind as she continued her walk. That was, until a hunting whistle accompanied the rolling cart. It's familiarity made the hairs on the back of Monica's neck stand up. The whistling inched up closer, almost as if it was directly behind Monica. Monica couldn't tell where it was coming from, only that it was close. She turned around, only to see nothing but a cart as she turned to her left. She locked eyes with Starr. Starr stood with her feet planted and a silencer barrel attached tightly to the end of her TEC-9.

Monica already knew what it was. She couldn't believe her luck. Already expecting the worst, she clutched the wood grip of her chrome custom 1911.

"You know what this is about," Starr spat.

Monica squinted her eyes. "That's all it ever was, wasn't it?" Monica responded.

"I didn't come for petty chitchat and flawed puns because that time is long past. Time is rolling, business is booming; that shit sound familiar to you?" Starr stated.

Monica gently pulled up on the hammer of her custom 1911 pistol. Starr quickly raised her arm, firing the silencer shots with a skilled arm. Spew spew was the sound Starr's TEC-9 cried out. Monica fired through her purse, creating a semi-muffled shot. She ducked for cover behind a wall. She noticed her purse now resembled Swiss cheese. "Shit!" she mumbled.

They exchanged gunplay one more time as Starr let out a barrage of bullets diagonally across the wall, just inches above Monica's head. Starr rushed toward her, hovering the TEC-9 over her. Monica kicked Starr in the knee, causing Starr to duck down and drop her TEC-9. Monica managed to bring her to the ground, hip-driving her into submission. Starr grabbed the butt of the pistol and clocked Monica upside the head like a drum solo. The elevator door peeled open from around the corner. Monica and Starr, grunting and punching on each other, poked their heads around the corner.

A police officer, with his hand on his waist pistol, crept down the hall. Starr and Monica slid the weapons underneath the destroyed purse the moment the officer hit the corner.

"Hi, ladies," he greeted them both, oblivious to what was just taking place between the two of them. "Have you seen or heard any suspicious activity, such as a weird noises circulating in this hall?" The officer gestured around. He was slightly turned on by the fact that Starr had one plump breast out from Monica tearing her shirt open while they fought. The officer noticed both Monica and Starr were sweating. He noticed scratches on their forehead, and a red lip from it being filled with blood. The destruction was so great; he didn't notice the tiny bullet holes above his head. The moment he turned to look above his head Starr ripped Monica's shirt, exposing her juicy breast as well. The officer raised an eyebrow.

"What are you ladies doing in this hall? What happened to your faces and clothing?" the officer asked. Police heat was the last thing on Monica's and Starr's minds to have as they knew it would lead them and the Double Gs into unwanted trouble.

"I'm so sorry, Officer. See, we're lovers and got a little carried away. We've been really, really naughty and we would enjoy making it up to you by any means necessary," Starr lustfully said. She and Monica slowly leaned in on each other, both with a facial expressions that said, "This is not over." They kissed each other, then continued to further the charade. The officer's manhood begin to stiffen. From the corner of Monica's eye, she realized the plan was working, but something else was rising.

She could feel Starr's nipples harden as if she was turned on. Monica begin to think she couldn't be so hated if she could turn her on. She herself became sexually excited. It was the same feeling you get when as a kid you got a toy you couldn't get. The officer tipped his hat and twirled his wedding ring. As much as he wanted to join in, he was a faithful man, knowing he had a wife and kids at home to lose and take care of.

"Okay, that's enough convincing for me. Just take it to your room. Probably kids and shit around here." The officer paced back down the hall. He stepped into the elevator and, as he waited for the door to close, he couldn't keep his eyes off of Starr and Monica.

As soon as he was gone, Monica and Starr continued to tear each other apart. They stumbled as Starr grabbed Monica by the hair and dragged her by it. They stumbled back into the room. In the midst of their struggle, Starr managed to retrieve both Monica's pistol and her TEC-9. She took the clip out of the TEC-9 and tossed it, then did the same with Monica's custom 1911. She cocked it back and out popped the bullet in the chamber.

"Let's finish this shit," Monica stated as she hopped back up on her feet.

Starr chanted as she tackled Monica onto the bed. She raised her hand like she was throwing a fist, only to land it on herself, ripping the rest of her clothing off. Once she was done, she ripped Monica's clothing off, violently. She rolled on top of Monica, turning her over on her back. She grabbed hold of Monica's hair as she leaned down with her ass at a ninety-degree angle. Licking and fingering Monica's sugar walls like her life depended on it, all the emotions she had that day were taken out between Monica's inner thighs. Monica moaned loud, basking in the glory of the shotgun platter she was being served. She couldn't believe their violent fight turned into a passionate escapade.

They both stared at each other, breathing uncontrollably, knowing they may be the most fucked-up lesbian couple ever. Monica reached out and caressed Starr's face in a loving way.

"I still love you," Monica whispered.

Starr's eyes widened. The words went through her, ear directly into her cerebellum, and secreted the max amount of dopamine like an explosion. She wasn't expecting Monica to say that after a full-blown shootout and fistfight. It caused her to flash back to the moment Diamond asked her to choose between the two. The choice was obvious now.

"I still love you too," Starr admitted.

Monica nodded. She moved in closer and stepped into Starr's embrace.

Chapter 30

Starr pressed the doorbell with urgency as if she was waiting far longer than she should have. The porch light came on and illuminated the darkness. Night was fast approaching. A car's engine could be heard rumbling close behind.

"Coming!" a female voice from inside shouted.

The door swung open. Diamond stood in the doorway with her feet planted, her arms folded, and a face of uncertainty. She locked eyes with Starr. "So is it done?" Diamond questioned.

Starr didn't respond. She was at a loss for words. There was no way she could explain what happened and how it happened that wouldn't piss Diamond off. She had chosen Monica. Not only did she not kill her, but she made love to her with greater passion than she ever did with Diamond. *This is the end of the rope,* she thought.

Diamond was pretty, but she was far from stupid. She could read Starr like MapQuest. She could tell something wasn't right. Starr didn't appear like someone who had just murdered someone they once loved or cared about. Starr's demeanor had her mind wondering. Diamond looked over Starr's shoulder. It was then she got the answer to her question. Monica, with a bruised face, sipped a steaming cup of coffee in the passenger seat.

Before Starr could say anything, it was clear what had happened. Starr noticed the shift in Diamond's eyes. It caused her to look down in shame.

"I'm sorry," Starr started to say but then was interrupted.

"Save it! How could you, after all I've done for you? After all she's done to you!" Diamond spat aggressively. Monica clocked Diamond with a squinted eye as she sipped on her drink.

"You just don't understand," Starr tried to explain.

"Damn right I don't! I thought you were better than that. I thought we were better than that. You choose this bitch over me?" Diamond let out a laugh of pity. "You used to be my bitch. Now you back with that bitch, and you think I'm not gonna express how I feel about this decision?" Diamond claimed.

"I know, but I feel something with her that I can't feel with you. I've tried, I really have. We can make love from morning to night, and it's not there. I feel empty inside with you. You understand?" Starr stated.

"I understand completely. Like when you love someone, and they say they love you too, but deep down you know they don't. So you hold back so you don't get hurt, but in the end, you never can really tell what's going to happen. Sort of like this," Diamond stated.

The statement hit Starr hard. Regardless, her mind was made up. "A person once told me it takes courage to follow what you want in life. Be outspoken, follow your heart, whatever it speaks to you. It spoke to me. Have you forgotten why Queen Fem even started the Double Gs?" Starr stated.

Diamond shook her head. She stared at the ground. "I remember. I told you that," Diamond remembered.

Starr leaned over and hugged Diamond tight. She kissed her on the cheek. "I want you to lead the Double Gs," Starr whispered.

Diamond's eyes widened. She was honored, but also worried. "What are you saying? Are you leaving the group?" Diamond spat.

"I just don't know. I need to get away for a while. I think you would run the group as powerfully as I could. I'll clear it with Queen Fem," Starr shot.

Diamond's eyes became glossy. She nodded. "I'm down. Double Gs for life, sister," Diamond said.

"Double Gs for life, leader."

Starr's words would linger in Diamond's head for several nights to come. Diamond watched as Starr swayed down the driveway into the dark car. Starr planted her hand on the gear, shifting it into drive. Monica locked eyes with Diamond she slowly smiled and threw up the middle finger. Diamond was pissed. She wanted to run up on Monica and wrap her hands around her throat but, before she could, the car drove off.

Chapter 31

Queen Fem sat in front of an illuminated television screen. A smile appeared on her face, hearing the news about the vacated bill. Pearly whites, with a gold strip in between the front two, revealed themselves as she had just watched the live broadcast of Rick Sinclair. The news stations and studios went into a frenzy as Rick Sinclair avoided all questions as he fought to break free of the stage's podium. Viral videos of crew members who recorded it on their phones had hits.

Queen Fem chuckled. "Good job, Double Gs." Queen Fem grinned.

Her disposable flip phone rang out, interrupting her news. She kept a disposable phone, so the dangers of it being tapped or tracked were slim to none. She answered and pressed the body of the cell phone to her ear. She nodded as she was fed information.

"I'll be there. You just make sure you're prepared for what's planned," Queen Fem stated.

She was fed more information. She leaned over, peeping out the window of the undisclosed building she resided in. Outside was a car with its engine running and its headlights turned off.

"Just let me know when it's done," Queen Fem spat before hanging up the phone. She leaned over, gently moving the curtains over to peep out the window in a way she would be seen. The car that waited outside flipped its headlights on. Queen Fem nodded.

As she made her way to her side door, the sound of her front door buzzer stopped her in her tracks. She knew it had to be Mirage.

Outside the door, a gloved hand with a silenced pistol had walked stealthily up to Queen Fem's buzzer. The gloved hand belonged to a masked man who had a death grip around Mirage's neck, with his free hand over her mouth, as he steered her toward the buzzer.

"Speak, bitch! Speak!" the masked man spat, after pressing it. He pushed the barrel of his pistol in her kidney to demonstrate he meant business.

"It's me. Let me up!" Mirage stated.

The masked man waited. The buzzer turned green; the door was opened. The masked man waved his pistol toward four more masked men, all armed with assault rifles. It was going down.

They all walked behind the masked man who held on tight to Mirage. Guns were aimed at every part of her body as they all walked down the dark hall.

They stopped in front of a black door; it had a gold panel with the numbers 357 in its center. The masked man shoved Mirage's shoulder with the barrel of his rifle. The tears in her eyes blurred her vision. She sniffed to keep her mucus from dripping. As she cleared her vision, she noticed a pendant on the mat below the door. It was of a golden shotgun. She felt a gleam of hope. She then grabbed hold of the doorknob and fidgeted with it.

"Please, I can't. I—" Mirage's sentence was cut short as she was pushed out of the way.

This was exactly what she wanted as one masked man hovered over her, pointing his weapon. Because they didn't pat her down, they never knew she had the small chrome Rossi attached to her ankle.

The masked man kicked the door open only to get a chest full of shotgun pellets.

The impact pushed him to the hall, killing him instantly. Mirage grabbed hold of the ankle Rossi revolver and took out two other men. Boom boom. They hit the ground hard.

The shotgun was not held by anyone but was connected by a rope, in a pulley system attached to the trigger so that when the door was opened, it went off. The last man sprayed his machine gun into the halls and room; Mirage rolled out of the way.

"Ahhh, motherfuckers!" The masked man shouted as he let off rounds like a madman.

Queen Fem stepped out of the closet swinging the butt of an AK-47 to the masked man's head the moment his assault rifle clicked out of ammo. It knocked him unconscious.

"You're a dead bitch," the man mumbled.

Queen Fem chuckled. "Maybe so, but today it's gonna be you. Right after I get some info out, though," Queen Fem calmly stated.

Queen Fem and Mirage dragged the masked man in a similar fashion to the way he had dragged Mirage. Once they tossed him in the trunk full of reptiles, Queen Fem gently slapped him on the cheek to wake him out of his unconscious state. His eyes were bulging out of his head as he struggled to even lift a finger.

"What the fuck are you doing?" the man asked.

"Until you tell me who sent you, it's gonna be very hard for you, you understand?" Queen Fem stated.

The man began to shout. "Fuck you!" he barked.

Queen Fem nodded. "I see you're trying to be a true ride or die, huh? Well, enjoy the ride, because it's gonna be long one," Queen Fem said without remorse. "Oh, and words of advice, all that screaming is just gonna deplete your oxygen and anger the snakes. Cheers." Queen Fem playfully gestured as she slammed the car trunk.

Chapter 32

The dark Dodge Dart pulled up to the side of a gray station wagon parked alone in an abandoned parking lot. A basketball court was positioned in front of the parking lot. The leaning rusty pole with a basket at the top didn't look like it had been used in quite some time by any neighborhood kids. Judging by the bullet holes embedded into the backboard, you could tell it was a bad part of town. Monica rolled the window down, leaving only her hazel eyes revealed.

The dark Dodge Dart rolled its window down all the way. A white man appeared, with pitch-black sunglasses on his face. He dropped the butt of a cigarette on the graffitied pavement below.

"Make this quick. McCarthy's team just shoved their own heads up their asses, and I'm supposed to pull them out," the mystery man spat.

"The last job we did, it was just that. We're done. I'm done," Monica stated.

The mystery man shook his head. A soft chuckle of disbelief crossed his mind. "Done? Ha, you're not done. Would've been if I didn't have to clean up after you, seeing as that little stunt you pulled made a heap of shit at the station. McCarthy's looking for you," the mystery man stated.

"Just tell him I disappeared and will take care of everything else like always," Monica stated.

The mystery man shook his head once more. "See, it's not that simple on this level. The notoriety of the Double Gs is higher than every other organization in this city right now. Besides, you said you want out," the mystery man stated.

"Don't even try to do that shit," Monica spat before holding a barrel through the window slit.

"What good will killing me do? Huh? Think before you act. Because, without me, you're fucking lost! Nobody in the feds will help you anymore. I'm the pathway to that bridge and once it's broken the only other way across is the wetlands," the mystery man stated.

"Cops and robbers get killed every day, and people come up missing every day," Monica stated, tugging at her trigger finger.

Starr, who was sitting in the driver's seat, got a ring on her flip burner phone. She placed it to her ear with a face of concern. She batted her eyes to the back of Monica's head. "Is that you?" Starr whispered, recognizing the voice.

"That's right. I need you to listen to me carefully. Are you and Monica in a parking lot?" Queen Fem asked.

Starr's eyes began to wander. *How could she possibly know where we are?* she wondered. Starr began looking around the parking lot. There was not a soul in sight. Nothing but the dark Dodge Dart. A rustle of wind caused her eyes to shift toward the bushes. The barrel of a rifle pointed directly at them. Monica was completely unaware as she zoned in on the mysterious man.

"Yeah. How do you know?" Starr spat.

Monica saw the unusual look on Starr's face and lowered her pistol from the window.

"A masked . . . Look, it's a long story. All you need to know now is that you need to get the fuck out of there. They're planning to kill that man, kill Monica, and frame you for it," Queen Fem stated.

Starr gulped as she wondered how she could get out of the situation. Her radar device showed multiple police cruisers fast approaching as Monica continued to chat.

"Change of plans on the location, too. They found the safe house. I'm moving underground. As for you, the only way out is to go down, catch my drift?" Queen Fem spat before hanging up the phone. Starr shoved Monica's arm to get her attention.

"That's that, you understand?" Monica said to the mystery man. She then turned her head toward Starr who shifted the gear into reverse. Monica was confused. "What are you doing?" Monica questioned.

"This is a setup. All it ever was," Starr spat.

"Who was that on the phone?" Monica continued to question.

"An old friend," Starr responded as she quickly revved the engine, spinning the vehicle in reverse just moments before the mystery man was killed through the dashboard of his dark Dodge Dart. His head slammed on the horn of the car, making it sound off.

"What the fuck? Who the hell is that?" Monica questioned. Her eyes began to survey the area. She saw a glare coming from the bushes right before she heard the shots.

Boom. Boom. The sniper man in the bushes shot Monica and Starr's car. Boom. Boom. Two more shots were let off. The back window was blown completely out by the powerful impact of the super sniper bullet. Starr raced off the road, speeding toward a short cliff.

Officers in the area got static on their radio. "Shots fired! I repeat, shots fired!" a voice stated. Inside of police cruisers, bulletproofed officers clutched shotguns and M16s as they put the pedals to the metal.

"En route, at Old Parkway Drive, parking lot C. All units in and around the area, proceed with caution! A federal agent has been hit!" the radio stated.

Back at the parking lot, the man in the bushes rose up. He tossed the sniper weapon to the grass, removed the clothing he wore, and replaced it with an FBI jacket and his badge. He walked over to the dead agent, snatched his sunglasses off of his warm, dead head, and put them onto his head. He smiled as police cruisers rushed past him toward Starr and Monica.

Shit's just getting started. Double Gs are going to be double dead, he said to himself proudly.

Monica and Starr grabbed each other's hands as the car flew over the Nevada rock.

Chapter 33

A purple glow painted the dark room with a king mattress in the center. Expensive champagne bottles were sitting up, and some were on the floor. Panties and more led to a pathway of red roses, although they appeared purple from the overbearing mood light in the room.

Close to the bed, the sound of a buzz occurred, similar to a vibrator. It was about twelve inches as it lay on the bed near Diamond, who had her head pressed against the back of the bed. She grinned and then gasped as a naked woman went down on her, twirling her tongue in her sugar walls like a roller coaster. Two more naked women with mouths full of breast were on the sides of her. She was being pleasured beyond her wildest visions.

Deep down, mentally, it was pleasurable, but it was more a way to forget about Starr. It wasn't exactly working as she expected. Every lick, every strap-on penetration reminded her of Starr, who did it like no other partner she had ever been with. The sheer thought of Starr brought a slight frown to her face. The women around her looked at each other. *Is this bitch numb? I know she feeling this,* they all thought. Her facial expression said otherwise. The women did it harder. Diamond gasped as her sugar wall cave flushed out juices that squirted on the naked women below her breasts. She smiled.

"There we go!" the woman spat.

Diamond waved her hands, and the women came closer, taking turns tongue-kissing Diamond. Diamond grabbed their breasts, licked them, sucked them. All the women in the world couldn't wipe Starr from her mind. Images of Starr and her making love kept flashing in her head. She even flashed back to the day Starr rolled over to cuddle her, whispering, "I love you, Monica."

Diamond opened her eyes. She became pissed all over again. She remembered the image of Starr getting back into her car as Monica sat in the passenger's seat, throwing the middle finger at her. Diamond came back to her senses and realized she had just thrown one of the women to the floor. All the naked women having an orgy in the room stopped fucking to just look at Diamond. She was a wreck.

"I need some different stimulation! Somebody, give me something different!"

The women looked at each other and shrugged before getting back to business. One of the women walked to the foot of the bed, attaching a strap-on to her snatch. "You ready for this shit, slut?" she spat playfully.

Diamond smiled. "That's Miss Boss Lady Slut to you," Diamond played along.

"Check this. This strap belonged to Rick, a legislator of Las Vegas. Sparkle and Glitter caught up with him and got a billed vetoed, just like Starr instructed. Double Gs about to branch out to an entirely new kind of power!" the woman proudly spat as she straddled Diamond.

The mention of Starr's name put a damper on Diamond's mood. Diamond pushed her off of her. "That's fine and dandy, but from here on out nobody shouldn't make moves like that unless authorized by me," Diamond stated.

"Who put you in charge?" the Double Gs member questioned.

"Starr did, until she comes back. Now, don't ever question me like that again," Diamond stated.

The Double Gs member nodded. The Double Gs member crawled on top of Diamond's nude body. Her breast touched her breast. She had a handful of yellow pills. She placed a few on her tongue as well as on Diamond's tongue. They begin swapping spit, as the Double Gs member circled Diamond's erect nipples. She then gently placed the strap-on deep, shoving all twelve inches inside. Diamond moaned loudly.

"Talk shit now!" the Double Gs member spat as she went deeper and harder. Diamond squinted her eyes. She began smiling and screaming as the girl thrust her hips, driving the strap-on as much as it would allow her to go. Diamond squirted like a water fountain repeatedly.

"Oh, God! Yes, please, keep going! Yes!" Diamond spat. Sweat ran down Diamond's forehead. The other naked women in the room begin playing with each other from the sight of the session. The pleasure reminded her of Starr. Although she knew she would possibly never have sex with Starr again, she shut her eyes, pretending it was her.

"I'm going to push you to the edge," the Double Gs member stated.

Diamond had a realization. The mention of the word "edge" made Diamond think of her ex-lover. Edge was second only to Starr as her top lover. In the midst of her sexcapade, it dawned on her that she should get in contact with her as soon as possible. Not only to fuck but, now with her new position, to have Edge as her right-hand woman, the way she was to Starr. She couldn't imagine how she could run the business without Edge or Starr.

Diamond's orgasm intensified. Her eyes rolled to the back of her head. She couldn't take any more of her hammer game. Diamond popped another yellow pill, then another, until her vision was blurry.

Diamond temporarily passed out on the floor from exhaustion. She wiped sweat from her forehead, as she held a phone between her shoulder and head. She lit a blunt.

"Hello?" a voice said.

Diamond took a quick puff and then placed it in the ashtray. "Hey. Hey. Hey. How you doing, girl?" Diamond spat.

"Shit, well, did you get my text, and what's up?" Edge said through the phone.

"No, I didn't. What text? Matter fact, hold on. I'ma just check. But I wanted to see if you wanted to kick it, you know, how we used to," Diamond suggested.

Edge was hesitant to respond. "Well, we'll see once you read what I sent you," Edge stated.

Diamond was confused when she read Edge's text. "Are you sure?" Diamond asked.

"Positive," Edge returned.

Now that they had Rick Sinclair on the Double Gs' side, he could not only provide Get Out of Jail Free cards, but he could help get to enemies. Diamond was curious. "Who are you taking out?" Diamond asked.

"Rick. We just found his office window, and have a clear shot on that motherfucker," Edge stated.

Diamond was shocked. It caused her to twitch, causing her foot to knock the ashtray down. The blunt hit the ground into a flammable sex oil spill. Diamond paid it no mind as she was in disbelief about the act of their major plug being killed. Diamond couldn't say no fast enough.

"Him? Firstly, I'm in charge. I—" Diamond's sentence was cut short by a tingling, burning sensation on her ankle. She looked down as a trail of flame traveled up her leg.

She quickly dropped the phone. The flames spread. Other Double Gs panicked as the flames caught some of them, trapping others as the flames consumed the entries and exits. The lustful heavenly scene turned to a torture from hell. Diamond thought this was a sign.

Grabbing her pistol, she shot the windows out. Boom! Boom! The glass shattered. The gun clicked from running out of bullets. Sparkle burst into the room and saw Diamond in distress. She leaped through flames and toward Diamond.

"Come on, sis!" Sparkle said as she held her hand out to assist. She pulled Diamond through the window. Glitter stood over the window with a large blanket.

"Come on, y'all!" Glitter shouted. The horns, bells, and whistle of fire trucks and the scream of ambulances came racing down the street.

Diamond turned her head at the sight of the window exploding as it blew her back against Glitter's car. Most of the women never made it out. The building was now quickly becoming a distant memory, Not even the pain she felt on her burned leg could compare to how much pain she felt seeing the house Starr had purchased for her destroyed.

Chapter 34

Edge and a Double Gs goon sat with their backs pressed against the short wall on top of a four-story building. The wind was gentle yet brisk. Edge's hair flipped and flopped back and forth. The Double Gs goon peeked from the cover over to a building of the same height no more than thirty yards away. The building was the office of Legislator Rick. He had a bandage over his eye. He paced back and forth, moving his arms as if he was having a conversation with someone. The Double Gs goon peeked at the office window through binoculars.

Edge still had her phone pressed against her ear. The explosion hit her eardrum like a shot. It startled her, but she continued to hold, waiting for a response.

"Diamond? What the fuck was that? Hello?" Edge spat. The Double Gs goon batted her eyes toward Edge. As she held the velocity device, the numbers on its display screen shifted and escalated drastically.

"We gotta make a move; the wind velocity is changing. It's picking up; soon it will be too high and beyond my skill set to make the shot," the Double Gs goon spat.

The Double Gs goon was a woman from Down South who was originally in the Marines for most of her adult life. After being discharged from the military for excessive drinking, she took up hunting. The same wood-finish custom sniper rifle she gripped tightly was the one she killed an estimated one hundred deer with. She moved to Las Vegas ironically to audition for a hunting show, one that was hosted by Prime at the time. She didn't make the cut because she wasn't exactly television material, as she had a large scar on her arm, and she would beat the shit out of any if not all male costars who hit on her. Being kicked off of the show, she realized she wasn't into men much, but preferred woman, as it seemed men were at the root of all her troubles. She met Edge by taking out a man she had requested to be killed. She was instantly snagged up.

Edge snapped out of it as the phone call cut off. She shrugged. She felt concern about what could have possibly gone wrong. At the same time, she was about business, and it needed to be handled. A man with as much power as Rick was hard to get to. If she passed up this opportunity, she could never get an easier, clearer shot.

Edge stuffed her phone in her pocket. She grabbed hold of the binoculars. She caught sight of Rick as he passed the window, walking and talking, back and forth. Edge unveiled the two-way radio she snatched up. "How's it looking downhill?" Edge spat in the two-way radio.

"All good in this neck of the woods," the voice responded.

Edge nodded as the Double Gs goon grabbed hold of the sniper rifle, positioning her arm in place, and putting her eye to the scope. The scope indicated needle points with different numbers written on them.

"Tell me every time those numbers change, okay?" the Double Gs goon spat.

Edge firmly grabbed the velocity device. The Double Gs goon seemed to shift the direction of the rifle continuously. Rick didn't keep still, as it was nearly impossible, with all the adrenaline drugs he'd ingested.

"Hold still, you bastard," Edge spat. As she looked through the binoculars longer, she raised an eyebrow at the sight of Agent McCarty. She smiled from ear to ear.

"Two birds with one stone. Can you hit both those pricks?" Edge requested.

"Most likely, unless they're standing stacked or right next to each other, only one can get hit," the Double Gs goon responded.

Edge rubbed her chin. *Decisions, decisions,* she pondered.

Chapter 35

The office was executive down to the rare gold cup holders. The walls were filled with medals, certificates, and degrees from business management to psychology. Rick was a drug addict and a sex addict, but he was far from a dummy. He had a plaques from societies and frat houses of Harvard. On campus was when his sex addiction was formed.

He paced back and forth in front of his sleek hardwood desk. Sun beamed through the large window behind it. Standing before him was Reddick, the tech agent and, last but not least, Agent McCarthy. They all had expressions that indicated just how badly they had fucked up.

"I understand all of that, but how can we fix this?" Reddick questioned.

"A leak this large is hard to cover with just a few silenced mouths, but three dozen hotel guests witnessed the entire thing. Not only that, but I was embarrassed beyond measure!" Rick lectured. "I feel like the only way to fix this is to blow my brains out!" Rick continued as a glare from the mirror of the rifle scope was seen behind him through the window.

As he peered out of the window, the Double Gs goon kept her aim. Rick missed the sight of her completely. He was too busy watching the trail of police cars headed in his direction as he gazed through the window. He flipped open his watch. "Shouldn't take them long to arrive." What he had cooked up was sinister. He found it amusing, grinning at his own reflection in the window before moving away from it.

"Why do we all have to take the rap for this? He did it. He should be the only one going to prison, not us!" the tech agent shouted.

Reddick looked at the tech man with his fist balled. He was ready to knock his block off.

"He's got a point. We shouldn't all be prosecuted for the same crime. Yes, we let it happen but, at the same time, we didn't and couldn't react in time. The device picked up the distress call. We simply were trying to save a man's life; that man was you," Agent McCarthy reasoned.

"Despite the bruises, I was enjoying myself with those twins," Rick Sinclair stated candidly. "And the device would get thrown out of court because we weren't sup- posed to be using it to begin with," Rick stated as he tapped the face of his watch.

Agent McCarty noticed it. He became suspicious. Something seemed out of place, but he couldn't put his finger on it. He wondered why Rick was so concerned about time.

"We boring you? Do the lives of your men not matter?" Agent McCarthy stated.

"Like I said earlier, I suggest you all remain calm. This will pass. I mean, you know how it goes, right? You'll beat this charge, but the longer you wait, the more guilty you'll look," Rick suggested.

The agents look at each other. Did they hear him correctly? they wondered. The expressions on their faces expressed their disdain for his words.

"You want us to turn ourselves in? As easy as that sounds, it's not gonna happen. They'll mix us with population, meaning all the arrests we made will get us creamed. I'm not going out like that," Agent Reddick exclaimed. "If anything, we should take out those twins.

They're the ones who embarrassed you; they're the ones who abused you. The Double Gs have been in charge fucking long enough," Reddick spat.

"You didn't get the message? Their spot was burned to the ground not too long ago. It was plastered all over the Net and news," the tech agent stated.

Chapter 36

The rumble below The Double Gs lookout's feet rubbed her the wrong way. For a street that was hardly ever busy, the utility hole cover began to vibrate on the cracked road pavement. The Double Gs lookout could feel something wasn't right when a red and blue flashing silent strobe light hit her eye. She quickly reached in her hoodie pocket for her two-way radio. She fumbled to grab hold of it. Before she can gain a grip on it, it plunged to the road and was destroyed by a passing police SUV. She locked eyes with the police officer in the passenger seat. He was angry, ready to do what he signed up to do. He gave her a brief smile and a thumbs-up, not knowing who she was. Her face remained stony. She thought she might have just screwed Edge and a member of the gang. She panicked but didn't let her sweat be shown.

She quickly glanced up to the four-story parking lot where Edge and the Double Gs goon were. There was no way she could get up there in time. "Shit!" the girl spat. She glanced down the road; a block away stood a payphone booth. She quickly rushed toward it.

"I am helping you," Rick stated as he turned toward the window.

Reddick caught the sight of the flashing lights. "Son of a bitch!" Reddick spat.

On the rooftop yards away, the line of fire was clear. The Double Gs goon had a clear shot of Rick as he stood still.

"Read me the numbers! Now or never!" the Double Gs goon shouted.

Edge turned the velocity device in the direction of the rifle. "Fourteen degrees, fifteen degrees, forty-five-degree angle, northeast," Edge explained.

The Double Gs goon caressed the trigger of the rifle similar to the way Rick grabbed the rod that closed the blinds. He stepped a few inches away from the window.

Reddick was pissed. "You turning us in? After all we did for you?" Reddick spat.

"This will help you! Don't you understand? You all are of no use outside!" Rick explained.

"Fuck you! If I'm going, you—" was all Reddick could say as a sniper bullet shot through Rick's shoulder and into Reddick's chest. He instantly dropped to the floor. Rick grabbed his shoulder, taking cover toward the wall. One shot after another tore into the office, desecrating the window and blinds, sending fragments and glass shards everywhere.

Boom! Boom! The tech agent was hit in the leg as he dived for cover.

Agents swarmed the office floors, hiking their way up the stairs and elevators to Rick's office. They kicked the door in only for some to get hit by wild sniper bullets. Agent McCarthy ducked for cover, crawling out of the room. Other agents ducked for cover. McCarthy noticed Reddick sprawled out on the floor near Rick Sinclair. "Fuck," he cursed.

On the rooftop, Edge and the Double Gs goon were clueless as to whether they'd hit Rick. "You think we got him?" Edge spat.

"Shit, I don't know, but we have to move!" the Double Gs goon stated. She packed her hunting sniper rifle in a long case and slung it on her back. As they ran toward the exit, Edge's phone rang. She ignored it until the Double

Gs goon was shot in the back of the head by an officer from the window. Edge took cover, squinting her eyes in brief mourning. She quickly took off as her phone continued to ring. She picked up.

"The feds are here. I'm so sorry I—"

Edge cut the girl's sentence short. "No shit! But forget all of that. Jazz is dead. Can you get to her car? That would be the best way to fix this fuckup!" Edge spat.

Shoes belonging to Agent McCarthy quickly rushed down a flight of stairs.

"Freeze!" an officer shouted as he pointed his weapon at McCarthy.

"Listen, the man you wanted is lying in a pool of his own blood upstairs. I'm not the one you're looking for!" Agent McCarthy stated.

The officer wasn't buying it. "I was ordered to neutralize you. Now turn around! Hands where I can see them!" the officer stated.

Agent McCarthy turned around slowly as the officer approached. "Screw that!" he barked. He grabbed hold of the officer. The officer shot his weapon at the top of the staircase, causing the bullet to ricochet and bounce back through his head. He instantly dropped dead, rolling down the rest of the stairs.

Agent McCarthy quickly rushed down the rest of the stairs into the street. He spotted the parking facility a few streets over and quickly rushed toward the four-story parking lot.

"I need another car, quick! You know how to hotwire one?" Agent McCarthy asked an agent he'd come across.

"Right there!" the agent spat as he pointed in the direction of an Explorer SUV.

The Double Gs lookout waited in the driver's seat, shaking. She had became scared to death. When shots rang out, she didn't know what was happening or about to happen. She stared at Agent McCarthy, whose stares were not nearly as startling as Edge's, who turned her head and locked eyes with him also.

Edge wanted the opportunity to kill Agent McCarthy. She knew he dreamed of taking down a Double Gs member and, because of that and a few other things, she wanted him dead.

Both drew their weapons at the same. Edge fired at Agent McCarthy, and he returned the favor. They took cover, returning fire. Guns were blazing at full capacity. Other agents discovered the parking lot from across the way.

"It doesn't have to be this way, Edge!" Agent McCarthy shouted.

Edge ran to the end of the parking lot. "Fuck you!" she spat.

McCarthy raised his weapon and aimed it in Edge's direction. Out of nowhere, he was hit in the arm. He ducked back behind a semi-destroyed concrete pillar as the bullet ripped through its outer surface.

Edge got in the car. "Go!" Edge spat to the lookout.

McCarthy attempted to stop the SUV, firing into the engine and dashboard. He missed. His eyes widened at the impact of it coming full force toward him. It passed him.

Boom. He dropped lower to the ground. Edge and the lookout took the back way.

McCarthy aimed and fired again. This time he aimed for the SUV's tires but missed. He turned his head toward the other agent.

"Help me. Fucking almost ran me over!" the agent begged.

Agent McCarthy rushed over, grabbing hold of the agent. "I gotta go!" Agent McCarthy shouted after helping the agent up.

He hit corner after corner as they attempted to escape. Finally discovering a vehicle pointed toward the office, McCarty galloped to the vehicle. A barrage of agents came out of the woodwork, spilling into the path with the barrels of their weapons pointed toward the direction in which Edge and the lookout fled. Officers came from behind, planting pistols to the back of McCarthy's head.

It was over, there was nowhere else to run and, even if Reddick wasn't dead, they knew he could be arrested now for resisting arrest, assault, and possible murder. Agent McCarthy dropped his head down in disgrace. An officer roughly handled him as he slammed handcuffs on to his wrists.

"You have the right to remain silent. . . ."

Agent McCarthy tuned the man out as he was escorted to the back of a black Dodge Dart. McCarthy swallowed roughly as he mentally prepared himself for what was to come.

Chapter 37

A SUV came racing down the road. It quickly drifted down a narrow alley. The lookout was in the driver's seat. Edge in the passenger's seat. Her phone was pressed against her ear. Her face appeared anxious all across the board, not only because of the situation at hand, but at the several brushes with death she'd just had. The lookout couldn't drive for shit and, what was worse, Diamond wasn't answering her phone.

"Come on, pick the fuck up!" Edge shouted into the receiver.

She looked up as the lookout looked her way. For the split second she took her eyes off the road, she nearly ran into a brick wall. Had it not been for Edge grabbing hold of the wheel, swerving out of the way, that would've been the case.

"Don't watch me; watch the fucking road!" Edge spat.

The Double Gs lookout rolled her eyes and sucked her teeth.

Realizing her words were a bit overboard, Edge lightened up. "Look, sorry, but you have to not worry about what happened back there. It's done and over, nothing can change it, and we just have to deal with it. The same goes for life: we can't spend all our time worrying about what happened; we have to look at what's to come. You following, youngster?" Edge stated.

The lookout was devastated. The hunter Double Gs goon was her friend, mentor, and secret lover. "They killed her! In cold blood!" the lookout spat as she began to swerve.

"Hey! Relax, all right? Just stay focused. We just lost the feds. We don't need to attract any more," Edge stated right before her phone rang. The screen read Diamond.

"Hey, I need you to slow down. Keep at the speed limit, okay?" Edge requested and then answered the call. "Hey, what the hell's going on?" Edge asked.

"Hey, this not Diamond; this Sparkle," Sparkle announced.

"Wassup?" The fact that another Double Gs member was calling her from Diamond's phone alarmed Edge. "Is everything okay? Where's Diamond?" Edge wanted to know.

"Shit's all fucked up. A lot of Double Gs died in a house fire. Diamond got burned bad on the leg," Sparkle stated dramatically over the phone.

Edge couldn't believe the words she heard. Could this be the end of the Double Gs? How in the hell could they bounce back after something like this? Question after question popped up in her head. Like spam and malware on a computer screen, she couldn't stop them from coming. Through all the thoughts, she kept a positive face for the young lookout to the side of her.

"Where is she?" Edge requested.

"Women and Children's. We got an affiliation with the hospital down Freemont. All the other hospitals in the city would turn us over to the feds," Sparkle explained.

"I'm on my way," Edge said as she closed the phone. She pointed to the side of the road. "Pull over. We need to change clothes, and I'll drive from here on out," Edge commanded.

Chapter 38

Esco cuddled his lover and soon-to-be wife, Chance. She was nine months pregnant. Any day or any moment now she could give birth to who would be Esco Jr. A boy was expected to pull through.

Esco lifted her shirt. He gently rubbed and kissed her belly, and softly pressed his head against it. His face glowed, and so did hers. Esco's hand went down to her maternity elastic sweatpants. He began fingering her. She moaned and gasped. Esco put his juicy fingers inside her mouth, then continued to kiss her. Their tongues danced in each other's mouths. Chance's nipples grew erect. So did Esco's manhood. He begin pulling and tugging at not only his pants but hers as well.

"Wait," Chance requested.

Esco looked as if he was figuring out a reason for them to stop. "What's the matter, baby?" Esco responded.

"Is this good for the baby? I don't want him coming out jacked up or missing an arm or something from all the ongoing ejaculation." She was concerned.

Esco smiled, pulling his pants up. "It's fine. He was made this way. More DNA means a stronger baby, just like his father," Esco joked. He opened his mouth wide, filling it with Chance's breast. She moaned when her pants became damp, then increasingly wet. They were soaked, dripping to the floor. Esco's eyes widened.

"Damn, I turned you own that much?" Esco playfully spat.

Chance wasn't playing anymore. She begin to breathe heavily. "My water broke! He's coming!" Chance shouted.

Esco panicked, grabbing hold of a towel and other things he thought he might need. "Shit, okay, relax, just—"

His sentence was cut short by Chance. "Just get me to the hospital!" Chance bellowed.

At the car, Esco kicked the back door open and gently placed Chance across the seat. He quickly ran to the driver's seat. At first struggling to fit the keys in the ignition, he finally managed, cranking it and putting it into drive.

"Take me to Women and Children's Hospital! It's closer, ahh! They know what they're doing!" Chance cried out.

Esco nodded and sprang into action.

"Push!" the doctor shouted as he and several others stood in the delivery room of Women and Children's Hospital. Esco wore scrubs, gloves, and a surgical mask. He was nervous yet excited that he actually created a being, someone who could breathe, someone who was a piece of him who, when he was gone, would be his legacy. He shed tears of joy as he leaned over and kissed Chance on the forehead. He grabbed her hand and held on tight. Chance slowly turned her head toward him. They gazed into each other's eyes. It was a cherished moment neither would ever forget.

A doctor propped Chance's feet up, raising her gown up. "Can you give me a push? I need you to try as hard as you can, all right?" the doctor requested.

Chance began huffing and puffing with each agonizing push. Esco held her hand tighter and tighter with each push. "You got this, sweetie. I've seen you get out of tougher shit. You got this!"

Esco's words were encouraging. She shouted, pulling through her greatest effort.

"There we go! You're doing it!" the doctor shouted.

The nurses noticed the rise in blood pressure from the machines going off. It grabbed Esco's attention. "What's going on with the machine?" Esco asked, but he was not given an answer.

"It's crowning!" the doctor shouted as he and the nurses prepared for the baby's arrival.

What followed next was unexpected.

The doctor's gloves were filled with blood. The baby's birth was turning into Esco and Chance's nightmare. The doctor, his shirt now filled with blood, was fully aware of what was going on. He got up and stormed out of the delivery room into the hallway.

"No, no. This can't be happening. This can't be fucking happening!" Esco shouted as he punched the walls, staining them with blood.

"I'm sorry. He didn't make it." The rest of the doctor's sentence was cut short as Esco stormed down the hallway. As he passed the burn center, he pushed a doctor to the floor, out of his path. In passing, he noticed a couple of familiar faces. *Double Gs,* he told himself. Instinctively, he reached for his weapon, but to no avail. He realized he had been so preoccupied with getting Chance to the hospital that he had forgotten to snatch up one. *Fucking bitches.*

The way he felt, he wanted to kill them all.

Esco made his way toward the room the Double Gs were huddled around. Just as he reached the entrance of the unit, he was stopped in his tracks by some approaching security guards.

"We're going to have to ask you to leave, sir," one of the security guards informed him. "And you're banned from stepping foot in here ever again, once your girlfriend has recovered," he added.

Esco nodded. He wasn't giving up. *When there's a will, there's a way.* Even if it meant staking out the hospital, he was all for it.

Chapter 39

Diamond lay in bed. Her entire right leg, from her inner thigh to the lower part down to her ankle, was wrapped and bandaged as it hung from a sling. Her hands and parts of her face were bound as well. Edge sat to the side of her with a look of concern. Diamond gently reached her hand out, placing it in Edge's palm.

"Thank you for being here with me," Diamond said.

Edge smiled. She had always seemed to hide her emotions from Diamond, but now was not a time to be coldhearted. Edge realized life wasn't something you should take for granted. It could end when you least expected. So from that daring escape, she swore to keep it real with everyone she met, rather being mean or nice across the board. It also meant no more hiding emotions. This was a new leaf for Edge. A new saga ready to be unfolded.

"I had to come be with you and show some love, you know that," Edge said as she leaned in and kissed Diamond on the lips.

Diamond loved it. She was the perfect replacement for Starr. She wanted Edge to be by her side, forever. "I don't know if you know, but the entire original clubhouse is gone."

Edge nodded. "I know. Sparkle told me shit's all screwed; but everything happens for a reason, right?" Edge moved in closer to Diamond. "It was a bad thing to happen but, at the same time, if it didn't we wouldn't be connecting on the level we are," Edge stated.

Diamond nodded. She cleared her throat and took a swig of the bottled water on the sliding tray connected to her hospital bed. "Before Starr left, she put me in charge and, well, I want you to be my right-hand woman. This world's too big to rule on my own. Just like kings, queens need a queen too," Diamond stated.

Edge smiled. "No doubt. I'd gladly take that position."

Diamond gestured for Edge to lean over.

"What's up?" Edge asked.

"You've been here with me in this hospital. You've bought me ice cream, we've watched scary movies, et cetera. I want to continue doing that"—Diamond smiled—"well, until death do us part. What I'm asking is, will you marry me?" Diamond stated.

Edge's eyes lit up. She couldn't believe her ears nor could she find words to express how she felt about the question. "Yes, oh, God, yes!" Edge beamed.

They hugged with passion, kissing and sucking each other's lips intensely. The ball was in motion. Edge and Diamond were now an unbreakable bond. Together, they would build Double Gs back from the ground up if they had to.

Later, outside of Women and Children's Hospital, they held hands as Diamond walked on a crutch to her car. Edge opened the door for Diamond, lifting her into the passenger's seat. A cheerful smile appeared on her face as she climbed into the driver's seat and pulled off.

From across the street. Esco's eyes were filled with pure hatred. He was thirsty and the only way to quench it was with blood. He scooted down low and watched as the car drove away. He then pulled out his phone and called Prime to let him know what he'd heard.

Chapter 40

Bells echoed against the backdrop of the Mandarin Oriental, a lavish, unique wedding venue. Nearly every single aspect of the building was of exquisite beauty. In the banquet and cocktail reception area, an array of glowing diamonds and jewels hung high from the ceiling. It was the most expensive wedding venue in all of Las Vegas, as it sat mere blocks away from the Strip's primary attractions. Excellent wines dating back to as far as 1965 sat untouched for the Double Gs.

"Double Gs!" they all chanted.

Diamond was excited beyond words. Though her leg was burned, she felt no pain. She wasn't on painkillers, nor anything of the like, but she was high on love and happiness. Edge was the one to tie the knot with. Although Starr still stood in the back of her mind, she'd gradually faded. When the name Starr was mentioned, it caused her to look into the night sky.

"Cheers to the Double Gs!" Diamond responded with joy. "We've lost some sisters, we've gained some sisters, but the remainder of us, either dead, departed, or standing right next to you, we're internally and externally sisters, in the spiritual form, always and forever," Diamond preached.

They shifted their bodies in unison from side to side, bowing them while keeping their glasses raised. "Always and forever!" the Double Gs sisters repeated. Most of them didn't see Diamond as a leader; they just respected her. Some downright distrusted her after the house fire, which killed a few of them and a few dancers. Once Diamond was out of the hospital, she visited the graves of nearly all of the Double Gs who'd been killed by the burning house and the street soldiers who'd been caught in the wrong place at the wrong time. The members respected that.

Sparkle and Glitter pressed and curled Diamond's hair as other Double Gs pampered her fingernails and toenails. She sat in her bra and panties as one of the Double Gs rubbed a special oil on her burned ankle and calf muscle.

"Look at you. You're fabulous." Sparkle playfully gestured.

"Thanks, sis." Diamond lit up. She was in an extremely good mood. In just ten minutes her life was turning over a new leaf. A new beginning.

Bubbles walked in, sniffling. "Aww, look at my big sis," she sang. "I don't think I've ever seen you more beautiful than today."

Diamond smiled from ear to ear. "Appreciate you."

"You're welcome, sis."

"Did you see Starr while you were out there?" Diamond asked.

"I haven't seen her all day since I've been here," Bubbles stated. "I'll take a look," she offered.

"Thanks, sis." Diamond began to put on her wedding dress. She wondered if Starr would even come or if she'd rip the invitation up that was sent to her home address. Although she still loved Starr, she was in love with Edge and wanted to spend the rest of her life with her. But Starr was still her friend and to see her would mean a lot to Diamond on her big day.

The traditional wedding starter song echoed throughout the church, reaching the back part where Diamond was preparing with the help of the Double Gs.

"It's that time," Bubbles announced.

Diamond smiled with her eyes.

"Today, we join these two beautiful women as they step into a union, a bond that a sword couldn't cut and acid couldn't melt. The sun was setting in the east, as our love in the west rose every single day," the pastor announced.

Edge was decked out in a traditional fitted tux as she stood across from Diamond, who wore a Vera Wang original. They stared into each other's eyes as they gripped each other's hands semi-tightly.

"This is the moment of truth. You ready?" Diamond proudly announced.

Edge smiled. "If you are." She grinned from ear to ear.

They had both written personal vows to each other and just finished reading them over the past hour. The ceremony was reaching an end. But in Edge's and Diamond's minds, a new beginning was just starting. The Double Gs family and business associates filled the white chairs planted neatly along the rows. Diamond and Edge wanted it to be weapon free, so not one Double Gs goon or sister was strapped.

"I love you, Edge," Diamond stated.

The statement hit close to home for Edge. She began to feel great guilt. "There's something I feel you should know," Edge stated.

Diamond raised an eyebrow, not sure if she was prepared to hear what Edge had to say, whether it was good or bad.

The ring bearer walked down the walkway with two rings placed on top of a pillow he held. He smiled as Diamond and Edge took the rings, sliding them onto each other's fingers.

The ring bearer walked away until he hit the end of the row. A weird man in all black sat at the piano playing smooth tunes that sounded more like funeral music than wedding music. Another single black rose sat on top of the piano in a clear vase.

"What was it you wanted to tell me?" Diamond questioned.

Glitter and Sparkle glanced at each other. They were both in earshot of Edge's and Diamond's every word.

Edge took a deep breath. Before she could get her words out, a loud bang filled the air. Out of nowhere, the ring bearer turned around, unveiling a pistol. He fired it into the back of Edge's head.

Edge's brain matter and blood painted Diamond's face and eggshell wedding dress, right before Edge's body flopped to the ground. Diamond's mouth dropped to the floor.

"Nooo!" Diamond cried.

Esco let off two more rounds in the direction of Glitter and Sparkle before fleeing. Sparkle dove to the ground. She wasted no time grabbing hold of her ankle pistol. Diamond briefly looked at her knowing she didn't want any weapons at the wedding, but she couldn't find a reason to be mad. Sparkle couldn't get a clear shot thanks to the stampede of people who blocked most of her view. Esco had managed to escape.

"Fuck!" Sparkle grabbed hold of her head. She along with several other Double Gs all bowed their heads at the sight of Edge.

Diamond's eyes were glossy. Sparkle threw her arm around her to console her. She noticed she didn't see Glitter anywhere in sight. She did a quick scan of the area. What she saw off to her far right caused her knees to buckle. "No, no, no, no, no!" she chanted as she rushed over to where her twin sister lay in a fetal position.

"Glitter? Glitter?" she called out as she dropped to the ground next to her sister. "Glitter, wake up," Sparkle pleaded. But her cries went unanswered.

Sirens could be heard wailing in the air. "Sparkle, we gotta go," one of the Double Gs called out.

Sparkle ignored her advice. Instead, she sat there cradling her sister, rocking back and forth.

It was actually Diamond's voice that penetrated. "Sparkle, I need you, sis. They gone," she said, referring to Edge and Glitter. "We not gonna do them any good if we get caught," she reasoned with Sparkle. "Don't worry; this isn't over. If it's the last thing I do, I'll find that bastard," Diamond cried.

Sparkle nodded. She popped a clip in her small pistol as an extra precaution and rose up. "You won't have to find him alone," Sparkle said. "I'm killing anybody he's associated with," Sparkle added.

Chapter 41

The doorbell sound broke Starr's beauty rest in the presidential suite at Horseshoe's hotel and casino in Lake Tahoe, Nevada. "Who is it?" she called out from the bed.

She looked around through cold-filled eyes and only saw a trail of clothing, evidence that Monica was in the walk-in shower. "Who is it?" she repeated.

All she could hear was a muffled noise. She flung the covers back and popped out of bed. She slipped her feet into her Gucci flip-flops and struggled to suite's entrance. The doorbell sounded off for a second time. "Coming, coming," Starr called out. Opening the double doors, she was met by a beautiful Somali server standing behind the tray cart with what she believed to be a full-course breakfast under silver tray tops.

"Good morning, Ms. Fields, may I come in and set up your table?" The Somali server's accent was strong. It complemented her sultry voice, thought Starr.

"Yes, come in." Starr moved out of the way and let the sever by.

"I am Lydia. I will be your server."

Starr smiled. "That's okay, you don't have to set it up or serve it. I have it from here. It's fine," Starr assured her.

Just then Monica came out of the room with only her hair wrapped up. She was so preoccupied with her hair that she hadn't even noticed the room service she had ordered had arrived, and the server was there. The

Somali woman turned away to avoid seeing Monica in her birthday suit.

"Oh, I'm sorry. I don't mean to offend you," Monica said.

The woman blushed.

Starr took the bill from the server's hand. She included a healthy tip. The Somali woman's eyes widened when she saw the hundred dollar addition Starr had tacked on to the bill.

When she spun around to thank Starr, she was met with her and Monica in a tongue fight with Starr's two hands full of Monica's ass cheeks.

"My apologies." The Somali server bowed as she back-pedaled. "Thank you for the generosity," she said before exiting the room.

"She was pretty," Monica announced.

"Yeah, I thought so too," Starr agreed.

"Too bad we're both taken, though," Monica joked.

"Yes, too bad." Starr grabbed her from behind and wrapped her arms around Monica's waist. "Hmm, you're getting thick," Starr noticed.

A nervous chill shot up Monica's back from the comment. *Please, God, don't let this be the day she finds out,* Monica began to worry. She still hadn't told Starr about the pregnancy, let alone who it was by. She also didn't let Prime know she was done with him as of yet. It was ironic that it was Starr who was the one she was supposed to cut off.

Monica tried to inconspicuously break free of Starr's hold. But the more she moved, the more Starr began to caress her. "What you tryin'a say, I'm gettin' fat?" Monica tried to make light of the situation.

"I'm definitely not saying that, but come on, babe, you tellin' me you haven't noticed those hips started to protrude more?" Starr asked.

Monica looked down at herself as if she were just seeing her hips for the first time. She ran her hands alongside the outer crevices of her frame and said, "I think I still feel the same."

Starr gave her an odd look. "So you're saying—" That was as far as Starr got before the only phone she could never turn off rang. "Hold that thought." She held her finger up to Monica.

What the hell am I gonna do? Monica's nervousness slowly began to turn into fear. *She's going to try to kill me and my baby, I know it.* Monica began to obsess. But the sudden outburst from Starr brought her thoughts to an end.

When Monica looked over at Starr, she was sitting on the sofa with her head in the palms of her hands. "Starr, what is it?" a concerned Monica asked. She was already making her way over to where Starr sat. "Honey, what's wrong?" She put her hand on Starr's back.

Starr shrugged it off and then hopped up. She took a long stretch and let out an eerie bellow. Shaking it off, she cracked her knuckles.

"Starr?"

"Somebody hit the organization," Starr abruptly jumped in.

A look of shock was Monica's new facial expression, although she was not clear on who had exactly hit the Double Gs. "Hit the organization?"

"Somebody from Freeze's crew hit up a wedding everybody attended, and there was a fire at the club," Starr informed Monica.

"Wait. What? Wedding? Whose wedding? And is everybody okay?" Monica rambled. She went from shocked to confused.

"Edge and Glitter are dead. Club burnt down. A lot of Double Gs were killed. Diamond was burned a few places." Starr paused and took a deep breath before she continued. "And the wedding was Diamond and Edge's."

The look on Monica's face matched the way Starr felt. Everything just told to her had Starr in total shock, from the club burning down to Diamond being in the hospital and niggas making a move on the Double Gs when they were a part of the G-files. What really rubbed her the wrong way was the fact that Diamond was nearly a married woman. Starr blamed herself. For everything. *None of this shit would have happened on my watch,* she believed.

All Monica could do was stand there while Starr collected her thoughts. She knew Starr was blaming herself and feeling some type of way behind Diamond's almost being married to the late Edge. She was no fool. Although she had chosen her, Monica knew Starr still loved Diamond, and the situation was still fresh.

Starr cleared her throat. The look on her face had already told Monica what she was about to say.

"I'm sorry, babe, but we have to get back to Vegas. The Double Gs need me."